Imminent Threat

A Detective Liv DeMarco Thriller

G.K. Parks

Copyright © 2022 G.K. Parks

A Modus Operandi imprint

ISBN:
ISBN-13: 978-1-942710-31-8

For Aunt Kathy, who always encourages me to keep my head up and continue writing...

BOOKS IN THE LIV DEMARCO SERIES:

BOOKS IN THE ALEXIS PARKER SERIES:

BOOKS IN THE JULIAN MERCER SERIES:

BOOKS IN THE CROSS SECURITY INVESTIGATIONS SERIES:

ONE

Closing his eyes, he listened. Thick-soled work boots pounded against the cement. The sound bounced off the drab cinderblock walls. When the nearest patrolling guard reached the end of the corridor, the buzzer sounded, followed by the click of the lock releasing, and the clang of the barred door sliding along the track.

Leaning over, he checked the time and made a mental note. He had their movements down to the minute, and tonight was no exception. Wilson Matthews hadn't been in this hellhole that long, but he already knew every guard in his cell block by name. He knew who patrolled and when. He knew how long it took each of them to make the rounds and who liked to cause trouble.

He rolled over on the paper-thin mattress, feeling the metal frame beneath his back. This was a far cry from his adjustable, memory foam bed at home, with its satin sheets and fluffy pillows. He had to get out of here. Tonight was the night. He wouldn't last another day like this.

His blood pumped faster through his veins as he thought about the woman responsible for his current predicament. Sure, he'd been warned she was an undercover cop, but that only excited him. He'd never faced another hunter before. His previous kills had all been prey. But Detective Liv DeMarco wasn't prey, at least not yet. That would change. Once he was free, she'd become his prey.

He thought about their brief encounters. That silky coral dress, the glossy waves of honey-brown hair, and those smoky blue eyes. He couldn't wait to see tatters of that dress holding her in place while tears streamed down her cheeks. The thought made him giddy.

He didn't like being trapped here or that smug look he'd glimpsed on her face the last time he'd seen her. That's when he concocted his plan. First, he had to gain his freedom. He couldn't chase her from inside a jail cell, and he liked the chase.

Rotting in here while he awaited trial was not an option. Luckily, his lawyer had given him a good idea. It wasn't a guarantee, but based on Matthews' previously spotless record, he thought it was worth a shot. For all any of them knew, he was innocent—the victim of a frame job. Given the players involved, it seemed plausible. That dirty Detective Gallagher had extorted him long enough, and now that Gallagher was dead and his secrets revealed, Matthews could weave a tale of woe of how he'd been targeted and framed by the dirty cop. He'd make this work to his advantage, one way or another.

If nothing else, he'd paint himself as the wrongly accused victim—abused by the very system that claimed innocent until proven guilty. Sure, Matthews was guilty, but not until a jury of his peers and a judge decided that. And as far as he was concerned, they never would.

Quietly, Wilson Matthews got up from his bunk, relieved to have the cell to himself. In thirty-four minutes, the next guard would make a pass. Since today was Tuesday, that would be Clemmons.

Officer Clemmons was a loudmouth bully, who would make the perfect patsy. Clemmons already had several complaints pending against him. He was a violent bastard who acted out of fear, using excessive force to beat the inmates into submission and to enact his own brand of justice on the men he considered to be the worst offenders.

Honestly, Matthews wasn't sure why Clemmons hadn't paid him a visit yet. It would have made his life easier, but he suspected the bully with the billy club didn't care about his alleged indiscretions. After all, the women Matthews hurt deserved it. They got what was coming to them, but civilized society pretended killing was wrong. Only, he knew better.

Snorting at the ludicrousness, he set to work. Since his attorney had made an impassioned plea at the bail hearing, the judge had placed Matthews in protective custody. He had his own cell and remained isolated from the rest of the general population. A man like him, with no prior criminal record, who had substantial means, and who'd been accused of killing women, might get shivved in the lunch line. This was the judge's attempt to keep him safe. But no one was safe behind bars. And Wilson Matthews was about to prove it.

Letting out a breath, he looked around the tiny cell. He didn't have much to work with. The sink didn't look sturdy enough, and he'd probably get sepsis from the toilet. The bed frame would be his best bet.

As quietly as possible, he slid the mattress off the frame, letting it droop to the ground. Then he moved the threadbare blanket and sheet, draping one end from the sink and leaving the mass tangled on the floor. Now for the finishing touches.

Since he didn't have any personal effects, like a few of his fellow inmates, he'd have to make do with what he had. Going to the sink, he reached into the drain and pulled out the thin piece of wire he'd pulled from the bed three nights ago and took the sharpened end to his scalp. He dug in, slicing across.

He knew what areas bled the most on the human body. The face and scalp bled a lot on account of so many veins close to the surface, but it wouldn't result in enough blood loss to cause concern. Leaning forward, so as not to drip on himself, he made a nice blood trail before smearing it onto the bedding.

Once he was satisfied his cell looked like the scene of an attack, he had one more thing to do. Again, he leaned out to see the clock. He could practically hear the rubber soles thudding toward him. It was time.

He grabbed the end of the bed frame and reared back. All he had to do was inflict enough physical damage to be convincing. He'd been working on this plan since he arrived. A bump here. A bruise there. But it was time to pull out all the stops. One good blow might be enough. But he wasn't sure.

With all his might, he threw himself toward the looped metal of the bed frame. At the last second, survival instincts kicked in, and he jerked to the side. He bit back the curse as his right eyebrow made contact with the bar. He could already feel it swelling from the impact. Tears ran down his right cheek while blood continued to dribble down the left side.

Now, he knew the thudding wasn't just in his head. It was now or never. If he wanted out of this shithole, he had to do it. He grabbed the frame again, this time in both hands, and positioned one knee on the lopsided mattress. Then with a scream that everyone in the cell block was sure to hear, he begged for mercy from his invisible attacker and slammed his head into the metal bar over and over again.

By the time the guards reached his cell, he was out cold.

*　　*　　*

My phone buzzed first. Then Brad's. My dad shook his head and reached for another helping of green beans. It wasn't that long ago when he used to be on the receiving end of such phone calls.

I pulled my phone out of my pocket and read the waiting text message. I held it out for Brad to read. My partner had received the same message. *Vehicular homicide.* Followed by the address.

"I'm sorry to eat and run, Mom, but we have to go to work." I skewered another piece of chicken and popped it into my mouth. "Thanks for dinner. This was great. But you and Dad didn't have to wait to eat this late. Brad and I would have been fine with leftovers."

"Olive, don't talk with your mouth full," she scolded.

Brad fought to keep his face neutral, but I could tell he was laughing on the inside. He finished eating and picked up his plate. "This was wonderful, Mrs. DeMarco."

"Maria," she corrected. "You've stayed in this house long enough to use my first name."

"Yes, ma'am." He swallowed at the scowl on her face. "Sorry, Maria."

"That's better."

Brad reached for my plate, but my mom told him to leave it. My partner didn't listen. He took our dishes to the sink, rinsed them, and loaded them into the dishwasher. "Are you sure I can't help clean up?"

"You have a crime scene to clean up, Detective Fennel," my father said. "You and Liv take care of that, and I'll deal with the kitchen."

"Yes, sir."

I grabbed my gear off the counter and handed Brad his holster and cuffs. Mom had rules about eating while armed. "Thanks for dinner. I love you."

"Be careful," Mom said. "Both of you. And Brad, don't forget about our lasagna date."

"I won't."

"Liv, honey," Mom said as we made our way to the door, "are you coming back after shift?"

"No, I'll be okay in my apartment, at least while we're working nights. When we get back on days, we'll see."

"Okay, but you know your room's always here for you." She gave me a hug and a kiss. "And the same goes for you, Brad. If you need a place to stay, the guest room is always available."

"Thanks, Maria. But I'm good." He kissed my mom's cheek and nodded to my father. "Good night, sir."

"Watch each other's backs," Dad called after us.

I got into the passenger seat and fastened my seatbelt while Brad adjusted the mirrors, glanced around the neighborhood, and double-checked the address on his phone. Normally, he didn't take this much time to get the car in motion, but it was his first day back. Our first day back together.

"Nervous?" I asked.

"Nope." He pulled away from my parents' house and headed for the crime scene. "Are you?"

"The complete opposite. I'm ready for things to get back to normal."

"You had to say it, didn't you? You realize you just jinxed us."

"I did not."

"You did too. Now we're jinxed. I should stop the car so you can get out, turn around three times, spit, and throw salt over your shoulder, or whatever it was your mom was telling us about your crazy Aunt Linda and her peculiar habits."

"Brad, stop."

He shook his head, but his eyes twinkled. "When we roll up on something insane, I want you to know it's your fault because you put it out into the universe."

"Me? You're the one making a big deal out of it. In case the universe missed it, you've really hit it home." I cocked an eyebrow at him. "Since when are you this superstitious?"

"I'm not. I just missed busting your chops."

I poked him in the arm. "Jerk." But I missed this too. "Speaking of, how are you feeling?"

"Right as rain. Did the cover story hold?"

"Everyone thinks you were out these last couple of weeks due to appendicitis, and Captain Grayson's already explained away your erratic behavior as the result of a high fever due to the infection. The rumors and hearsay have already died down."

"Just in case, I have a nifty scar in roughly the right place to sell the story."

"Emma would probably disagree. Your appendix is lower and closer to the middle."

"Well, she's a nurse. We're not dealing with nurses. We're dealing with cops. It'll be fine."

I stared out the windshield, but the nervous energy radiated from my partner. I understood first day jitters when coming back from sick leave. I also understood how hard it was to adjust after coming back from an undercover assignment. For Brad, this was both, and almost no one on the force knew the truth.

"Why was my mom talking about lasagna?"

"She's teaching me how to make it."

"No way. I don't even know how to make it."

"Emma does."

"Yes, but Emma helped her perfect the recipe years ago."

"So get the recipe from Emma."

"Not the point, Fennel."

He snickered. "I guess your mom likes having me around. I always told you parents like me."

"You're good with everyone."

He parked behind a blue and white that still had its lights flashing. "Almost." For a moment, we sat in silence. I'd give him as much time as he needed. It was hard to flip a switch. After a few measured breaths, he reached for the door handle. "Let's get to work, Detective DeMarco. And since you're so sure we're not jinxed, you can take the lead."

"Chicken."

"I'm pretty sure that doesn't go in your mom's lasagna."

After narrowing my eyes at him, I let myself out of the car. The area hadn't been roped off, so I wasn't sure where the accident occurred. A couple of patrol officers were standing on the sidewalk, filling out reports and speaking to two women.

The supervisor on scene nodded when he saw me. "You caught the case?"

"Yep." I surveyed the area, feeling my partner lingering half a step behind me. "Where's the body?"

"In the hospital morgue by now."

"That was fast."

"Not really. After the accident, those two women called 9-1-1. When the paramedics arrived, the guy was circling the drain. They hauled ass, but the docs pronounced him as soon as they rolled him into the ER."

"Damn." Brad rubbed his chin. "Has the notification been made?"

"The hospital handled that. The deceased was Garrett Rollins, fifty-two, married, father of three. He was on his way home from work." He pointed to the grocery store half a block away. "According to the witnesses, the walk sign illuminated. He was halfway across when a silver hatchback ran the light. They said the driver was swerving everywhere. She blew through the intersection, smacked into Rollins, turned the wheel, probably to compensate or as a delayed reaction, banged into those three parked cars, and kept going."

"Did they get a plate?" I asked.

The sergeant shook his head.

"What about make and model?" Brad asked.

"Nope."

I studied the traffic light. "What about the red light camera?"

"I already requested the footage," the sergeant said.

"Thanks." That was a start. "Did you run the vic's name through the system?"

"Clean. No record. No known criminal affiliations. Honestly, I think this was just a freak hit and run. Some drunk got behind the wheel and destroyed someone's life."

"Probably." Brad nudged me. "I'm going to check out those parked cars." After making a few detailed notes, I went to see if my partner had found anything. Silver paint had transferred to two of the parked cars. "We'll need the lab to check that out. That might give us make and model. Also," he pointed to the broken pieces of plastic and glass on the ground, "the driver's got at least one busted headlight and side mirror."

"That'll make it easier to ID the car when we find it. I bet traffic cam footage will give us everything we need. But just in case, I'll talk to the witnesses and see if they have anything to add."

They repeated the details the sergeant had already shared, but that did little to help us identify the driver. While we waited for the traffic cam footage to come through, Brad and I headed to the hospital. The victim's personal effects hadn't been claimed yet, but the doctor said Garrett's wife had been called. She was on her way.

My partner bounced on the balls of his feet. He didn't want to speak to her. Making the notification was always the worst part, and since the hospital had already taken the lead, Brad hoped we could delay the inevitable a little while longer.

"Are you sure you're okay?" I asked.

"Yeah, fine." But he didn't look so good.

"Do you want to sit down? I'll get you some water."

"It's not that."

"What is it?"

"Nothing."

Before I could pry any further, my phone rang. The car and driver had been positively identified from the traffic cam footage. I repeated the address and name while Brad jotted it down. "Great, thanks."

"Let's go pay this asshole a visit," Brad said.

TWO

"There's the car." Brad pointed to the banged-up hatchback, haphazardly parked near the curb. The driver's side had several deep scratches. The remnants of the side mirror dangled from a wire. From the way the dents looked, I didn't think it was possible for the driver to get out on that side.

Grabbing my flashlight, I approached the car from the passenger's side. The butt of the car partially blocked the rightmost lane, while what was left of the front end was parked on the sidewalk. The turning light continued to blink. At this time of night, traffic on the residential street was nonexistent, so no one had called to complain about the car.

"I got blood." Brad aimed the beam of his flashlight on the walkway leading to the brownstone.

"Me too." The airbag had released, probably on impact. Red smears covered the white plastic. More blood had dripped onto the passenger seat and door handle. "The traffic cam footage didn't show anyone else in the car."

"That's probably from when the driver got out." Brad headed for the townhouse. "That's a lot of blood. Whoever was driving needs medical attention."

The front door was ajar. Cautiously, Brad went in. I couldn't see past him, but when he swore, my hand went for my gun. "Police," I announced into the darkness, the beam of my flashlight sweeping from left to right. "Is anyone home?"

"Is anyone else here?" Brad bellowed. He knelt beside the woman. Blood dripped from her nose and mouth. But I didn't see any other injuries on her. He pressed his fingers against her neck and shook his head.

I radioed for an ambulance while he gave her CPR. He continued with the chest compressions until the EMTs arrived. Once they took over, we cleared the rest of the townhouse. But Macy Lowan lived alone.

"She's dead," the lead paramedic said.

"From the accident?" Brad asked.

"I don't know. But this is too much blood for just a broken nose."

"What are you thinking?" Brad asked.

"I can't speculate."

"Off the record?" I nudged.

"You'll have to ask the ME."

"We'll need a blood alcohol panel and full toxicology report. We should also have CSU print the car. It wouldn't hurt to make sure her prints are on the wheel." I looked around the apartment, but I didn't find much in the way of booze. There were no empties in the recycling or abandoned bottles on the counters. Macy didn't keep any vodka or tequila in the freezer. All I found was a bottle of champagne in the fridge.

"Hey, Liv," Brad held up a tiny baggie he'd found in one of her pockets, "look at this."

"What is it?" The baggie had a rabbit sticker on the front of it.

The EMT gave it a look. "I've seen that before when we've been called to a couple of ODs. It's some designer drug. The Narcan has no effect on it. I don't know what the hell it is."

"But it's killing people?" Brad asked.

"It's called Red Rabbit," the other paramedic said. "It's a blend of ecstasy, ketamine, and god knows what else. I saw a notice about it. It's a party drug." He peered down at the dead woman. "If she took this before driving home, it's amazing she managed to stumble out of the car and through her front door. That shit would probably knock someone on her ass, if not out cold."

"That would explain the hit and run," Brad said.

"She was hit by a car?" the paramedic asked.

"No," I said, "before coming home tonight and dropping dead, she killed someone."

The lead paramedic rubbed a hand over his face. "That's karma."

"She's one cruel bitch." Brad exhaled.

An hour and a half later, the coroner arrived. He couldn't determine cause of death, so he'd have to perform a full autopsy on Macy Lowan. In the meantime, CSU checked her car and photographed everything we'd need. While they worked, Brad and I searched her apartment. We didn't find any indication she was an addict. She didn't have any pills or paraphernalia anywhere. Her apartment was clean.

Her employment history was spotless. She had committed no prior offenses. Macy Lowan didn't have a single DUI charge. What on earth possessed her to drive under the influence tonight?

"She's had three speeding tickets in the last ten years. And two parking tickets," Brad read from the MDT. "Nothing indicates she had a problem. Maybe tonight was just a bad night."

"Tell that to Garrett Rollins." I tapped against the center console. "Then again, Lowan might have always been careful. People like to party. They go out to decompress. She might have liked to drink and use drugs recreationally. Perhaps her designated driver fell through or she thought she was okay to drive when she wasn't. Regardless, her mistake cost her and someone else their lives." My heart ached for Garrett's family. They'd never be the same.

"I wonder if the accident's what killed her," Brad mused.

"What are you thinking?"

"I'm not sure. I didn't see any defensive wounds on her, but if she was high as a kite, she might not have had the wherewithal to fight back."

"The coroner didn't notice any trauma to her body, aside from her face and forearms. Both of which he seemed confident had been caused by the airbag."

"Yeah." He frowned at the screen before blowing out a breath, his head shaking from side to side.

"Do you want to tell me what's going on with you? We said no more secrets, remember?"

"The other night I went out to get some air. I got tired of being cooped up at home."

"Okay."

"Yeah, well, I don't exactly remember how I got home."

"Brad—"

"I know. That was stupid."

"Did you drive?"

"I know better than that. But the hit and run got me thinking that I could have wandered out into traffic or worse. I've just been having a rough go of it lately."

"It's only been a few weeks. If you need more time—"

"I need to work. I just got into a weird headspace. I'm good now." He met my eyes. "Promise."

He'd had a lot on his mind lately, but I wasn't going to push. Instead, I tried to cheer him up. "On the bright side, I think we just set a record for closing a case."

"That depends on how quickly we get through the paperwork."

I checked the time. "We should have it done by shift change."

"There you go again, jinxing us."

I rolled my eyes, but I couldn't keep this up much longer. "In all seriousness, are you okay?"

"Better than." He glanced at me. "How 'bout you? Are you sure you don't prefer having Jake Voletek as your partner?"

"Bite your tongue. I meant what I said. I want you. We just have to find our rhythm. But we're getting there. Do you know what would get us there even faster?"

"What?" he asked suspiciously.

"If you tell me why my mom's teaching you how to make her secret lasagna."

He laughed. "My lips are sealed."

THREE

We'd only pulled up to the precinct when the hospital called to notify us that Garrett Rollins' wife was there. I let out a sigh. So much for putting off that conversation. "Why don't I go speak to the widow while you get started on our report?"

"Are you sure, Liv?"

"Yeah, no problem."

He handed me the key he'd just taken from the ignition. "I don't mind going with you."

"I know, but there's no reason for it. I got this."

"All right. I'll drop by narcotics and see if they know anything about Red Rabbit or our hit and run driver." He gave me a small smile. "We'll divide and conquer."

I went around the car and got behind the wheel. After adjusting the seat and mirrors, I headed for the hospital. This had been some shift. Two bodies, one crime. I couldn't help but think they were both victims. Lowan made a bad decision; one neither of them should have had to pay for to this extreme.

I didn't know what to say to Mrs. Rollins. Nothing would make this situation any better, so I'd keep it simple. All she needed to know was the basics. I'd stick to the facts, express my sympathy, and get out of there.

Once the vehicular homicide was squared away, I'd have

to notify Lowan's next of kin. That would be another horrible experience. Perhaps my partner was right. Maybe I did jinx us.

The woman working at the hospital information desk pointed me to a private waiting area. I found Mrs. Rollins sitting in the corner, her elbows on her knees, while she held a cup of coffee in her hands. She wore a sweatshirt and a pair of pajama pants. I wondered if she was aware she only partially changed out of her bedclothes.

"Mrs. Rollins?"

She looked up, her face devoid of makeup and her eyes glazed over. "Uh-huh."

"I'm Detective Liv DeMarco. I'm working your husband's case."

She nodded a few times, her gaze dropping to the floor. "Do you know what happened?"

"Yes, ma'am. The red light camera caught the entire incident."

"And the driver?" She swallowed, the cup in her hand shaking.

"The driver's been identified. I'm sorry for your loss."

"What's going to happen to him? Has he been arrested?"

"She," I corrected, "and no."

"Why the hell not?"

"I'm sorry, ma'am. But that's not possible." I glanced around, but the room was empty. The hospital administrators had left her here to process her grief in private. "The driver's dead."

She looked up from the floor, finding my eyes. She opened her mouth, thought better of saying what came to mind, and looked to the side. "Do you know why she hit my husband?"

"Drugs were involved."

"Of course." Anger leached from her words. "I always told Garrett to be careful. Walking home late at night, in the dark, that's not safe. It's not safe for anyone. I was stupid. I thought he'd get mugged or jumped, not hit by a car."

My phone vibrated against my thigh, but I ignored it. "Is there anyone I can call for you?"

She bit her lip to hold back her tears and shook her head. "I haven't told the kids yet. I refused to believe this was real. But they showed me Garrett." Her face contorted, and I reached for a tissue box on the nearby table and held it out to her. She shook her head, too stubborn to give in to the tears. "At least the person who did this can't do it again."

"Yes, ma'am." I pulled out my notepad. "Would you mind answering just a few questions?"

"Go ahead."

The case was open and shut. But I asked if she or her husband knew the driver or if he had any enemies. Unsurprisingly, the answer was no. I wrote down the case number and gave her my card. "You can pick up a copy of the police report at the precinct. It should be ready by this afternoon. But there's no rush. You can get it if and when you need it."

"Why would I need it?"

"For any insurance claims or civil proceedings."

"Who am I going to sue? You said the woman who did this is dead."

"That's something you can worry about later. If there's anything I can do or anything you need, don't hesitate." I stood. "Again, my condolences." Slowly, I made my way across the room, pausing when I heard her sob. A member of the hospital staff nearly collided with me as I opened the door. He nodded and stepped back, gesturing for me to go ahead. At least she wouldn't be alone.

Taking a breath, I reached for my phone. *One missed call from ADA Winters.* I hit the button, but the caller didn't leave a voicemail.

I dialed Logan back and found an unobtrusive place to stand between an artificial potted plant and the coffee machine. He answered on the second ring.

"Hey, Liv. Thanks for getting back to me so quickly. I'm sorry to call so early."

"Is it early?" It felt like midnight, but I'd worked graveyard, so my days and nights had flipped.

He let out a practiced chuckle. "I take it crime doesn't sleep."

"Not this morning. What's up?"

"Last night, Wilson Matthews was attacked."

"How is he?"

"They transported him to the hospital for tests. They're keeping him for observation. He's alive, but he took quite the beating. The doctors found bruises all over his body in various stages of healing. Whoever did this has been beating on him for a while."

"Did he report the abuse?"

"Not that I know of."

"What hospital?" I asked.

"City General."

"That's where I am. Are you stalking me, counselor?"

"No, but maybe I should have consulted my find a friend before I called you."

"Not funny. Do you know what happened? What's his condition?"

"The last I heard, he's stable."

"Then it must not have been Matthews who was attacked."

Logan snorted. "His attorney claims Matthews sustained a pretty nasty concussion. From the way his cell looks, his attacker might have intended to hang him, but his screams drew too much attention."

"So he was attacked inside his cell."

"I think so."

"How could he be attacked in his cell after lights out? He should have been alone. You swore to me the judge tossed him into solitary. Did that change?"

"Not that I know of." He let out an uneasy laugh. "To be quite honest, at this point, I don't know much. I just got in. Matthews' attorney is already petitioning for another bail hearing, citing unsafe conditions."

"Dammit. Who could have attacked him?"

"I don't know. It's under investigation, but I just wanted to give you the heads-up."

"Thanks."

"Are you okay?"

"How can you ask me that? Matthews killed fourteen women. If he goes free, he's going to run or kill again. Both, probably."

"I'll see what I can do."

"Same here." I hung up, my head spinning from the unexpected nosedive my morning had taken. "Stupid jinx."

The woman at the information desk looked up when I approached. "Is there anything else I can do for you, Detective?"

"Actually, I heard a prisoner was transported here last night. His name is Wilson Matthews. Can you give me his room number?"

She glanced around before leaning over the keyboard. "I assume this is urgent police business."

"It is."

"Figured." She looked up. "Room 623."

"Any updates on his condition?"

Again, she looked around, shifty-eyed. "He was admitted for head trauma. He's stable but remains under observation."

I tapped the desk in front of the partition as a silent thanks and conducted an about-face. The short elevator ride didn't give me much time to think. The hospital smelled like disinfectant and cafeteria food. It wasn't an appetizing odor. But I'm sure Matthews must be enjoying it.

After getting out on the sixth floor and following the signs which led me down two different hallways, I spotted the room. One guard sat outside the door while another corrections officer remained seated inside. I pulled out my badge as I approached the bored CO.

"Something I can do for you?" he asked.

I peered into the room. Matthews' wrists handcuffed to the bedrail. From what I could tell, he appeared to be sleeping. A large, white bandage had been wrapped around his head, securing a cold pack in place. From the red that had bled through, he had at least one laceration.

"Not really. I just thought I'd stop by and see if you needed anything. Coffee? Water?" I glanced at the cup beside him.

"I'm good."

"Great." I rocked back on my heels. "That's Wilson Matthews, the serial killer."

"You a groupie or something?"

"I'm the reason he's in handcuffs."

The CO snorted and held out his hand for me to shake. "Bet you were hoping he was dead."

"How is he?"

"I'd say the fucker got off easy compared to the things he's done. He'll be back behind bars as soon as the doctors clear him."

I wasn't so sure about that, but I kept my mouth shut. "Do you have any idea what happened to him? I heard he was attacked inside his cell. Wasn't he in isolation?"

"He was. Is. It was the damnedest thing. His howling woke up the entire cell block. But by the time we got to him, he had blacked out. No one else was around."

"What about the cell door?"

"Locked."

"Were you the first to arrive?"

The guard frowned, growing suspicious of my questions. "No."

"Who was?"

"Officer Clemmons, but he's a good guard. A good man."

"Is that Clemmons?" I nodded to the man inside Matthews' room.

"No, that's McCall."

"Did Matthews say what happened?"

The guard let out a displeased grunt. "He says Officer Clemmons attacked him."

"What do you think?"

"No way."

I peered one more time into the room. Matthews shifted slightly, but his eyes remained closed. That bastard planned this. I just didn't know how.

FOUR

The sound in the hallway roused him from his dreamless sleep. Wilson Matthews opened his eyes, glad to wake up in a room with natural light and soft, adjustable bedding. His head throbbed and buzzed. He knew he should be in pain, but he couldn't quite feel it. The IV drip probably had something to do with that.

The guard at the end of his bed, Henry McCall, stared at the television screen. The speaker was attached to a remote which belonged to the bed, but the guard had taken it, probably for security reasons. Matthews didn't bother to look at the screen. He knew McCall would be watching the morning show. The man came to work every day and jabbered on and on about the segments and hosts while he patrolled.

Instead, Matthews noticed a blur of brown streaked with golden honey highlights. He started to smile, but moving his facial muscles triggered a sharp pain behind his eyes so he kept his expression neutral. Slowly, he glanced in her direction. He couldn't believe she was here.

Detective DeMarco remained outside his room, oblivious to his stare. The heart monitor beeped as his pulse and blood pressure increased. Her presence aroused him.

McCall shifted in his seat. Quickly, Matthews closed his eyes, his face and posture as relaxed as he could make them. But he yearned to get out of bed. He wanted to hear her footsteps echo against the tile and inhale her scent. From what he remembered, she had smelled faintly of vanilla and strawberries. Perhaps it was her shampoo or some lotion she used. Regardless, he enjoyed it. Most prey wore bolder, obvious perfumes—flowers and musks, but not the feisty detective.

Cautiously, he lifted his eyelids just enough to see a tiny slit of light. At that moment, she turned to look into the room. Again, the monitor beeped. This would be fun. Now all he had to do was wait until after the bail hearing. Surely, no judge in good conscience could let a man with an otherwise spotless record, like Matthews, die inside a cell while awaiting trial for crimes he swore he didn't commit.

He listened as the soft thumps against the tile grew fainter and fainter. Then he let himself go back to sleep. This time, the medicines allowed him to dream of Detective DeMarco in the coral dress, bound to her bed while he took his time to punish her for all the lies.

*   *   *

I was still in the elevator, on my way back to the lobby, when ADA Winters answered his phone. "He can't get out on bail, Logan. If he goes free, he's going to run. And once he escapes, he'll kill again."

"I know, Liv. You already said that."

"It's worth repeating."

"I'll do my best, but it's not up to me. It's up to the judge."

"Then you have to make him understand what's at stake." I told Winters everything the guard had said. "I don't believe a corrections officer attacked him."

"You said Clemmons did this?"

"That's who Matthews accused."

"You should know, Clemmons is already under investigation. Other inmates have filed complaints against him. There are two allegations currently pending."

"Why is this guy still working? He should be suspended until the investigation is complete."

"It's called staff shortages and overcrowding. Since there was no proof, he was allowed to remain at work."

"Has the bail hearing already been set?"

"It's this afternoon. It goes before Judge Hessler."

"Dammit." Hessler would rather allow a guilty man to go free than allow an innocent man to rot in a cell. Philosophically, I found that admirable, but as a cop, I didn't agree, particularly in this case. "Is there anything I can do? Do you want me to speak to the judge? Provide a statement?"

"I'll make the same argument I made last time. That was good enough to have Matthews' bail denied once. It should be enough. Realistically, nothing has changed. The circumstances and evidence remain the same. Matthews' attorney will try to confuse things, but I'll do my best to keep that from happening."

"Call me with the verdict."

"I will." His voice grew softer. "Whatever happens, this isn't your fault. You built a solid case. He's going down for those murders." There was something else Winters wasn't saying, but I wasn't sure what it was.

"Thanks, Logan."

"Based on your tone, I take it that doesn't make you feel any better."

"I'll feel fine once I know Matthews is back inside a cell."

"Hopefully, this little field trip won't last more than a day or two. Just hang tight."

Once I made it back to the precinct, I went straight to my desk. The news had left me in a daze, but I had to focus on my current case. The Rollins murder was squared away, but I still needed more information on the driver.

The ME's office hadn't called yet, but I knew it would take hours before we got the toxicology report back. It could be days before we heard anything about the autopsy, and that's only if they deemed it important enough to rush. Given the givens, Lowan's death didn't seem like a priority.

I pulled up her profile, but she was clean. Her prints weren't even in the system. We'd IDed her from her license.

"Hey," Brad appeared behind me, "what's wrong? You look like you've seen a ghost. Rough notification?"

"They all are, but that's not it."

He took his usual seat across from mine. "What's wrong?"

I shook the question away. Despite everything, I nearly smiled. I missed seeing him there. "Where were you?"

"I was upstairs talking to the guys in narcotics. Red Rabbit's been circulating for a while now. It's nothing new. Lethal overdoses are rare. Most are complications related to spikes in body temperature and dehydration. The same kinds of complications we see with MDMA use."

"Do they think Lowan got a hold of a bad batch of Red Rabbit?"

"Possibly, or she just had a bad reaction. We won't know more until we get the autopsy back." He held a folder out to me. "I'm almost done with the report on the hit and run."

I scanned it, adding in a few details from what Garrett Rollins' widow had said. "That's one case closed." I shut the folder and pushed it to the side. "I ran Lowan again. Nothing indicates someone intentionally wanted to harm her."

"That was my impression too."

"Have you reached out to her next of kin?"

"I couldn't find anyone. She lost her family in a car accident when she was fourteen. She went into the system, bounced from foster home to foster home until she graduated, but her good grades got her a full ride. Room and board, tuition, everything. She took on a work study and had a part time job. Based on her financials, she scrimped and saved everything she could. When she graduated last year, she moved to the townhouse and got a marketing job."

"What about significant others?"

"According to her social media, she's been single for the last ten months. I'm waiting for her phone records to come through, but I'm not sure any of this is necessary."

"Probably not, but it doesn't hurt to be prepared."

Brad stretched back in his chair and yawned. "Do you want to tackle anything else before we call it quits?"

"I think we've done all we can for now. We'll pass the rest off to next shift in case they need something to do."

He finished making a few notes, straightened his desk, and logged off his computer. "How about we get smoothies on the way home?"

"Actually, I'm gonna hang around here for a while. You go on ahead. I'll find another ride."

"Are you sure?" He scrutinized me. "Is everything okay?"

I wasn't sure if I should tell him Wilson Matthews had requested a new bail hearing. Brad hadn't worked the Matthews case, but he had crossed paths with the serial killer while investigating Ian Gallagher, a corrupt cop. Since the two were tangentially linked and Brad was already having a rough time, I thought it was best to avoid having this conversation, if possible. "It's fine. I just need to talk to Voletek about one of the cases we worked."

Brad jerked his chin toward the double doors. "Did you plan that out?"

I laughed. "No, but he must have a sixth sense whenever someone says his name."

"In that case, I'll hang out 'til you're finished. Then we'll get breakfast."

Before I could open my mouth in protest, Voletek approached our joined desks. He went behind Brad's chair, grasped my partner's shoulders, and drummed on them for a moment. "Hey, man, you're finally back among the living." Voletek grinned, releasing his grip on Brad before resting his hips against the side of the desk. "I was about to say you're in my seat, but it's good to have things back to normal. How ya feeling?"

"Better," Brad said. "I hope you kept my partner out of trouble, Jake."

Voletek smirked at me. "More or less."

"I'm wondering about the less." Brad eyed me, silently urging me to discuss the case in front of him.

"Have you heard from ADA Winters this morning?" I

asked.

Voletek shook his head. "I don't like that face. What's wrong, Liv? Did someone put the wrong address on a warrant or something?"

"Worse." And now I had to let the cat out of the bag. "Wilson Matthews petitioned for another bail hearing."

"There's not a chance in hell he'll get it." Voletek eyed me. "Don't worry, princess."

"Don't call me that."

"That's the last time. I promise. At least for today. But seriously, when we arrested him, he had the murder weapon on him. We proved he had dates scheduled with the murdered escorts. And given his more than ample means and lack of close community ties, no judge is going to let a flight risk like that out on bond."

"I hope you're right."

Brad's gaze flicked from me to Voletek and back again. "Is that why you look so distraught, Liv?"

"Maybe."

Brad sighed. "Matthews might get out."

"Like I said," Voletek interjected, "I don't see how that's even possible. He's a suspected killer."

"Circumstances have changed," I said. "He was attacked while in isolation. He claims a guard is responsible."

"Has he said anything else?" Brad asked. "Is he making any new claims or offering information in exchange for a deal?"

I narrowed my eyes, picking up on my partner's sudden apprehension. "I don't think so. Winters didn't mention anything about it."

Brad nodded a few times. "Come on, Liv. It's been a long night. Let's get something to eat. Then I'll drop you off at home. With all that's going on, you should probably get some sleep. I know I'm exhausted."

"Well, you did lose an organ." Voletek feigned a jab to the side of Brad's stomach but stopped before making contact. "Is an appendix even an organ?"

"It's a vestigial organ, so yeah, I guess that makes it an organ. All I know is I'm a couple of pounds lighter." Brad gingerly patted his side.

"That's just from being sick, not the surgery." Though, my excuse was also a lie. "And it's not like you had a couple of pounds to spare."

"Which is why we need breakfast. Now," Brad said.

"Fine." I pushed away from my desk.

"Here," Brad handed Jake the file we'd been working on, "see what you can do with this."

"Gee, thanks, guys."

"Don't mention it." I winked at him and mouthed thank you. Voletek nodded and slid behind his desk.

FIVE

Brad stared out the windshield, one hand on the steering wheel, the other holding his smoothie. The muscles in his forearms bunched, and the veins in his hands protruded from beneath his skin. If my partner gripped the wheel any tighter, he'd leave permanent indentions.

"This is why I wasn't going to mention it to you. It's your first official day back, and you have enough on your plate," I said. "I didn't want to stress you out."

"We said no secrets, Liv."

"I know. I wasn't keeping it a secret."

"Yes, you were."

"Are you mad?"

He let out an exasperated grunt. "I should be, but I get it."

"I was going to tell you."

"When?"

"After Logan tells me how the bail hearing goes."

"Has the FBI contacted you about their investigation?"

"Not lately. The last time I spoke to Agent Anderson, he said he was still looking into Detective Gallagher's phone records." I resisted the urge to gnaw on the paper straw. Instead, I drank more of the fruit-laden green smoothie and tried to see things objectively. "Voletek's right. No judge would let a serial killer wander free until his trial date. Murderers rarely get released while awaiting trial, and Wilson Matthews is the worst of the worst. So we shouldn't worry."

"Probably not." Brad sighed. "So why do you look so freaked out?"

"Logan's phone call. He wouldn't have bothered to tell me about this if he didn't believe there was a strong possibility Matthews will get bailed out."

Brad waited for me to finish my smoothie before handing me his cup to hold. "Detective Gallagher extorted Matthews. He offered to cover up the serial killer's crimes in exchange for cash. Lots of it." He pulled into the parking garage two blocks from my apartment and rolled down his window to grab a ticket. "But the Feds haven't found a paper trail linking Matthews to Gallagher. The extortion was always paid in cash. Gallagher was careful."

"And so is Matthews. The calls from Matthews never originated from the same number. That's why Voletek and I had such a hard time pinning him down. He mainly used VOIPs and burners. The Feds can't even establish a consistent line of communication between the two men."

"Right." Brad stopped circling when he found an empty space on the third level. He cut the engine and took the cup from my hands. He stared into my eyes. "Do you think my investigation into Detective Gallagher's corruption is going to get out?"

"I don't know. But I don't care about that."

He raised his eyebrows. "You don't?"

"Okay, maybe I care a little, but only because I don't want any of Gallagher's buddies to come knocking. Who knows what a bunch of vindictive assholes with badges might do?" Images of Brad beaten and bloody came to the forethoughts of my mind, but I forced them away.

"I don't want that either." Brad sucked absently on the straw. "And I sure as shit don't want any of this to bounce back on you."

"Maybe we have it wrong. We don't even know if anyone knowingly aided Gallagher in destroying evidence and selling out witnesses. He might have been working alone."

"The Feds are playing it so close to the vest, I have no idea."

"When I arrested Matthews, he never mentioned Detective Gallagher. I don't know why he would now."

"Gallagher's dead. I'm sure by now Matthews must have heard about it. That means he can say whatever he wants and no one's going to contradict him."

"Wouldn't that implicate Matthews as the killer he is?"

"What you don't know is Gallagher threatened to kill Matthews if he uttered a word about their arrangement to anyone. But now, Matthews has nothing to fear by coming forward." Brad put his cup on top of the dash and stared out the window. "I wish I'd known who Wilson Matthews was or what he was doing when I first encountered him. Maybe I could have stopped him from killing those two women."

"That's not on you. Matthews wasn't your mark. He was mine."

Brad exhaled slowly. "Maybe, but I knew the types of people Gallagher worked for. I should have assumed the worst."

I studied my partner, seeing the creases in his brow and the tensed muscles in his neck and shoulders. "What do you think will happen if Matthews runs his mouth?"

"I don't know. He could try to blame the murders on Gallagher. Since Gallagher investigated seven of the original twelve murders and probably tampered with the crime scenes, it might not be that hard to garner support for that idea."

"Especially since Gallagher came to my apartment intending to kill us both."

"Maybe I have it wrong," Brad said. "Matthews might try to make a deal instead. He could have an insurance policy against Gallagher, but since Gallagher's six feet under, I'm not sure the prosecutor's office cares. It'll depend on what else Matthews has on Gallagher—his associates, other crimes, things like that."

"You don't think Matthews will get immunity."

"Hell no. He's a psycho. No one's going to cut him loose.

Y'know, even if Matthews talks, it'll only prove just how corrupt Detective Gallagher was. The truth can't hurt us. Not really. At least in terms of my investigation."

"Tell that to the hole in your side."

"I'd take this any day over the possibility some corrupt scumbag's waiting to compromise us or a witness again. Gallagher did that. He betrayed the badge and his fellow cops. You, me, all of us. Maybe this is a good thing. If Matthews talks, the truth will come to light. All the measures Captain Grayson and IAD have gone to in order to protect me won't be necessary. This could be our silver lining. We could finally wash our hands of this."

I wasn't sure our fellow brothers and sisters in blue would take kindly to Brad investigating one of our own, even though Gallagher posed a danger to all of us. But someone had to do it. It was the right call, and I'd stand by and support my partner no matter what. "I hope you're right, but that doesn't mean Matthews should walk around freely, even if it is just temporary. He's dangerous. His freedom won't be good for anyone. If he gets acquitted, I don't want to know how many more kills he'll rack up before he gets caught again."

Brad assessed me. "We never really talked about your case or how it connected to mine." He reached out and brushed my hair behind my shoulder, glancing at the fading scar at the back of my neck. "Our psychic connection is a little rusty. Tell me what's going through your mind because I'm out of my depth here."

"Even after Voletek and I arrested him, Matthews seemed so sure of himself. He was certain he'd get out. He told me he'd see me soon."

"You can't let this prick get inside your head."

"He's not."

Brad gave me that annoying look which said he knew better.

"Okay, he is, but after everything that happened with you and Gallagher, I'm more afraid of Matthews causing additional fallout. He's the scorched earth type."

"He'll burn everything around him. And he knows I was your partner."

My jaw dropped. "What?"

"Gallagher told him. He wanted to convince Matthews he could make the case you were building against him disappear. Gallagher thought I was his ace in the hole, or at least that's what he wanted Matthews to believe."

"Okay, now I'm freaking out."

"Don't." He ran his hand down my arm and gave my hand a squeeze. "Gallagher didn't have any way of stopping you. He just wanted to convince Matthews he did in order to get paid. But once he realized it was too little, too late, he decided to do everything he could to make sure Matthews went down hard. He had to discredit the prick in case he decided to talk. For all we know, maybe Gallagher has some hidden evidence stashed away that ADA Winters could use against Matthews."

"Brad, stop. Matthews knows you. He met you. He knows we're connected. What if he gets out and targets you?"

"Why would he?"

"I don't know. But I know Matthews wants to hurt me. That's one way to do it."

"Matthews is more likely to make a move on Voletek. As far as Matthews knows, I'm a disgraced ex-cop."

I thought about the sting Voletek and I had set up and the way Matthews had stared with jealous annoyance as Voletek flirted and touched me. "Maybe."

"See? Plus, Matthews insists he's innocent. He can't offer information in exchange for a deal without confessing his sins, and he sure as hell can't go after a cop without dire consequences. We'll be okay, Liv. He can't hurt you."

"Again, you're probably right." I just wished I could convince the uneasy feeling in my stomach that Brad was right. I'd never been so stuck in my head before. Recent events had me on edge. I should probably schedule another appointment with the department shrink to discuss this newfound anxiety, but for now, I'd have to chalk it up to a crazy day. After all, this was Brad's first day back. It'd take some adjusting.

"Most serial killers keep trophies. Did you find anything like that when you arrested Matthews?" Brad asked.

"No. A search of Matthews' apartment and car didn't turn up anything." He'd covered his tracks pretty well, but if he was free to move about, he'd make sure anything we missed disappeared.

"It's not important," Brad insisted. "Let's just keep our fingers crossed that ADA Winters can convince the judge to keep Matthews locked up until his trial date and all this worrying is for nothing."

"You're right. There's no point in jumping to conclusions. You should head home and get some sleep. Who knows what next shift will bring?"

"It'll be fine as long as you don't jinx us again." Brad opened his car door.

"Where are you going?"

"I need to stretch my legs, so I thought I'd walk you home." He remained beside me as we headed down the stairs. "Are you meeting Emma for yoga?"

"Not today. I have to wait for the mechanic to call about my car. He said it should be ready by this afternoon. The part came in yesterday."

"All right." He stopped in front of my apartment building. "If for some reason you don't get it back, call me, and I'll pick you up for work."

"Thanks, but he promised it'd be ready today." I bumped against Brad's arm. "I'll see you tonight. If you play your cards right, I'll even bring you lunch."

"I'll bring the coffee."

I opened the apartment door. Turning back around, I asked, "Do you remember how I take it?"

"I'll just have to wing it. If I screw it up, I'll drink it. No big deal."

"Jerk," I teased.

"Sleep well, Liv."

"You too."

But I didn't sleep well. The bright, daytime sun didn't help with my sleep issues. It'd been a while since I'd worked graveyard. I'd adjust, but it would take some time.

I twisted and turned before beating my pillow into submission. Thoughts of bloody crime scenes, that smug look on Wilson Matthews' face, and the sight of paramedics working on Detective Gallagher while my partner nearly bled out on my carpet only a few feet away swirled through my head, mixing with images of Macy Lowan dead in her foyer.

You probably should have gone home, my internal voice said. Mom liked it when I stayed with them, but I was a capable adult. Still, I hadn't been able to shake off the bad juju since the night Brad had been attacked inside my apartment. Emma had even tried burning sage to cleanse the place, but neither of us actually believed that would work. So it didn't.

After more readjusting and pinning the drapes to the wall to keep out the light, I finally fell asleep. A few hours later, I awoke with a start. Images of Jake Voletek dead in my bathtub with his wrists slashed while Wilson Matthews stood over him holding a knife dripping with blood were seared in my brain. It was just another nightmare. I'd been having them frequently enough but never one like this.

Taking a deep breath, I grabbed my phone off the dresser and sent a text to Jake. *How's it going?*

He replied back a few seconds later. *Are you asking about the Lowan case or Matthews?*

I let out a sigh. *Either.*

The answer's the same. Nothing yet. Tox should be waiting for you when you get in, but it hasn't crossed my desk.

I thanked him and eased back against the pillow. Brad was right. I couldn't let Matthews get in my head. Every perp made threats. This was no different, but the conviction behind the killer's words when he said he wouldn't remain in custody had me convinced.

I knew the score. Matthews wasn't done yet. If given the chance, he'd finish what he intended to start in that hotel.

Moments before I drifted off, my phone rang. This time, it wasn't a dream. My car was fixed and ready for pick-up. I got up, showered, dressed, and waited for someone from the dealership to come get me. Brad had told me to leave my car with the guys in the garage, who worked on the patrol cars, but since my mom had convinced me to get the extended warranty, I'd taken it to the dealership when the check engine light came on last week. According to the guy, one of the sensors was broken.

"It's fixed now. You shouldn't have any more problems with it," he said.

I signed the form and picked up my keys. "I hope you're right."

I'd just gotten to the door when my phone rang again. *ADA Winters.*

Steeling myself for whatever was to come, I glanced back at the car guy. More than anything, I hoped his statement would hold true for everything else in my life and not just my vehicle. "Tell me you have good news."

"Not quite. We have a problem."

SIX

I paced back and forth inside ADA Winters' office. He watched from his seat. His blue eyes trailing my every movement.

"Detective DeMarco, please." He gestured to the chair.

"Sorry." Whenever he started using titles and last names, I knew he was serious. "I just don't understand this. Doesn't the jail have cameras? Wouldn't the attack have been caught on video?"

"One would think." He slid the information toward me. "I've had investigators look into it. This is all we've gotten so far. The inside of Matthews' cell is too far away to be caught on the nearest security camera, so we have no way of knowing what happened inside."

"But the camera would catch anyone who entered that cell block. Officer Clemmons wasn't there."

"Maybe." Logan's shoulders hitched upward. "Maybe not."

"No, this isn't some debate, counselor. That is a fact. Clemmons doesn't appear on the footage until after Matthews starts screaming. As far as I can tell, no one entered Matthews' cell."

"Matthews' attorney could make the argument that

Clemmons, as a veteran corrections officer, knows where all the security cameras and blind spots are inside the jail. And since this wouldn't exactly be his first offense, it wouldn't be that much of a stretch."

"It's a stretch. No one unlocked Matthews' cell until they entered to render assistance."

"The guards have access to records. The data could be compromised."

"Bullshit." I shook my head, hoping to make sense of this lunacy. "I thought you said Clemmons was under investigation. That doesn't make him guilty."

"He has two pending complaints against him, but he has priors."

"Jesus." I flipped through the copy of Clemmons' personnel file. "For what?"

"Use of excessive force."

"And they kept him on?"

"It was a while ago. A different time."

"He attended anger management and underwent additional training. Maybe he's reformed."

Logan gave me a look. "Sure, I can make that argument, but these two recent complaints suggest otherwise."

"They could be fabricated." I looked at the dates they'd been filed, but both had been prior to Matthews' arrest.

"I doubt that'll fly without proof."

"What are our options?"

His expression told me we didn't have options. "I pointed out the severity of the crimes Matthews is charged with, his personal wealth, and his lack of any real ties to the community."

"Given that Matthews quit his job, has no family in the city, and is staring down multiple life sentences, I'd say that's an understatement."

"The judge took all of it into consideration, but it wasn't enough."

"Can't we get Matthews transferred to another facility while he awaits trial? If he said Clemmons did this, let's get him away from that one bad apple. Or what if Clemmons gets suspended? That'll solve the problem, right?"

"The hospital found bruises all over Matthews' body.

Someone's been beating on him regularly. He said it's not just Clemmons. He said the other guards are involved too. They take turns."

"Again, there's no proof to these claims."

"Proof?" Logan's eyebrows went skyward. "The doctors photographed the damage." He flipped open another file and spread out the images for me to see.

I stared at them. "Those don't look like bruises from a beating. Getting punched or kicked looks different." I'd seen enough marks on Brad lately to know the difference.

"The guards carry clubs."

I examined the photos. "I don't believe it."

"Shit like this happens, Liv. That's why we need reform and additional prisoner protections."

"Is that what Judge Hessler said?"

"Yeah, right before he set bail at five million. Since most of Matthews' assets have been frozen, he can't pay it. He'll have to find a bondsman, and that won't be easy."

"That might buy us a few days. Max."

"In the meantime, the judge has ordered he remain in custody under medical care until his injuries heal."

I'd already read the medical records his attorney had presented on his behalf. Matthews had bruises covering forty percent of his body. His ribs and collarbone had hairline fractures which had already started healing. The night of the alleged attack, he sustained a concussion and possible linear skull fracture. "I know this sounds crazy, but Matthews is playing us."

"He didn't fake those injuries."

"Maybe not, but no one saw how any of them happened or when. It's a jail. A lot goes on. The other inmates would be all over this if the guards were responsible."

"Unless they're afraid."

"Someone would squeal." I stared at the photos again. "I think these were self-inflicted."

"How is that even possible?"

"I'm not sure. I'm probably wrong, but that's what my gut's telling me." I sat back in the chair. "Look at the facts. He's in solitary. He has a cell to himself. He doesn't get near the other inmates, and with all the cameras in that area, I don't see how the guards could lay hands on him without something getting filmed."

"I'll keep digging, but it's probably too late. Judge Hessler already set bail. Getting it revoked will take some sort of provocation. We'll have to wait for him to commit another crime or attempt to flee."

"That's not an option," I said.

"The only other thing I can do is request to have the trial date moved up." But Logan knew that was a bad idea. I just wasn't sure why.

"What happens if you do?"

"Discovery gets cut short. We have less time to build our foundation and investigate any potential snafus. From what I know of defense counsel, that's exactly what he's hoping I'll do, which means he has a trick up his sleeve. I just don't know what it is."

"Damned if we do, and damned if we don't."

"Yeah." Logan pointed to the clock on the wall. "How did it get this late? It's no wonder it's so quiet out there." He jerked his chin toward his open office door. "Everyone else must have gone home for the night. Am I keeping you from anything?"

"I have to go to work in a few hours."

"How about we order dinner, and you tell me everything there is to know about Wilson Matthews and the investigation?"

"You know everything I do about the case. We kept you looped in every step of the way. It's all aboveboard."

"I know. You do good police work. You always cover your ass." His eyes narrowed. "I'm sensing there's a problem you're not telling me about. What is it?"

"Detective Ian Gallagher worked seven of the murders, all unsolved."

"Gallagher, the cop who was recently killed, believed to have been murdered due to his gang ties?"

"That's the rumor."

"You're afraid that's going to taint the case?"

"Could it?"

"I don't see how. Gallagher had nothing to do with your case or the arrest."

I peered out the door to Logan's office before closing it. "This is off the record, but I know for a fact Gallagher extorted money from Matthews in exchange for concealing evidence of his crimes. Now that Gallagher's dead, I'm not sure if Matthews plans to come forward with this."

Logan stared at me. "How long have you known about this?"

"I found out after he was arrested."

"Did Matthews tell you this?"

"No."

"Does this have anything to do with the FBI looking into police corruption at your precinct?"

"Yes."

He rubbed his eyes and rocked back in his chair. "I'll call them in the morning and see if they have anything to share regarding the Matthews case. Then I'll reassess. But I don't see how this would change anything."

"Thanks. I just don't want you to be blindsided, especially on the off chance it could result in Matthews going free."

Logan opened his drawer and pulled out a stack of takeout menus. "Is he your first serial killer?"

"No, but he's the first killer I've encountered who takes such a perverse joy out of stalking his victims before bleeding them dry. He's a sicko. He does it for sport. I don't want to see more women suffer because a cop or a corrections officer screwed up. And given the way he is, the only reason he'll stop killing is if someone makes him."

SEVEN

According to the coroner's report, Macy Lowan bled to death. I hadn't expected that. The toxicology report showed she had MDMA in her system. But given the blood around her nose, mouth, and eyes, the coroner ran more than just a basic drug test to figure out the cause.

"The coroner found blood thinners and anti-coagulants coursing through her," I said. "It looks like the accident killed her too."

Brad rubbed his chin, but his eyes remained fixed on his computer screen. "Why was she taking those medications? She was young. Normally, that kind of stuff is prescribed to an older crowd."

"I don't know." I dropped the report and flipped through the files that had found their way to my desk. "We don't have her medical records, so I'm not sure. She could have had some kind of condition."

"She probably shouldn't have been drinking or using drugs, if that's the case."

"Obviously." He didn't snort or offer a response. Clearly, something had his attention. "What are you looking at?" I asked.

"Nothing."

"So, naked women?"

It took a moment for my words to register, and then he tore his gaze away from the screen. "What?"

"Never mind. It's no fun when you're not paying attention."

"I'm paying attention now. What about naked women?"

I stifled a chuckle. "I see what your priorities are. For the record, I was asking if you were looking at naked women."

"The autopsy report didn't include photos."

"Not that. Jeez. It was a joke."

"For it to be a joke, it'd have to be funny."

"It was freaking hilarious." I jerked my chin in his direction. "Are you okay?"

"I'm just tired. You look about as good as I feel."

"Hey, now. That wasn't very nice."

He grinned. "How do you know it wasn't a compliment? Maybe I'm feeling fantastic."

"You just said you're tired, and you look like shit."

"Now that's just uncalled for." He pushed away from the desk. "I guess that means it's time we take a break. You want some more coffee?"

I picked up the travel mug Brad had brought me and gave it a shake. Empty. The sludge in the break room wasn't particularly appealing. "No, I'm okay."

"We could go for a ride and get some." He looked around the bullpen, but unlike our last shift, things were quiet.

"Yeah, all right." I closed the report and grabbed one of the handhelds. "We might as well have lunch or whatever meal one eats at four a.m." I grabbed the bag from the fridge and handed it to Brad as we made our way down the stairs. Tonight, it was my turn to drive.

Brad poked his head into the bag, eyeing the logo on the takeout containers. "Ooh, fancy."

"You can thank Logan Winters. He paid for it."

"You went to see him?"

"Uh-huh." I adjusted the mirrors and fastened my seatbelt. "You're good with uncured bacon, right?"

"Yes, Liv." He tucked the food back into the bag. "What did Winters say? Did the judge set bail for Wilson Matthews?"

I focused on the nearly empty road ahead of me. "Yep."

"Fuck. Doesn't he realize Matthews is a killer? He doesn't deserve to walk around freely."

"There were extenuating circumstances."

"Like?"

"Matthews claims he was abused. I don't know if it's true. But the judge gave him the benefit of the doubt. He has to come up with five million dollars if he wants to get out." I glanced at my partner. "I told Logan about Matthews' connection to Gallagher. He's going to reach out to the FBI, in case they found anything."

"Did you tell Winters what happened to Gallagher?"

"No, if Agent Anderson thinks he should know, he can tell him. But I don't see how it's relevant."

Brad's eyes remained on me. "Is that why you couldn't sleep? You were too busy with the ADA?" Although his words were meant to be teasing, his tone wasn't quite right.

"It was a few different things. The sunlight, the weird hours, y'know circadian rhythm issues, and then it was nightmares, and my car, and dealing with Matthews." I turned to look at him. "What's your excuse for not sleeping?"

"The same, minus the car. What did you dream about?"

"Voletek dead in my bathroom."

He let out an unexpected snort, which even surprised him. He placed his hand over his mouth and shook his head a few times. "Did you kill him?"

"No." I laughed, smacking my partner in the arm. "That's not funny."

"How often do you dream about Jake?"

I smacked him again. "Stop. The dream really freaked me out."

He sobered. "I know. They have a tendency to do that."

Before I could ask what his nightmare had been about, he pointed to the neon diner sign up ahead. "I bet if we ask nicely, Beatrice will reheat our burgers for us."

"You can ask, but I'll eat mine cold. I don't want anyone

spitting in my food."

"She wouldn't do that. She likes us. We're her favorite customers." He gave me that boyish grin he always used on her.

"All right, Dimples, but you're asking."

"Dimples? I don't have dimples. What happened to Brown Eyes?"

"Beatrice doesn't call you Brown Eyes. She calls you Dimples." I pulled the unmarked into one of the many vacant spots. "I don't think she's talking about your face."

"Liv—"

I pressed my hands to my ears. "I don't want to hear it, Romeo."

He scowled at me before grabbing the bag and exiting the car.

The bell above our heads chimed, and Beatrice looked up. "Sit anywhere," she said. "I'll be right with you."

"No rush," I said. "We're just here for coffee."

A moment later, she met us at our usual table in the corner. With practiced ease, she placed two mugs on the table and poured from a ceramic carafe before putting it down. "I haven't seen you guys in a while. I wondered what happened to you."

"Work," I said.

Brad smiled up at her. "We missed coming here. But this was an unplanned visit. Liv needed coffee."

I picked up the mug and inhaled deeply. "It smells great."

"You're in luck. I just opened a new bag of this organic Sumatran blend. Everyone's raving about it."

I took a sip. "I can see why."

Brad picked two packets of raw sugar out of the bowl and poured them into his mug before taking a sip. "Incredible. Is there any chance we could convince you to come to the precinct to make our coffee?"

She laughed, watching as he unpacked the takeout bag and placed the containers on the table. "Y'know, most people who come here don't arrive as prepared as the two of you. This is a diner. We do sell food. It's kind of our thing. You didn't have to bring your own."

"I'm sorry about that," he said. "We can get the coffees to go if it's a problem."

"Not a problem, at all. In fact, I wish a few of our pickier customers came as prepared as you." She peered down at the lettuce wrapped burgers which had been placed on top of our salads. "Do you want a plate?"

"We don't want to be any trouble," Brad said.

"No problem, sweetie." She grabbed two plates from behind the counter. "If you want to unwrap them, I can heat 'em up for you. Just a quick zap."

"Are you sure?" he asked.

I glanced at my partner. He was a smooth operator. He didn't even have to ask. "We don't want you to get in trouble. It's no big deal. Cold is fine."

She waved away my protest. "At this time of night, no one's gonna bat an eye. It's not exactly peak hours."

Brad slid our bacon, mushroom burgers out of their lettuce leaves and onto the plates. Beatrice swiped them off the table with a flourish and returned a minute later. "Is there anything else I can get you?"

He gave her a huge smile. "Just the check."

She eyed the handheld radio I'd placed on the table beside me. "Busy night?"

"We'll see." But I hoped not.

Knowing how often we had to run out in the middle of a meal, she brought us the check. Before I could even offer to pay, Brad handed her a twenty and thanked her again for reheating our lunch. She left us to eat in peace.

"I said I'd bring you lunch. You should let me pay for this."

"Next time." Carefully, he tucked the burger back into his lettuce wrap and took a bite. Blotting his lips, he said, "God, that's good."

I cut my burger into bite-sized pieces and sprinkled it on top of the salad. Then we ate in almost total silence. Brad appeared famished, as usual. He'd just downed the last bite of his burger and speared a cucumber from his salad when dispatch notified us of a body found inside a bar. Keying the radio, I told dispatch to show us responding and closed the container on my lunch.

"Thanks, Beatrice." Brad waved to her as we headed out. "Have a good night."

"You too."

The bar was only a few blocks away. I didn't bother with the siren. The call was about a body, not a crime in progress. I didn't see any reason to wake the neighborhood.

"It's after four. All the bars have shut down for the night," Brad said. "Who found the body?"

"Maybe it's an after-hours place."

He checked the address. "That's just a dive. They don't have anything going on after hours."

I parked in front of the bar. They had hosted a live band earlier. I wondered if that had something to do with the body inside. But this place didn't look popular enough to have been the scene of a stampede.

Two uniformed officers were near the door, speaking to a woman wearing a black apron and holding a mop. She kept gesturing toward the back corner of the bar. The mop in her hand swung emphatically with each of her movements.

"Ma'am, we need you to calm down," Officer Deagan said. "Speak slowly. What happened?"

She gestured again, her answer an endless string of Spanish.

Officer Gruper asked her to calm down and speak slower in her native language.

"I was cleaning and found her in the bathroom." She made the sign of the cross and clutched the crucifix that hung from a gold chain around her neck.

"Have you cleared the scene?" I asked.

The two officers shook their heads. "Not yet. We got here a minute before you did."

"Is anyone else here?" I asked the woman.

"No. I clean up after everyone goes home."

"We'll make sure." Brad headed toward the bathrooms.

Since the bar was closed, it only took a minute to determine the place was empty. "Have you found anything, Fennel?" I asked.

He stepped out of the men's room, his hand near his

weapon. He shook his head and pushed against the ladies' room door. The door moved about six inches before stopping. He took a step back. "Police. Is anyone in here?"

The cleaning woman spoke more frantically, but I only caught drips and drabs of what she was saying. My Spanish was rusty. I hadn't had any formal classes since college, and I'd never even been close to fluent. Despite that, I got the gist. There was a dead woman in the bathroom.

I peered through the crack in the door. On the floor was a young woman. "Shit. She could still be alive."

Brad shouted to the officers to call for an ambulance and forced the door open, moving her body out of the way with the edge of the door. As soon as it was wide enough, I slipped inside and felt for a pulse.

"Tell them they don't need to hurry. She's been dead for a while." Her skin was already cold. Blood dribbled out of her nose and from the corners of her eyes. On the counter, I found white dust and a crinkled baggie with the same rabbit logo I'd seen the previous night.

"Dammit." My partner rubbed a hand over his face. "What is in this shit?"

"I don't know." Her shirt had ridden up on her side. Slipping on a pair of gloves, I lifted it higher to find a large blue bruise.

"That looks fresh." Brad turned to examine the back of the bathroom door, but with all the graffiti and carvings, it was hard to tell if that's what had hit her. The bathroom was sole occupancy with a toilet and sink. He peered into the toilet.

"Anything?"

"No blood, but this place is disgusting."

"That goes without saying. It's a public restroom. CSU's going to hate this if they have to investigate." I didn't want to think how many DNA samples and fingerprints they'd have to analyze and rule out. I searched the woman's pockets, but I didn't find a wallet or ID. "Do you see her purse?"

"No."

"What about a phone?"

He checked the trash. "Nothing's in here. Does she have

any cash or credit cards?"

"Not on her." She wore makeup but no jewelry. "Maybe she was attacked and mugged." I pointed to her right hand. "Two of her nails are broken." A clamminess settled over me. "I don't like this. Do you think the cleaning lady saw anything?"

"Probably not." Brad pushed his way through the tiny opening. "I don't see any security cameras in the hallway."

I followed him out of the bathroom and headed for the officers. They'd finally gotten the cleaning lady to sit down at one of the tables. Quietly, I spoke to Deagan. We'd need the bartender and owner rounded up. He went outside to notify dispatch while I knelt near the woman.

Gruper remained close. His Spanish was much better than mine, so he translated, even though she seemed to understand everything I said.

From what I gathered, she washed the dishes while the band played. Only after the bar closed did she come out to clean up. She hadn't seen the woman prior to finding her in the bathroom.

"Do you remember if anyone got violent or aggressive?"

"That happens most nights," she said in English. "Too much booze, not enough common sense."

Brad joined us after thoroughly checking the entire bar. "Are there any security cameras inside?"

"I don't know," she said.

"Did you find anything?" I asked him.

"No. Maybe she didn't come out with a purse."

"Maybe not, but she looks young. She'd need an ID to drink."

Brad turned to the woman. "Does the bartender check IDs?"

She nodded.

"Every time?"

"Yes."

He narrowed his eyes at the emergency exit near the bathrooms. "Gruper, did you guys check out back?"

"We didn't have time to check anything before you arrived."

"Stay here," I said. "Guard the body. Wait for the

paramedics. Do what you can to keep the scene contained."

Officer Gruper gave me a strange look. "Isn't it already too late for that?"

"Do your best." I stepped away from the woman and followed Brad down the narrow hallway to the rear door. The door had a lock on the knob. Whoever left last could have flipped it on his way out. "That's not the type of security I'd expect from an establishment like this."

"This isn't exactly the classiest of places."

"True, but they have cash and liquor. Plenty of punk-ass kids would be happy to knock this place over."

The door groaned as Brad opened it, the rusty metal hinges protesting. A street lamp illuminated most of the rear of the bar. Two dumpsters leaned against the chain-link fence that stood on two sides.

I did a visual sweep of the area, but I didn't spot any blood. Cigarette butts littered the ground beside several broken bottles and crushed beer cans. I made my way past them, stopping to examine the four dilapidated lawn chairs. Most of the vinyl on the seats had worn away, leaving a dirty black film from constant exposure to the elements.

"Used rubbers." Brad pointed to several discarded condoms on the ground. "Whoever came out here to party must have done so days ago. These aren't new."

"Lovely."

The chain-link fence rattled. We turned toward the sound, but it immediately stopped. Silently, Brad signaled. Someone or something had to be over there. He motioned for me to keep talking while he reached for his weapon.

"Do you think someone was dealing out here?" I asked.

"Possibly. From what we've found, I'd say people come out here to party."

I followed him toward the fence, hoping to spot some security cameras. "It seems pretty private, and it's easy to gain access from inside and outside the bar." The sound of an approaching siren drew my attention.

"We should head back inside." Brad continued to edge closer to the dumpster. "We should get those two officers to start a search for her missing handbag."

"That's a good idea." I edged around one side of the fence while Brad went around the other.

"Police," he announced, just as a figure darted from behind the trash can, shoved my partner, and raced toward the street.

EIGHT

Brad let out an oomph, jerking backward more from reflex than injury.

I sprinted after the shadowy figure with Brad at my heels. "Stop right there."

But the person kept running. The figure raced around the side of the building, banging into the wall as he made the turn. He pushed off with his palm, righted himself, and kept going. He'd just made it to the street when the approaching ambulance nearly collided with him. The driver hit the brakes, which made a squealing, whooshing sound. The suspect froze in surprise.

I yanked him backward and onto the sidewalk. He crab-walked closer to the building, his entire body trembling.

"Are you okay?" I asked.

The suspect nodded, rubbing his head and knocking off the hood from his jacket. He was just a kid, probably not even old enough to drive.

Brad holstered his gun, his hand trembling almost as much as the kid. "What were you doing back there? Why did you run?"

The kid swallowed a few times, while the EMTs stepped out of the rig. "Is he okay?" the driver asked.

"I don't know. He hasn't spoken a word. He might be in shock." I knelt beside him. "Do you have any weapons on you?"

He stared at his shoes, shaking his head.

"My partner's going to pat you down. We just want to make sure."

He nodded, his voice stuck in his throat.

Brad checked him, but the kid didn't have anything on him.

"Can I take a look at you?" the EMT asked.

The kid blinked and stuttered, "I don't have any money."

"Don't worry about that." The paramedic crouched in front of him while I took the other paramedic aside to tell him about the body in the bar. Officer Deagan led him inside while Brad and I stayed behind to make sure the kid didn't run again.

"What's your name?" Brad asked while the EMT checked the kid's vitals.

"Vincent." He looked from my partner to me. "Price."

"Really?" Brad gave me a look.

"Yep."

"Why'd you run, Mr. Price?" I asked.

"I didn't want to get in trouble."

"Were you causing trouble?" Brad asked.

"No, sir."

"What were you doing near the dumpsters?"

"Nothing much."

"Then why run?"

"You're cops. I know what happens to kids like me when the cops show up."

"Were you inside the bar tonight?" I asked.

The kid shook his head.

"You ever been inside?" Brad asked.

"No, sir."

Again with the sir. I gave Brad a look. "Wow, first he shoves you and now he calls you sir."

"It's the jacket," Brad said. "He didn't see how nice it was when we were standing out back in the dark. Right, Vincent?"

Bewildered, the kid said, "You guys are weird."

"We get that a lot." Brad jerked his thumb toward me.

"Mostly, she gets that a lot."

The kid looked at me. "Really?"

"What were you doing back there?"

"Nothing."

"C'mon, we saw the empties and the condoms. Were you drinking and getting some action?"

"Nothing. I swear." His eyes went wide, and he looked to the paramedic for help. "I don't do drugs. I wasn't drinking. You can breathalyze me or whatever. I wasn't doing anything wrong."

"So why did you run?" Brad asked. "Why would you think you'd get in trouble?"

The kid shrugged. "You're cops. That's just what you do."

"You almost got splattered to the windshield like a bug. That's not smart. And being out this late, it's not safe either. Is there someone we should call for you?" I asked.

The kid looked even more agitated. "I wasn't doing anything illegal. I come out after the bars close and go through the trash. I pick up the bottles and cans and take them to the collection center. They pay me."

"If that's true, where's your bag of empties?" I asked.

The kid scratched his head a few times. "It's that black trash bag next to the dumpster. I put it there while I was looking inside the bin, but then I heard the door squeak, so I jumped out and hid."

"Why?"

"I got scared, okay? It's dark out, which means the freaks are out. Pushers and hos. I don't want to get involved in shit like that."

"Did you see a woman tonight?" I described the woman we found in the bathroom, but the kid hadn't seen her. "What about any drug dealers? Do you know anyone who's pushing Red Rabbit?"

"I didn't see anyone, except you."

Brad offered him a hand up. "Show me where you put the bag with your bottles and whatever else you found while dumpster diving. If you run again, I'll put you in cuffs. Got it?"

"Yes, sir."

Brad put a hand on the kid's shoulder and headed around the side of the building. I gave them a minute to talk, figuring the kid might be more willing to open up to Brad. Quickly, I ducked back inside to see what the paramedic had to say, but as I'd said, the woman was dead. He couldn't say anything for certain, but off the record, he said she'd probably been there for at least a couple of hours. Her facial muscles were already starting to show the onset of rigor mortis.

The coroner would be able to narrow down time of death, but she probably died right before the bar shut down for the night. No one else would have wanted to use the restroom, and even if they did, they would have eventually given up when the incessant knocking and badgering had done nothing to revive the woman.

"Can you speculate on what killed her?"

The paramedic shrugged. "That's out of my wheelhouse."

"Mine too." But the bruise on her torso and her broken nails convinced me she'd been attacked. The rest would require a professional.

While Officer Gruper contained the scene and kept an eye on the cleaning woman who was currently our only witness and potential suspect, I went to see how Brad was doing. The kid, Vincent Price or whatever his real name might be, remained beside the dumpster while Brad went through the black trash bag.

"Does his story check out?" I asked.

"I'd say so. However," he pulled out a tiny neon crossbody bag, "I'm not sure the collection center's going to pay for this." My partner opened the purse, but it was empty. "Did you take the money?"

"No, it was like that when I found it," the kid said.

"Where'd you find it?" I asked, and the kid pointed to the dumpster on the left.

"Why keep it?" Brad asked. "It's not your color." He examined a stain on the side that might have been blood.

"I thought I'd clean it up and give it to my girlfriend. Her birthday's next week."

"Dumpster gifts, just what every girl wants." I glanced at

Brad. "Don't get any funny ideas."

"I'd never dream of it." He focused on the kid. "Did you find anything else, Vincent? A cell phone? Credit cards? Anything like that?"

"No, just the empty bag. I figured whoever had it didn't want it anymore."

I opened the lid and peered inside. This was not how I wanted to spend my night. I pulled out my flashlight and leaned in. Everything inside the dumpster appeared to be properly bagged. I'd have to get inside and sift through the bags to see if anything had fallen to the bottom or gotten mixed in with the refuse.

"Liv, wait. I see something." Brad came up beside me, shifting the bag nearest the edge toward the middle. A flat, rectangular object caught the light. Reaching down, he turned sideways, grabbing the item between his fingertips. He pulled it up to show me. "The photo matches the vic. Kara Dornan. Twenty-three." He frowned, flipping the driver's license over. "This is a fake."

I took the fake ID from him, careful to only touch the edges and held it out for Vincent to see. "Do you recognize her?"

He studied the photo. "No."

"Are you sure?"

"Yeah." He narrowed his eyes. "Why?"

"She's dead." I nodded toward the neon purple bag. "I'm guessing you have her purse."

"Shit." The kid looked like he might try to run again, so Brad grabbed his shoulder.

"You're sticking with us until we get this sorted out."

The kid gulped, but he didn't resist as Brad led him back to our cruiser. Brad opened the rear door and waited for the kid to get in.

"We haven't read him his rights. We didn't put him in cuffs. Do you want to arrest him?" I asked.

"No. I don't think he's dangerous." Brad jerked his chin toward the garbage bag in my hand. "He doesn't have any weapons or ID on him. We'll run his name and see what pops, but I'm guessing that's as phony as the license we found."

"Or his parents are huge fans of monster movies."

"Also possible." He sighed at this disaster of a night and shook out his hand, hoping to get the tremor under control. "But something tells me we're going to need this kid's cooperation."

As soon as the crime scene was squared away and the ME arrived, we headed back to the precinct. The medical examiner would get back to us with cause of death. Officers had pulled the trash from the bins in case they found anything else belonging to the victim or the killer. Techs were already working on analyzing the bar's security cameras, and the owner had been brought to the precinct for questioning. The rest of the staff would be rounded up in short order.

"Do you want something to drink or eat, kid?" Brad pointed to a chair inside the interrogation room.

"I dunno. I guess a cherry coke, if you have it."

"I'll see what I can do. We'll be right back." Brad turned to me and whispered, "See if you can find anything on him."

"Yes, sir." I saluted.

"Please, Liv."

I dropped the teasing. "No problem. I got this. Are you okay? He pushed you kind of hard."

"I'm good." He pointed to the break room. "Do you think we have cherry coke?"

"Vice might if we don't."

Sliding behind my desk, I looked up the name Vincent Price. Nothing came back. Deciding to risk it, I did a quick social media search. I got several hits, but only one with a photo that matched our suspect. He was fifteen and a prep school student. After some digging, I found his dad's phone number. But when I called, no one answered.

I returned to the interrogation room, finding my partner laying out a smorgasbord of snacks. From the looks of it, he'd gone a little crazy at the vending machines. Beside a can of cherry flavored cola were several varieties of candy bars, two kinds of chips, a sandwich, and an apple. Vincent kept eyeing the bag of ridged chips while he sipped his soda.

"Help yourself," Brad said. "I figured you might have worked up an appetite."

Vincent picked up the chips and tugged the bag apart before digging his hand inside. I took a seat beside Brad. "Your dad didn't answer when I called."

"He can't. He's at work. They aren't allowed to have their phones on the floor," Vincent said around a mouthful.

"We can call a child advocate," I said.

Brad looked at me, silently communicating with his eyes how apprehensive Vincent got when I suggested that. "Maybe we can hold off for a while, Liv."

"He's a minor. He's fifteen."

"He's not in any trouble." Brad turned to the kid. "Right?"

"No, sir."

"Then tell us why a prep school student is out in the middle of the night sifting through garbage," I said.

Vincent finished the chips and reached for a candy bar. He stopped, unsure if he should take it. "I need the money. It doesn't bring in much, but it helps."

Brad nodded, and Vincent tore into the candy bar. "Walk us through your night. What time did you get to the bar?"

"It was around four."

"Did you see any cars out front?" I asked.

He shook his head, chewing more enthusiastically. The kid wouldn't have gone around back while a police car was parked out front. So he must have gotten there before Officers Deagan and Gruper.

"How'd you get there?" Brad asked.

"I walked. I have a route I take. I start with McGinty's, then move on to The Ale House, Slick's, Jumpin' Joes, Pub Brew, and a few others."

"Do you do this every night?"

"Most nights, after my dad leaves for work."

"Where does he work?" I asked.

"The mattress factory." He tucked the wrapper around the uneaten portion of the candy bar. "He doesn't know about this. I'd really like it if you didn't tell him."

"We can't make any promises," Brad said. "Did you see

anyone else near the bar? Outside? Inside? Leaving?"

"Nope, just the two of you."

"What about the other days?"

"On the weekends, a lot of people hang out back there. Like I told ya earlier, dealers and hos. They usually clear out by five, so I circle back around if necessary."

"Do you know who's dealing Red Rabbit near that bar?" Brad asked.

"I don't even know what that is."

I wasn't sure if the kid was lying, but if everything he said was true, he probably didn't know what it was.

"What about molly or ecstasy?" Brad asked. "You ever try any of that?"

"My school's real strict, especially on those of us who play sports. I wouldn't risk it."

"Are you on scholarship?" I asked.

"Why does that matter?"

I held up my palms. The question wasn't meant to be offensive, even though Vincent took it that way. "I understand not wanting to do anything to jeopardize your opportunity." I held out the copy of the fake ID we found in the dumpster. "Are you sure you don't know this woman?"

"I've never seen her before."

I described what she'd been wearing, but the kid insisted he didn't know her. I checked with the techs who were analyzing the bar's exterior cameras. Vincent showed up two minutes before the police and headed straight to the dumpster. None of the cameras covered the back, but that was enough to verify his story. Given TOD, he had nothing to do with the victim's death.

After he finished his soda and snack, a uniformed officer took him home with instructions to wait for his dad to show up. That might not have been protocol, but we'd exhausted that lead.

"We don't even know if she was murdered." Brad pulled out his desk chair and sat down. "She might have ODed."

"Regardless, she died under suspicious circumstances. We have grounds to investigate. You saw the bruise and her fingernails. Plus, her stuff got taken. The thief probably dumped her bag and ID as soon as he went outside." I checked with the techs, but they hadn't noticed anyone suspicious on the feed. Since the cameras only covered the front, the perp could have tossed her bag and ID in the dumpster, jumped the fence, and bypassed the cameras.

"I'll place a request for additional CCTV feeds." Brad picked up the phone and dialed.

While he did that, I ran the name on the fake ID, but that didn't give me any leads. The ID wasn't great, but in a dark bar, it might have been convincing enough. I spoke to the bar owner. He hadn't worked since last Tuesday, and he didn't recognize the girl.

I asked about dealers and the kinds of things that happened right outside the door, but he claimed not to know anything about any of it. His attorney showed up in the middle of my questioning and told me without evidence I had no reason to harass his client. When I couldn't take banging my head against the wall for another second, I let the owner walk. We'd have better luck with the bartender and staff.

The bartender recognized her. "She ordered a seven and seven. A couple of them. Maybe three."

"Was she with anyone?" Brad asked.

"Not that I could tell. She seemed really into the band."

"Did she come to the bar often to listen to music?"

"I don't think so. I've never seen her before tonight."

"Did you see any guys hitting on her?" I asked.

"Plenty."

"Any of them get rough?" Brad asked.

"I don't know. I just serve drinks."

"Well, since we found her dead in the bathroom, I'm guessing the answer to that question is yes." I waited, but the bartender didn't amend his story.

Brad glared at him. "I want you to really take a moment to think about it before you answer. Did you see anyone follow her into the bathroom?"

The bartender looked from me to Brad. "Stark."

"Who?"

"His credit card says J. Stark. He's a regular, always wears a leather bomber jacket and relaxed jeans with a chain hanging out of his pocket. He slicks his hair back. I saw him grab his beer and head for the bathrooms right after she got up from the bar, but I don't know where either of them went after that. I didn't see them again."

"What time was that?" I asked.

"It must have been close to two. I'd just made the announcement for last call."

"Do you know anything about J. Stark?" Brad asked.

The bartender shook his head.

"All right. Hang here for a sec."

I followed my partner out of the interrogation room and back to his desk. He ran the name through the database, pulled up everyone with a record who had that last name and first initial, downloaded the photos to a tablet, and headed back inside the interrogation room. If this didn't work, we'd have to call for a sketch artist.

Three photos in, the bartender made a positive ID.

NINE

I banged against the door. "Jimmy, open up. I know you're in there." I waited. "Come on, man. Don't make a girl beg." I kept my palm over the peephole. "Fine, I'll beg. Please. I need something. I need you." I strained to hear footsteps and glanced at Brad, who shook his head.

"Maybe he's not home," he whispered.

"Dude, seriously, I'm desperate here. I got cash or whatever else you might want. Come on. You told me I could come over and party anytime." I knocked harder against the door. "Don't tell me you got some skank in there."

That's when I heard a door slam somewhere inside the apartment. Heavy footsteps approached. "Jeez. Give me a minute." The deadbolt flipped, and the knob twisted. The moment the door opened, Stark shoved a gun in my face. "Who are you?"

I held up my hands. "Whoa. Take it easy. I'm just looking to score."

He took half a step out the door, and Brad surprised him from the side, grabbing the gun. I yanked the guy by the front of his shirt and spun him face first against the wall.

"Police." I removed a second gun from where he'd tucked it into the back of his pants. "I hope you have a permit for these."

"What the fuck?"

"Is anyone else home?" I asked while Brad cautiously entered the apartment.

"My girlfriend's in the bedroom." He tried to turn around to face me.

I pushed him harder against the wall and slapped my cuffs on him.

"Ma'am, put some clothes on." Brad's voice carried. About ninety seconds later, he led the woman into the living room and told her to sit on the couch. "The rest of the apartment's clear."

"Great." I eased some of the pressure off of Stark.

"What's this about?" Stark asked. "You can't just barge into my house in the middle of the night without a warrant."

"It's morning." Brad held up the firearm he'd taken from the guy's hand. "We just had a few questions, Mr. Stark, but you answered the door with a gun in your hand. You can't do shit like that."

"You didn't identify yourselves. I have a right to defend my home." He had us there, but the bastard wouldn't have answered if I'd played it straight.

"Why'd you come to the door with a gun? Are you expecting trouble?" I asked.

He glared at me. "What do you want?"

"Where were you a few hours ago?" Brad asked. "Say around two a.m.?"

Stark's eyes burned with rage. The woman on the couch perked up at the question. "Yeah, Jimmy, where were you?"

"Shut up, Marietta."

"He wasn't with you?" Brad asked her.

"No," she stared at her boyfriend, "he said he was working late. He had some late night deliveries to make." She focused on me. "Where was that lying, cheating sack of shit?"

"What time did he come home?" Brad asked.

"Three. He's been here ever since." She continued to stare at me. "Where was he?"

"Marietta, shut your damn mouth," Stark snapped, "or I'll shut it for you."

"He was at a bar," I said. "Weren't you, Jimmy?" He jerked forward, but I shoved him back toward the wall.

"Bitch, you don't know what you're talking about."

"Your credit card says otherwise." I studied him, wondering if the anger he displayed was meant to mask fear. "Tell us about the girl."

"What girl?"

"Were you with a girl? I swear," Marietta moved to stand, but Brad blocked her path, holding up a hand, "I told you what would happen if I caught you with another ho."

He looked past me. "I wasn't with anyone. Now shut your damn mouth before you get me into trouble."

"Looks like you got yourself in enough trouble," I said. "Unless you can explain everything, you're under arrest."

"Explain what?"

Brad stifled a grunt. "Sir, did you go to a bar tonight?"

"No."

"Your credit card was charged, and witnesses place you there. Would you like to rethink your response?" Brad asked, a challenge in his tone.

"Fuck you."

"Arrest him, Liv."

I informed Stark of his rights while he continued to mouth off. "Do you understand your rights as they've been read to you?"

He sneered and spit on me.

Brad lunged forward, but I held up my palm and wiped the glob of saliva off my cheek.

"Answer the question," I growled.

"I don't have to do anything, bitch."

Brad crossed the room, yanked Stark away from the wall, and hauled him toward the door, glancing at me to make sure I was okay.

"I'll be there in a sec." I could see the anger in my partner's eyes. "Watch his head when you put him in the car. We don't need any accidents."

"Yep." He escorted Stark from the apartment.

I turned to the woman, who appeared angrier than my partner. "What's your name?"

"Marietta Linley." She tucked the robe tighter around her body. "What did Jimmy do this time?"

"Why don't you tell me?"

"Nuh-uh." She shook her head. "I'm not playing that game with you."

"May I look around?"

"The apartment's in his name. I'm not on the lease. I can't give you permission, but you can do whatever the hell you want."

"Do you mind if I ask what you're doing with him?"

"Honey, I ask myself that every damn day." She sat up a little straighter. "What did you want to question him about? What do you think he did?"

"He's a person of interest in a murder investigation."

She inhaled sharply. "Murder?"

"Yes."

"Well, shit, I knew he was doing something shady with all those late night deliveries, but I didn't think it'd be that." She fidgeted with the sash on her robe. That's when I noticed the fresh scratches on her wrist and forearm.

"What kind of deliveries?"

"He works for one of those third party services that brings takeout to people."

"Were you here all night?"

"Naw. I was hanging out at a friend's place until midnight. Then I came back here, but Jimmy was gone by the time I got home. I texted him." She pointed to the device on the kitchen counter. "Do you mind if I get my phone? I can show you."

"Go ahead."

She crossed the room, unplugged her phone, and returned to the couch. I sat beside her, hoping to get a better look at the injuries on her arm. She scrolled through the text chain and showed me the messages.

"How'd you hurt your wrist?" I asked.

"Cat scratch." She shook the sleeve down over her hand.

"It's no big deal."

"I don't see a cat."

"It was my friend's cat."

"May I see your phone?"

She hesitated, frowning at the device. "Why?"

"I want to see what time you and Jimmy were texting."

She handed me the phone, and I scrolled up, keeping one eye on her.

"You texted through a social media app, not through direct text messages."

"It was direct. I don't put my private business up for the world to see."

"Would you mind showing me your profile?"

She sighed dramatically. "Fine." She swiped on the screen a few times. "Is that it? Are we done here?"

"Not yet. Would you mind coming with me?" I asked, even though it wasn't a question. "I need you to verify a few details at the precinct."

"I don't know anything. I have nothing to do with Jimmy's business, legal or otherwise."

"That might be." I pointed to the screen. "But you have location tracking set on your phone. It automatically checked you in when you went to the bar last night."

Her face read *oh shit* in big bold letters. Her eyes darted back and forth, debating between lying and running. In the end, she let out a huff. "Fine, but I'm telling you the truth. I have nothing to do with Jimmy's business. I don't know what he was up to or who he was with inside that bar. I never went inside. I waited for him to come out, and then I dragged his drunk ass home."

I followed her into the bedroom, afraid she might try to climb out a window or retrieve a weapon if I left her alone. Calmly, she tugged on a pair of pants, put on a bra, and pulled a long sleeve shirt on over her head, making sure to keep her arm concealed from my view. After she got her shoes on, I led her out of the apartment and down to the waiting car.

For everyone's safety, I put Brad's cuffs on her and stuck her in the back seat with Jimmy. Immediately, they started to argue.

Brad gave me a look. "You want to wait for another car to pick one of them up?"

"They're both restrained, and we may learn something insightful. It's up to you."

"Fine, but I'm driving. And if they don't behave, I won't hesitate to pull the car over."

"Whatever you say, Dad."

He narrowed his eyes at me, muttering to himself about the unpleasantness of domestic spats and road trips. I didn't think this qualified as either, but he was right. The fifteen minute ride back to the precinct was particularly unpleasant. According to Marietta, Jimmy had problems not sticking his dick in every willing hole, and Jimmy thought Marietta was a needy and jealous woman who'd cut a bitch for looking in the general direction of her man.

Once we passed them off to intake, Brad folded his arms across his chest and stared at me. "All right, Liv, explain to me why we just endured that R-rated reality show."

"Marietta lied to us. Her phone showed her at the bar at 1:23."

"That's right around the time the bartender saw Jimmy follow our vic into the bathroom."

"Yeah, and if Marietta's lying about being there, she's probably lying about more than that, like how she got the scratches on her arm."

"Scratches?"

"She tried to cover them with her robe, but I spotted them. She said a cat did it, but she doesn't have a cat. And I don't think her friend does either."

"You think she caught Jimmy with Kara, attacked Kara, and Kara fought back."

"Do you have a better theory?"

"Not yet." He squirted hand sanitizer into his palms and rubbed them together. "Let's do some more digging."

TEN

"Marietta Linley, twenty-five, no prior felonies. The same can't be said for Jimmy Stark. Twenty-seven, assault and battery, possession with intent, and armed robbery."

"She sure picked a winner." Brad stretched back, fighting to keep from yawning. "The bartender doesn't remember seeing her inside the bar. I checked the surveillance footage from the door, but it doesn't look like she ever went inside."

"Let me see."

He turned his monitor toward me and hit play. The bar's exterior showed Marietta arriving after one a.m. She circled the entrance a few times, checked her phone, sent a few text messages, which she had already let me read, and waited. When Stark finally left the bar, a few minutes after two, she leapt at him. Her hands flying wildly in the air while she screamed. He grabbed her wrist before she could strike him.

"Pause it there." I leaned closer. "I don't see any scratches."

"You've seen Stark's fingertips. He has his nails trimmed down to nubs. Stark didn't scratch Marietta." He hit play, so I could watch the rest of the footage. "Based on this, we know the scratches happened sometime after she arrived outside the bar, which means her friend's cat couldn't have scratched her either. She lied."

"Are you surprised?"

"Not really."

I watched Stark and Marietta move out of frame. "They didn't call a car to take them home. Instead, they headed toward the bar's side entrance, near the dumpsters and alleyway. That door doesn't have any cameras covering it. It's possible Marietta entered the bar, found Kara in the bathroom, and roughed her up." I watched the woman on the screen. One thing was clear. She was pissed as she jerked away from Stark's touch. Just his presence agitated her.

"We'll have to wait for the DNA analysis. But since Marietta isn't willing to comply with our request, we need a court order to compel her." He straightened his monitor. "I'm not saying you're wrong."

"Which usually means you think I am."

"From Marietta's initial reaction inside the apartment, I don't think she caught Jimmy cheating. But she probably suspected." He stared at the monitor. "Maybe after Marietta texted Jimmy, Kara tried to sneak out the back and got caught."

"That might explain why her purse was in the dumpster and why the bartender never saw Marietta enter the bar." I sighed. "But Marietta seemed surprised by the murder. If she were responsible, wouldn't she have had a lie prepared?"

"I don't think Marietta or whoever assaulted Kara intended to kill her. They fought, but I'd wager when the attacker walked away, Kara was still breathing. I think the real culprit in Kara's death is Red Rabbit, just like Macy Lowan."

"Did the ME get back to us with any other details regarding Lowan's death?"

"Not yet. I tried calling Carrie, but I was told she's working days."

"Are you two back together?"

"No."

I quirked an eyebrow at him. "So why would your ex-girlfriend feel inclined to do us a favor?"

"We're still friends. I'm sure she'd bump our case up the list, if I asked. Plus, she was never really my girlfriend. We didn't have labels."

"Too bad she's working days." I clicked on our case file from last night's scene. "Lowan and Kara both exhibited excessive amounts of bleeding and bruising. But neither showed any of the usual signs of an overdose. I'm not sure the drug is what killed them. Wouldn't we see a lot more bodies popping up?"

"What if it's a tainted batch or an intentional poisoning?" Brad asked.

"The same drug killing two different women in two completely different locations on two separate nights seems unlikely."

"Unless the same person poisoned them." Brad keyed something in. "Maybe they're connected. They could have the same dealer or hang around the same neighborhoods."

"It's possible. But we don't even know Kara's real name. We're just calling her that based on the fake ID. Her prints aren't in the system, and since she used a fake ID, she must be below the legal drinking age, probably nineteen or twenty. I already checked missing persons, but she didn't pop up. I asked the techs to run her through facial recognition, but they said it'll take days."

"What about the missing persons calls that came in tonight? They wouldn't necessarily be logged in the system yet. We should check to see if any parents or college students called to report a missing woman. Can you check with 9-1-1 dispatch while I check downstairs to see what came in on the direct line?"

"Sure, no problem." I phoned the call center while Brad went downstairs to the front desk.

I went through every call 9-1-1 received, comparing the descriptions to the body we found. None even came close. I leaned back in my chair and took a deep breath, hoping to release some of the tension from my neck. Letting my head loll back, I watched Brad enter through the double doors.

"Anything?" he asked.

"No hits for Kara."

He retook his seat, cocking his head to the side. "Do you want me to rub your neck?"

"And my back." I held up my palm before he could come around the desk. "I was joking."

"Are you all right?" He couldn't see my scar from where he was sitting, but I knew that's what he meant.

"Yes." I pointed to the time. "Shit. Winston's going to have our asses if we don't get the hell out of here. Our shift ended twenty minutes ago, and we haven't even finished questioning Marietta and Jimmy yet."

"We can't until an attorney shows up. You know how this works. Once they request a lawyer, we're done." Brad cocked an eyebrow. "Since when do you worry about working overtime?"

"Since my partner's already on thin ice."

"I'm good if you are." Instead of packing up, he searched for any open investigations regarding Red Rabbit. "Did you know Arthur Sullivan's working a Red Rabbit case too?" He reached for his phone and dialed Sullivan's extension. He drummed his fingers while he listened to it ring. "Hey, Liv, would you happen to know Sullivan's schedule?"

"How would I? Captain Grayson might be my dad's best friend, but that doesn't mean he tells me every minute detail regarding the inner workings inside the intelligence unit. He didn't even tell me that stuff when we worked intelligence."

Brad put down the phone. "I'll take a run upstairs and see what's what."

"I'll come with you."

As usual, Sullivan's desk was messy. Brad grabbed one of the sticky notes and pulled the pen from his pocket. He'd just finished scribbling a note to Sullivan when the detective snuck up behind us.

"Don't tell me the two of you transferred back here," he teased. "Loyola and I are really tired of playing second fiddle to you." He winked at me and held out his hand to Brad. "It's good to see you up and walking, my brother." He pulled him into a one-armed hug and clapped him on the back. "How ya feeling? No more fever dreams?"

"Not lately." Brad crinkled up the sticky note and tossed

it in the bin. "I'd be better if you could clue us in on Red Rabbit."

Sullivan narrowed his eyes. "You catch something I should know about?"

"Actually, two somethings." Brad filled him in on what had occurred over the last two nights.

"Well, I'll be damned." Sullivan dropped into his chair. "That's two more to add to the list."

"You have a list?" I asked.

"Unfortunately." He found a folder and opened it. "With the addition of your two cases. This makes eight victims we've seen in the last three weeks. When Loyola and I caught the first case, we thought we were dealing with some kind of contagion, ebola or some other infectious disease. We even called hazmat." He brought up a photo of the first victim. "She bled from her eyes and mouth."

Brad cringed. "I did not need to see that."

My stomach clenched. I'd seen enough that most crime scene photos didn't make me flinch, but bleeding from the eyes was all kinds of creepy. I looked away from the photo. "Red Rabbit caused that?"

"Yeah, that's how it got its name. It gives a lot of users pink eyes, like those white bunnies in pet stores. This," he gestured at the photo, but neither Brad nor I looked at it again, "is just an extreme case."

"So these complications are overdoses?"

"Not exactly," Sullivan said. "The autopsy reports showed every one of the victims had consumed anticoagulant rodenticide in a large enough dose to prove fatal. We suspect the pills are laced with rat poison or something similar, and a bad batch is circulating."

"Even if it wasn't a bad batch," I said, "the car accident and an assault would have caused internal injuries to the victims. Since rat poison is basically a blood thinner, that might have been enough to cause Lowan and Kara to bleed to death."

"Do you mind sending me a copy of the files and autopsy reports when you get them?" Sullivan asked.

"No problem." Brad clapped him on the shoulder. "Thanks for filling us in. If you think of anything else that might help, let us know. Okay?"

Sullivan made a finger pistol and pointed it at Brad. "You got it." He smiled at me. "Hey, DeMarco, keep an eye on this guy before he gets himself into any more trouble."

"I'll do my best."

We'd just gotten back to our desks when Lt. Winston entered the bullpen with a briefcase in one hand and a coffee cup in the other. Several cops wished him a good morning, getting nothing but grunts in return. The lieutenant twisted the knob to his office, spilling coffee on his shirt and cursing. Finally, he opened the door and stepped inside. He spotted us on his way to get napkins from the break room.

"Detective Fennel, in my office, now."

The phone rang, and Brad grabbed it. "Just a sec, lieutenant." He pressed the phone to his ear. "That's right. A DNA sample."

The lieutenant turned the force of his death stare on me. "Don't go far, DeMarco. I want to speak to you too."

"Sir?" I moved to stand.

"Sit tight. I'll let you know when I'm ready for you." He marched into the break room, grabbed some wet paper towels, and blotted the stain on his shirt, only making it worse. Continuing to curse, he returned to his office. "Now, Fennel. Tell your girlfriend she can wait."

Brad hung up the phone and looked at me. "We got the court order to compel Marietta into providing a DNA sample. Also, the ME's sending over samples of the foreign DNA and blood found beneath Kara's fingernails. It might be a match."

I jerked my chin toward Winston's office where he stood in the doorway, blotting his shirt and appearing ready to blow a gasket. "Do you have any idea what this is about?"

"No, but since he wants to talk to me in private, I can only imagine." He pushed away from the desk. "Say something nice at my funeral."

"That's not funny."

"It wasn't supposed to be."

I couldn't help but wonder if this had anything to do with Brad's hush-hush investigation into police corruption.

Then again, I hadn't been able to shake the feeling that the other shoe was about to drop.

"DeMarco," Lt. Winston barked, "join us."

Crossing the room at a fast clip, I slipped past Winston and into his office. Brad was seated in one of the chairs in front of Winston's desk, so I took a seat in the other while the lieutenant pulled the door closed.

"Do you have a watch?" he asked.

"Not on me."

"But the clock in the bullpen's accurate. And the display on your computer, also accurate. Just like on your phone. So you know what time it is, right?"

"Uh, I guess."

"You guess?"

I glanced at Brad, whose expression told me I gave the wrong answer. "Yes, I know what time it is."

"Okay, and you know my policy on overtime, right?"

"I'm sorry, sir. But we caught a case halfway through shift. A body was found inside a bathroom."

"I'm aware."

I glanced at Brad who gave me a barely perceptible headshake. He hadn't spoken to the lieutenant about this. "We're in the middle of an investigation. We interviewed the bartender, who gave us the name of a man he last saw with the victim. We followed up and made two arrests."

"Arrests?" Winston paced behind his desk. "On what grounds?"

"Stark pulled a piece and pointed it at Liv," Brad said.

Winston looked at my partner and let out a sigh of exasperation. "That barely explains one, not both."

"Marietta, Stark's girlfriend, has scratches on her arm, consistent with the torn fingernails and defensive wounds we observed on the victim," Brad said.

Winston rubbed a hand down his face, agitated. "It's ten a.m. Your shift ended two hours ago, yet you're still here. Do you want to know where I've been for the last two hours? Getting my ass chewed because the two of you can't seem to stay in your damn lane." He pulled a copy of Officer Gruper's report from inside his briefcase. "The desk sergeant handed me this two seconds before Captain

Elswin from narcotics pulled me aside." He placed his palms flat on the desk and leaned toward us. "He says the case belongs to him since this is a drug issue, not a homicide. I contacted the medical examiner. He has yet to rule on the exact cause of death. But the victim wasn't stabbed, shot, strangled, or suffocated. White dust and a baggie were found near the body. So why are two of my homicide detectives looking into this? What makes you think this is murder?"

"Weren't you listening? Tonight's victim was attacked," I said. "We didn't find any of her belongings. Initially, we suspected it might have been a mugging gone wrong. Frankly, I'm surprised the robbery commander didn't jump down your throat too."

Winston's stone cold stare grew even icier.

"Lieutenant—" Brad began, hoping to save me from myself, but Winston held up a hand to keep him quiet.

"Detective DeMarco, you need to watch yourself. This is my unit. You work for me. I decide what investigations you work. I also have to make sure you color inside the lines. That means you don't work past shift without permission. You don't go chasing down suspects when we're dealing with a drug issue. You want to go after the dealer, you talk to narcotics. You understand?" He let out a huff. "Have you even identified the victim yet?"

I glanced at Brad. Again, he shook his head. "Not yet. Like I said, her belongings are missing. We found a bag we believe belongs to her in the dumpster outside the bar. We also found a fake ID with her photo in the same dumpster."

"That's also where you found some kid scrounging around. Did you arrest him too?"

"We questioned and released him."

"He's a minor. You can't interrogate him without a guardian present." Winston's cheeks turned puce, and the vein at his temple visibly throbbed. "Dammit."

"Sir," Brad tried again, "it wasn't like that."

Winston pointed a meaty finger at my partner. "Shut your mouth, Fennel. You're already on my shitlist. I suggest you think long and hard before you get yourself in deeper." Winston took a few deep breaths, letting out a humming noise before he spoke. This time, his temper was in check and his voice a lot calmer. "Listen, you're both good cops. Some would argue great. But here's the thing. DeMarco, ever since you got off patrol, you've mainly worked undercover. You know how to collect evidence and build a case. But when you're on the inside, the rules are a little different. Everything's heightened. Your primary objective is to stay alive. It's different from the outside. We have a strict set of rules and guidelines that have to be followed."

"I know that, sir."

"Even if you forget, Fennel's supposed to remind you." Winston reached into his desk drawer, pulled out a bottle of aspirin, and popped two into his mouth, knocking his head back and swallowing. "That's why I'm at a loss here. What am I supposed to do with the two of you when this one goes rogue, disobeys orders, and disregards the terms of his suspension?" He gestured at Brad. "I didn't get a chance to talk to you yesterday on your first day back. But things have to be different. You will follow orders, or you're out."

"I will," Brad said. "You have my word."

"We'll see." Winston turned to me. "You think you're untouchable, just like Voletek. To some extent, that's true. But your father's retired now, which makes you accountable for your actions. No one in the commissioner's office is going to save your ass. So a friendly word of advice, DeMarco, be careful and watch your step."

"I didn't do anything wrong. Kara," I shook my head, "tonight's Jane Doe, was attacked and killed. Her death might not have been intentional, but that young woman on the bathroom floor had her entire life ahead of her. I want to find out what happened. We owe her that."

"Last shift," Brad said, "we responded to a hit and run. When we located the driver of the vehicle, she was dead. We found an empty baggie near her body. Tonight, we saw the same baggie next to another victim. The baggies had the same rabbit logo."

"Which makes this a narcotics case," Winston pointed out, "just like Captain Elswin said."

"Do you want us to turn a blind eye and hand this off without another thought?" I asked.

Winston scratched his forehead and chuckled. I wondered if he was on the verge of a stroke. "No, DeMarco. What I want is for the two of you to come to me, tell me what's going on, and ask for permission before you go pissing all over another cop's territory." His gaze shifted from me to Brad and back again. "I'm your commanding officer. I will go to bat for you. But I can't do that if I don't even know what's going on. I don't like getting caught with my dick in my hand, which is precisely what happened this morning. This department values trust. The entire reason I requested the two of you join my team was because you're dedicated and determined. You have excellent closure rates, no major fuckups, and you know how to get the job done. You have to trust me to make the right call. If I say drop a case, you do it. If I say go after it, then you nail the son of a bitch. Do I make myself clear?"

"Yes, sir," Brad said.

"Good." Winston looked at me. "Do you have a problem, DeMarco?"

"No, sir. I'm just not sure where that leaves us on this case."

"I told Elswin we'd loop him in. Next time, catch me up to speed beforehand." He jerked his chin toward the door. "Get everything together and present it to him. Then get the hell out of here. The city's got enough problems without the department going over budget."

Brad and I left the office and went back to our desks. He leaned in close and whispered to me, "Winston knows."

"Knows what?"

"He knows what I've been up to these last six weeks. And he's pissed."

ELEVEN

The next day, we were called to work early. When I arrived, I was surprised to find Brad waiting for me. He handed me the DNA results. "You were right," he said. "Marietta Linley attacked Jane Doe, a.k.a. Kara. Marietta's DNA was found beneath Kara's fingernails."

I scanned the details. "What about cause of death?"

"The ME hasn't had time to perform a full autopsy yet. A dead Jane Doe isn't a priority. But the preliminary exam and toxicology indicates she died the same way Macy Lowan did."

"Macy Lowan was in a car accident. Kara was attacked. That's vastly different. We need to know what part the assault played in her death. If she hadn't been attacked, would she have survived?"

"I don't know." Brad nodded to an officer who signaled to him from across the room. "Kara was high when she died. She tested positive for MDMA. She also had a large dose of rat poison in her system. We still aren't clear on precisely when she was attacked. From the footage we've seen, we can't prove Marietta ever entered the bar."

I didn't want to stand here and theorize with my partner. "I need to take another crack at her and possibly

Jimmy."

"I figured as much. They're waiting in interrogation rooms one and two."

"Did their attorneys show up?"

Brad chuckled. "Damnedest thing. They changed their minds. We even got it in writing that they are willing to waive their right to counsel."

"Why would they do that?"

"I don't know, but no one's gone near them since we booked them. Lt. Winston thought it'd be best to let them stew. Maybe some time in lockup convinced one or both of them to be more forthcoming."

"Have you spoken to the LT since this morning?" I asked.

"Nope." Brad led the way down the hall. "Who do you want to tackle first?"

"I'll try my luck with Marietta."

"Do you want backup?"

"No, I want to speak to her woman to woman."

Brad didn't appear convinced this was a great strategy, but he kept his mouth shut. Instead, he pulled open the door handle and waited for me to enter. I took the report from him and sashayed into the interrogation room.

Marietta looked up when the door opened. "I'm hungry. Where's my sandwich?"

I turned to the officer who'd been stationed inside the room with her. "Can you get her something to eat?"

"Sure, Detective. Are you okay in here?"

"I'm great." I took a seat across from her. She wore handcuffs and an unhappy frown. "How are you?"

Her eyes narrowed. "What am I still doing here? You said you just had a few questions. The next thing I know, I'm getting manhandled by some butch lady cop and tossed into a cell."

"I'm sorry about that. It's protocol. My lieutenant doesn't like us working overtime. How about we go over a few things from last night, and I'll see if I can get you out of here? Does that sound good?"

"Sure." But her expression told me she suspected this was a trap.

"Let's cut to the chase. The DNA results came back. I know the scratches on your wrist weren't caused by a cat. They were caused by a woman. I need you to tell me what happened."

"The bitch was crazy. She grabbed onto me. I was just trying to get away."

"What bitch?"

"I don't know her name. I don't know anything about her."

"Where did this altercation occur?"

"Out back, near that side door. Bitch latched onto my arm and wouldn't let go. I had to shove her off of me so I could get away."

"When?"

"I don't know. Around two." Her eyes narrowed to slits. "Is that the chick Jimmy's banging?"

"Did you see them together?"

Marietta shook her head. "No. He came out of the bar alone, and we fought. He was supposed to be home hours ago, not off fucking some groupie. He always does this. I warned him the last time that that would be the last time. But there he was, preying on the mindless band bimbos. That's probably the only reason he even went to the concert."

"Did you enter the bar at all last night?" I asked.

Marietta shook her head. "I texted Jimmy and told him if he didn't come out right now that I'd go back to his apartment and burn the place down." She licked her lip. "I'm not saying I'd really do that, but he believed me and walked his ass right out that door. After we argued for a bit, he said he had to go back inside to get his credit card from the bartender. While I was waiting for him at the side door, this crazy bitch comes running at me from out of nowhere like her hair was on fire and grabs my arm."

"Her hair was on fire?"

"No," Marietta looked at me like I was stupid, "but that's how frantic she was acting. She grabs my wrist, and she's screaming at me. She said she was burning from the inside. She looked possessed. Her eyes were red and freaky looking, like in those exorcism movies."

"You didn't try to help her?"

"Are you fucking crazy? She's clawing at me and screaming about burning. I'm lucky I got away alive."

"How did you get away?"

"I shoved her. She banged against the dumpster. That's when Jimmy came back. She took one look at him and ran back inside the bar."

"Was she bleeding?"

Marietta paused, her eyes darting back and forth as she thought. "I don't know. Why?" She rubbed her bound hands together, massaging the bandage over her wrist. "Did she have some kind of disease? Is it contagious? Am I infected?"

"Are you sure you don't know who she is?"

"I've never seen her before."

"Why did you lie to me last night?"

She looked away. "I know how it sounds. But I didn't hurt that girl, and I definitely didn't kill anyone. I didn't want to get in trouble for whatever dumbass thing Jimmy might have done, so I said it was from a cat."

"Did you lie about anything else?"

"No."

"Okay." It was time to regroup. "Did you notice if the woman who attacked you had a purse or cell phone?"

"She had a neon purple bag. When I shoved her, she dropped it."

"What did you do with it?"

Marietta stared at me. "Answer my damn question. Is she contagious? Do I have some kind of flesh-eating demon thing inside of me now?"

"No, ma'am. The demons you have inside of you are yours. You didn't catch them from anyone else."

After the momentary confusion wore off, she glared at me. "You fucking asshole."

"What did you do with her stuff?"

"I didn't do anything with it. I wasn't gonna touch nothing that belonged to her. In fact, the first thing I did when we got home was shower."

The officer returned with a sandwich and a bottle of water. He put them on the table between us. She reached for it, unable to unwrap it with her bound hands. "You can take the cuffs off while she eats," I said.

"That's so kind of you," she said sarcastically.

"Ms. Linley, what you fail to realize is that woman is dead. If what you said is true, you might be the last person who saw her alive. I need to know what happened."

"I don't know."

"What happened to her purse?"

Marietta took a huge bite of the sandwich and chewed with her mouth open. "I already told you I didn't touch it. If you don't believe me, ask Jimmy. He's always doing shady shit." She took another big bite and washed it down with the water. "Maybe he took her stuff."

With the officer guarding Marietta, I left the interrogation room. Brad had been inside, monitoring the situation from the observation room. "Do you believe her?" he asked.

"I don't know. You remember the things Jimmy said in the car last night and the way they were together at the apartment. Marietta's the jealous type. She's convinced Jimmy's screwing around on her. When she saw Kara, she might have snapped and attacked her. Did officers go back to question the bartender and staff after we arrested Jimmy and Marietta?"

"Yep."

"And?"

"No one remembers seeing Marietta inside the bar last night. It's possible her story checks out." Brad watched through the glass as she bit into her sandwich. "She's pissed at Jimmy, but she still loves him. She could be covering for him."

"Or she's hoping we'll blame him. Either way, let's see what Jimmy has to say." I reached for the door handle before Brad could grab it. Chivalry wasn't dead. My partner was the epitome of it, but I didn't want Jimmy to think I needed a man to help me get inside the room. I was a strong, independent female, in case he'd forgotten that in the last several hours.

Jimmy Stark was leaning back in his chair with his arms folded over his chest. The silver bracelets caught the light. I dismissed the officer in the room and took a seat. Brad lingered just outside the open door. He didn't want to leave me alone with Stark after our suspect exhibited such rude manners the previous night.

"You joining us, Fennel?" I asked.

My partner entered the room and pulled the door closed behind him.

"I didn't know you were waiting for an invitation," I said.

Brad caught on and played along. With Stark, it'd be easier to pull off a good cop, bad cop routine, especially if he bonded with Brad over putting up with nagging, ballbuster women. My partner pulled out the chair beside me, flipped it around, and put it adjacent to Stark. Then he sat down.

"I just spoke to Marietta. She's one feisty lady," I said.

Jimmy worked his jaw for a moment. "Yeah, so?"

Brad let out a chuckle. "Man, you don't want to know the things she's been saying about you."

Jimmy didn't take the bait. Instead, he stared at me. "What's any of this got to do with me? I don't even know why I'm here."

"The body of a young woman was found inside the bar. The bartender said he saw you follow the dead woman into the bathroom."

"I didn't do anything to anyone. You have nothing. I was in the wrong place at the wrong time. Big deal."

"We ran your guns," Brad said. "It turns out they aren't registered. That's a crime, and with your record, I don't think a judge is going to go easy on you."

"I was holding them for a friend."

"Your friend's not here," Brad said. "With the way your luck's going, you might want to consider getting some new friends."

Jimmy shrugged. "I know how this works. When am I getting out of here?"

"No, Mr. Stark, you don't know how this works. A woman is dead. Your girlfriend said you robbed and killed her." I pretended to read a statement from the notepad I'd tucked inside the folder.

"What?" He showed genuine surprise. "I didn't kill anyone."

"Did you have sex with her?" Brad asked.

"Marietta would cut my nads off."

"What were you doing at that bar last night?"

"Drinking. They had some punk rock band playing live. They dress a little too emo for my taste, but their songs are okay."

"Marietta said you were making deliveries."

"Yeah, at midnight. I got a call to pick up a few pies from that all night pizza joint and deliver them to a law office."

"Which office?" Brad asked.

"Rialto and McKinney." Stark gave us the address. "Building security can verify that. They didn't let me inside, but they took the pizzas."

"What time did you leave there?" I asked.

"12:28. The time gets recorded on the delivery app."

"That's your day job?" Brad asked.

"It's a gig economy. I work when I want, as much as I want. It's easy pay. Generally, the tips are great." He scratched his chin. "After that, I thought I'd go have some fun. Marietta had gone to see some of her friends, and I just wanted to go somewhere and blow off some steam. I love her, but she's a fucking handful and a half. Most days, I don't know why I put up with her shit."

"That's when you arrived at the bar?" I asked.

"Yep." He stretched his arms out and leaned back in his chair. "I ordered several drinks and watched the show. Since the bartender IDed me, he can tell you I was there."

Brad was growing impatient. "He also said you were talking to the dead woman and followed her to the bathroom."

"I did not."

"Okay," I said, "maybe you didn't follow her. But you spoke to her at some point." I showed him her photo. "This woman. Do you remember her?"

"Yeah, she kept flirting with me. I told her I was taken."

"Did she tell you her name?"

"She said it was Kara."

"What did you two talk about?"

"Mostly the band. She was really into them. That's why she was at the bar. She wanted to see them perform. She was really excited, bouncing up and down and bopping along to the beat."

"Did she exhibit any signs of distress?" I asked.

Jimmy thought for a moment and shook his head. "After the band played their last set, she finished her seven and seven and left. I don't know where she went. I wasn't paying that much attention to her. I guess it must have been around the same time Marietta texted me."

"We know Marietta met you outside the bar," I said.

Jimmy nodded. "She tracked my location. I forgot to turn off the find my friends thing. I knew I had to get my ass outside or she'd come in and make a scene. Her screaming and yelling probably woke half the neighborhood. But I calmed her down, and we left."

"Just like that?" I asked.

"Yeah." Jimmy narrowed his eyes. "Wait, I had to run back in to get my credit card. Then we left."

"Did you see Kara again?"

"Nope."

"How about a neon purple crossbody bag?"

"What the hell is that?" he asked.

"A woman's handbag." Brad held his palms about a foot apart. "It's like this big. We found one outside the club. We've pulled prints from it."

I knew that wasn't true.

"Oh, yeah," Jimmy corrected. "It was beside the trash. I picked it up to see if it belonged to anyone."

"What was inside?" I asked.

"Nothing, so I tossed it in the dumpster."

Brad and I exchanged a look.

"Am I seriously going to get in trouble for throwing out someone's trash?" Jimmy asked.

"That's not why you're in trouble. That bag belonged to Kara. Are you sure you don't want to tell us what really happened?"

"I told you everything that happened." He rocked forward. "Now it's time you release me."

"That's not happening." I leaned closer. "Marietta said Kara attacked her in the alley. Would you care to elaborate on that? If you were defending Marietta, we'll take that into consideration. But we need to hear your side of things."

"I don't have a side of things. I told you what happened. I didn't see Kara again after I left the bar." Jimmy glanced at Brad, hoping his tale had swayed my partner's opinion.

"C'mon, man, help yourself here. If Marietta did something to Kara or you had to protect your woman, just say so. We'll understand. That will all be taken into consideration."

Jimmy stared at me with dead eyes. "I changed my mind. I want to call my attorney."

TWELVE

"Who do you think is lying?" Brad asked.

"I don't know."

"Me neither." He swiveled from side to side in his chair. "My gut says they're both lying."

"Your gut's probably right." I rewatched the surveillance footage from outside the bar. "Jimmy used the side door to go back in to get his credit card. Why didn't he use the front?" I checked the timestamp. "He and Marietta were out of sight for almost fifteen minutes. Anything could have happened during that time."

"Let it play." Brad watched the feed. By then, lots of people were leaving the bar. "Maybe Marietta's right, and Jimmy is cheating. He might have led her around back in order to keep her from seeing the girl he was with."

"That would mean he wasn't with Kara, but according to the bartender, Jimmy followed Kara down that hallway."

"Maybe it wasn't to hook up." Brad shrugged. "Jimmy makes late night deliveries. Maybe he's delivering more than food."

"You think he's dealing?"

"He had two unregistered weapons on him when we arrested him. What does that say to you?"

"But we searched Jimmy. He didn't have any pills on

him or anywhere inside his apartment."

"The bar had a live band playing. He could have moved his entire inventory. Kara might have just gotten unlucky and ended up with a bad dose."

"We can assume Kara had already taken the pills when she ran into Marietta. I think Kara realized there was something seriously wrong and tried to get help."

"And Marietta only made it worse." Brad tapped his fingers against the desk while he thought. "Jimmy might have followed Kara to the bathroom to sell her the pills, or they went out back to make the deal. It's also possible she scored from someone else in that alleyway outside the bar. Perhaps that's why Jimmy was headed that way too."

"He wasn't high when we knocked on his door."

"It might have worn off by then. Vincent told us pushers and hos hang out at the side door. So we can't rule anything out."

"Great theory, but we can't prove any of it."

"CSU printed the bathroom and the door leading out. Marietta's prints are nowhere to be found."

I rubbed my temples. "What are we supposed to do?"

Brad sighed. "We have to read in Captain Elswin on the progress we've made and give him our updated theories. Narcotics should know the dealers in that neighborhood. They can round them up for us."

"Gag me." I climbed out of my chair and picked up a copy of the files and my report. "Do you still believe Kara's death isn't the direct result of whatever Jimmy and Marietta might have done?"

"The high dose of rat poison in the drugs is what killed her. The scuffle she got into with Marietta before her death may have sped things up, but I don't think she would have survived anyway. You heard what Sullivan said. The victims in the cases he's investigating didn't show any signs of physical trauma, yet they still bled to death. Remember the photos?"

"Don't remind me. Those images will probably give me nightmares."

After updating the narcotics captain on our most recent findings, he took the folders from me. "We'll take it from here."

"But sir, we're in the middle of investigating."

"What else is there for you to do? My team will do the best they can to find out who was dealing at the club that night, but I'll be honest. It's probably a crapshoot. We've yet to collar anyone for dealing in these designer pills."

"Fennel and I will continue to investigate."

"Investigate what? You have a case of he said she said. You have limited surveillance footage, no reliable witnesses, and not much physical evidence."

"The DNA matches."

"Yes, and we'll pursue that, but the assault is only one factor. At best, you might be able to charge your suspects with manslaughter, but even that will be hard to prove. This is a drug case. We'll have better luck finding Jane Doe's dealer and tracking the supplier if we treat this as such. I'll pass this off to Detective Ashmore. He's been leading our Red Rabbit investigation these last few weeks. If we can offer Jimmy Stark or Marietta Linley some sort of deal or immunity in exchange for names or descriptions, they might be able to tell us exactly what we want to hear." He nodded to me. "Thanks for doing such a thorough job. You saved us a lot of legwork. Your father taught you well."

"Thank you, sir." But that wasn't what I wanted to say. Defeated, I returned to homicide and went through the double doors.

"What's wrong?" Brad asked.

"Narcotics took over our case. We're done."

THIRTEEN

"When can I go home?" Wilson Matthews asked his attorney. "My bail's been posted. Why are the guards still watching my every move?" He jangled his wrist, which was chained to the bedrail.

"Soon. There are a few formalities to take care of and some forms that need signing."

"Then I'm free?"

"With a few conditions." His attorney eyed the corrections officer who remained stationed at the door. "Have you had any problems?"

"No." Frankly, Matthews couldn't be entirely certain of that. He'd spent most of these last few days in a dreamlike state. He wasn't sure how much was due to the concussion and how much was due to medical interventions. But for a man who hadn't slept well in almost a month, the last few nights had been glorious. "What are we waiting for?"

"The paperwork's on its way. After that, we just need the hospital to release you."

"Why are they keeping me here? What's my condition?"

The attorney frowned. "They didn't tell you?"

"I have a concussion and a couple of hairline fractures. Anything else?"

"Isn't that enough?"

Wilson snickered. His father always said he was an overachiever. "More than enough." He hadn't meant to do this much damage. It would take time to fully heal. That was precious time he didn't want to waste. But even sitting up in bed had caused his head to hurt and the nausea to set in. Perhaps he'd take a couple of days to plan more thoroughly.

With most of his victims, he took his time to figure out their routines and habits. He knew how they operated and where. He always had a solid plan and contingency, until he didn't.

Acting rashly and uncharacteristically is what put him in this position in the first place. One emotionally driven kill had untethered his life. When he tried to correct his mistake, he overcompensated. His second lapse in judgment only compounded his problems, which made everything else spiral out of control until that lying bitch and the man who'd been practically dry humping her in a crowded bar turned out to be undercover cops, whose sole agendas had been to find him. They succeeded, but now they'd pay the price.

To dole out punishment to the deceptive detective he'd need a strategy. Unlike the rest of his prey, Liv DeMarco had been trained to fight, to react, to survive. He'd need an advantage, and his overzealous attempt to gain his freedom had turned into a detriment. His throbbing headache was just a reminder that he needed to proceed cautiously. He had to regain control.

"How long until I'm fully recovered?" Wilson asked.

"They said it could be a couple of months for the skull fracture to completely heal, but it doesn't look that severe. You should be back on your feet in a couple of days."

"When's the trial?"

"Don't worry about that." The attorney eyed the red gelatin as it jiggled slightly on the tray. "You have no reason to be nervous, Mr. Matthews. While you're entitled to a speedy trial, the court system is slow. You have time to decide what you want to do. If you want to enter into a plea deal—"

"I'm not guilty." Matthews' eyes turned cold and hard. "I didn't do the things they said. I'm not a monster."

Subconsciously, the attorney swallowed. "Of course, you're not. But like I told you from the beginning, I don't care about your guilt or innocence. That's not what trial is about. The prosecutor has to prove his case beyond a reasonable doubt." He glanced back at the corrections officer in the hallway. "We'll discuss this in more detail when our privacy is guaranteed. In the meantime, enjoy your lunch. You'll be going home soon."

* * *

The next few days dragged. On the bright side, Brad and I hadn't been called to any more scenes. Instead, we caught up on some paperwork and checked to see if any progress had been made on our open cases. We clocked in and out as if this job were just any other office job.

Lt. Winston didn't leave us any messages. In fact, he hadn't spoken to either of us since that morning in his office. Brad didn't go into the details of their conversation, but suffice it to say, Winston had discovered my partner's involvement in assisting IAD and the FBI's investigation into police corruption. And since Detective Gallagher used to be one of Winston's homicide detectives, I couldn't help but wonder how Winston had come upon that information.

Since it was another slow night, I looked into Gallagher's other unsolved murders. Seven of them linked back to Wilson Matthews, but if Gallagher let Matthews walk, there had to be other killers he extorted and murders he covered up. I'd just started making a list when Brad's elbow slid off the desk and his arm hit with a thud.

He bolted upright, blinking rapidly and looking around.

"That's the second time you've fallen asleep at your desk this week. Are you okay?"

He didn't look okay. The skin beneath his eyes was dark and puffy. His eyes were bloodshot, and he looked sloppier than the Brad Fennel I remembered from two months ago. "Fine, just bored."

I didn't buy it. "Why don't you go lie on the couch in the

break room for a while? I'll cover for you on the paperwork. If a call comes in, I'll wake you."

He considered his options, glancing at the other cops stuck working graveyard. "I just need a little stimulation."

"Call over to vice and find out what massage parlors fit the bill."

"Not that kind of stimulation." He stretched. "You want some coffee? I'm gonna get a refill."

"No, thanks." I picked up my travel cup. "Emma convinced me to exchange the caffeine for antioxidants and vitamins."

"While that's a great thought, the green smoothie just isn't cutting it. Not tonight." He picked up the cup I brought for him and sucked on the straw to let me know it was empty. "What was it? Kale and pineapple?"

"With a bit of spinach and banana to round it out."

A rookie passed our desks on his way to the copy machine, catching the last part of our conversation. His lip curled up at my words, and Brad chuckled.

"What do you say, Atwood? Liv would be more than happy to bring you one tomorrow."

Officer Atwood looked like a deer caught in headlights. "Uh...no. That's quite all right. I'll stick with diet cola."

"That stuff will rot your insides."

"At least I won't shit green or turn into some New Age hippie."

"Is that what you think?" Brad asked. "After spending two tours in the middle of nowhere with nothing to eat but MREs and other things that should never be consumed in a civilized world, I bet you'd change your tune on fresh fruits and veggies."

"No, I mean yes. I just...I...uh...I'm sorry, Detective." Atwood glanced at me. "I like pineapple and bananas. Maybe just leave out the kale, and it wouldn't be so bad."

Brad laughed. "Relax, man. I'm just screwing around." He held out his hand. "I'm sorry."

The rookie blushed, shaking Brad's hand. Then he quietly excused himself and continued to the copier.

"You shouldn't do that," I warned. "The rookies scare easily. They have enough to deal with. They shouldn't have to worry about some crazed detective."

"You're the one who brought the smoothies. I'd be perfectly content and awake with nothing but coffee." Brad picked up his mug and went into the break room. When he returned, he had an apple in his hand.

"Okay, seriously, where do you keep getting these apples?"

"They're in the fridge. Bottom drawer. Voletek put them there. I thought he did that for you."

I stared at the apple, which had gotten a little shriveled. "Those must be from the farm." While I was explaining how Voletek acquired those apples, the phone rang. "This time, you jinxed us."

"How?"

"You said you wanted stimulation." I picked up the receiver and listened. "All right, we'll be there." I scribbled down the address and hung up. "We have another body in a nightclub. According to witnesses, the guy just dropped."

"Shouldn't we loop narcotics in and see if they want to take it? It might save us some time and paperwork."

"Actually, that was narcotics looping us in. They put a task force together, along with intelligence. Captain Grayson's taken over, and he specifically asked for us."

Brad gulped down half of the coffee and slipped into his jacket, pulling the back loose to make sure it concealed his cuffs and holster. "Narcotics, intelligence, and homicide. This can't be good."

"Probably not."

On our way there, Brad asked, "Do you think they know anything else about the last victim? Kara or Jane Doe, whatever we're calling her?"

"I don't know. No one from the ME's office has gotten back to us, but I think Ashmore made sure everything got rerouted to his desk."

We pulled to a stop behind two other unmarked cars and entered the club.

"What do we have?" I asked the two men standing above the body. My partner looked around at the shabby seats and dirty tables, studying everything else in order to avoid looking down at the corpse.

"Hey, DeMarco." Detective Loyola nodded to me and then my partner. "It's nice to see the two of you back to work."

"It'd be better if we didn't have a body," I said.

Loyola snorted. "Probably should have thought about that before you transferred to homicide."

Sullivan sighed. "We got another possible poisoning." He tapped the toe of his shoe beside an evidence marker. A bunny sticker had been pressed to the front of a tiny baggie. "Looks like the same shit again. Same insignia from the previous scenes. I don't know who's moving the bad dope, but we gotta stop it."

"I'm gonna go out on a limb here and say COD is an overdose of rat poison." Loyola rubbed his chin. "The coroner's determined that's the most likely outcome in these recent deaths, but this shit keeps spreading throughout the city. It's not just a single isolated club."

"Do you think these deaths are intentional?" Brad asked.

"I'm not sure how, but it's possible," Loyola said.

"Wouldn't the body count be higher if this came from a tainted batch?" I asked. "I don't know how many pills get cooked up together, but it has to be more than ten or twelve, right?" Based on the dried blood around the victim's nose and mouth, he'd bled to death. The autopsy would reveal more. But it was no secret anticoagulant rodenticide in large enough doses was lethal to humans. And whatever amount the victims ingested was lethal enough to kill them almost immediately.

"It's tough to say. We don't know how many pills the victims took or if other factors played a part in their deaths," Sullivan said.

"What did the ME have to say?" I asked.

Loyola and Sullivan exchanged a look. "We have eight autopsy reports. Every victim's different. One victim was on birth control. Another took migraine medicine. But some were perfectly healthy," Sullivan said. "It's making figuring this out even more difficult. We think it might have to do with the number of pills they took at one time, other drugs they took that night, and the amount of alcohol consumed."

"What about physical attacks?" Brad asked. "The car accident victim, Macy Lowan, sustained injuries which continued to bleed. Kara Dornan, the dead woman found in the bathroom, appeared to have been in some kind of altercation."

Sullivan pulled out his notepad. "Kara?" He turned back a few pages. "You mean Carla Doucette. She was nineteen years old." He jerked his chin toward the body on the ground. "She was a student at the same university as our most recent vic."

"Two from one school. That has to mean something. Do you have any leads on who's dealing this shit?" Brad glanced toward the narcotics detective who was questioning the staff. "Narcotics hoped to shake something loose from the suspects we brought in."

"They gave us a few possible leads, but none of them panned out," Loyola said. "Detective Ashmore's convinced there's a new player on the scene, who came up with this designer MDMA. The rabbit logo is part of his branding, but narco still doesn't know much about him or who he is."

"I remember hearing something about that when I volunteered over there," Brad said. "But that was before people started dying. Narco should know something by now."

"Apparently not," Sullivan said. "That's why we're here and why Cap took over the task force and called you two in to assist."

"Does intelligence have any theories on what's going on?" I asked.

"Word on the street is Red Rabbit is exclusively a party drug. It's only being dealt in bars and clubs. We aren't even sure exactly what's in it. This stuff causes some kind of insane high. All the previous victims have tested positive for MDMA, ketamine, and rat poison. The rest varies, which might indicate it came from different batches or they were experimenting with a bunch of stuff before they died."

"Have we gotten a hold of any pills yet?" Brad asked. "That'd be the best way to find out what's in them."

Loyola and Sullivan shook their heads.

Brad looked at me. It didn't make much sense that undercovers hadn't been able to find a dealer to secure the latest designer drug. "That's odd."

"It's more than odd," Sullivan said.

Brad focused on the baggie. "This is the ninth victim. Have you found any connections among them?"

Loyola puffed out his cheeks before exhaling. "This one and the girl you found in the bathroom connect to the university. I don't know about the others."

"Macy Lowan graduated college last year," I said.

"Isn't this her alma mater?" Brad asked.

Sullivan chuckled. "This is why Captain Grayson asked you to assist on the task force. Be honest. Which one of you has a photographic memory?"

"Neither," I said.

"Did you memorize the case files?"

Brad snorted. "Liv hurts me if I don't have perfect recall."

"I do not."

"Hey, whatever works. Maybe you can teach me that trick, and I'll whip Artie here into shape." Loyola nudged Sullivan with his elbow. "Regardless, with three units working this investigation, we might actually make some headway before more people die."

"Or Grayson's just trying to woo the two of you back to intelligence by dangling a juicy case in front of your noses," Sullivan teased.

"With the way things are going, it wouldn't take much," Brad muttered. He crouched down beside the body, the conversation edging a little too close to reality. "He looks like a frat guy." He indicated the ring on the victim's finger. "Have you IDed him yet?"

"Paul Gwynn, twenty-two, college senior." Sullivan chuckled. "You want to take a stab at which fraternity he belongs to, or should I continue?"

"I'd hate to show you up. By all means, please continue."

"Wiseass." Sullivan jabbed the end of his pen into Brad's ribs. I cringed, but Brad didn't flinch. His face and posture gave nothing away. Only a handful of people knew what had happened, and we all swore to keep a lid on it. Sullivan didn't notice and continued to tell us everything he'd learned about the latest vic, which wasn't much.

"Where are his friends?" I asked.

"Officers escorted them to the precinct about an hour ago. From the statements they gave, none of Gwynn's friends know where he got the drugs. But after they arrived, he disappeared with some girl he met on the dance floor. Gwynn and the girl were gone for about an hour."

"What time was that?" I asked.

"A little after one a.m. The next time Gwynn's buddies saw him, he was totally wasted. He collapsed right here. They thought he had too much to drink, but when they couldn't wake him, the bartender tried to revive him. That's when they realized he was dead and called it in. Paramedics arrived, but by the time they got to him, he was already gone. The responding officers shut down the club, roped everything off, and questioned everyone inside."

"That was at what time?" Brad asked.

"Around three."

A small group remained in the far corner, seated at several tables. From the way they were dressed, they worked here. "What happened to the girl?" I asked.

"Gwynn's friends think she left. They didn't see her again, but they were all pretty wasted. They might not have recognized her. I'm not sure any of them got a good look to begin with." Sullivan closed his notepad.

"What about the rest of the clubgoers?" Brad asked.

"Officers questioned them, collected their contact info, and cut them loose." Sullivan jerked his chin toward Detective Ashmore. "He has everyone's details."

"Why isn't the ME here yet?" I looked around, but I didn't see anyone from the coroner's office.

"They're dealing with the victims of a building collapse. They'll get here as soon as they can," Loyola said. "Until then, we're babysitting the scene and taking statements."

"Did Gwynn give his friends any drugs?" Brad asked.

Sullivan tucked his notepad away. "They said no. I'm not sure I believe them, but they didn't appear to be in any physical distress and sobered up while patrol kept them here, so I think they'll be okay."

"Let's hope so. Do we know anything else about the mystery girl?" I asked.

"We don't, but Ashmore might." Loyola jerked his chin toward the narcotics detective heading our way. "Hey, Bryan, did the club manager have anything else to say?"

Ashmore shook his head. "Nothing we can use. Gwynn and his frat bros are regulars, as are a lot of college kids. The club caters to them. The management does what it can to keep drugs out, but these dumb kids just want to come here and get drunk and stoned. We've raided the club a few times, but the management's good about not serving minors and turning away fake IDs. The few busts we've made have been for MDMA, Special K, and the occasional amphetamine."

"What about surveillance footage?" Brad asked.

"They handed everything over. Inside. Outside. I checked it out, but I didn't see the exchange or the dealer." Ashmore pointed to the cameras. "Dim lights, neon strobes, and large crowds make it pretty damn hard to see or identify anyone or anything. We'll have the techs go over it again, just in case."

Brad nodded. "What about Red Rabbit?"

"You know almost as much as we do." Ashmore stared at my partner with cold, hard eyes for a few long seconds. The tension continued to build, and I struggled to come up with a question or comment to diffuse the situation. Before anything came to mind, Ashmore cracked a smile and winked. "I'm just busting your balls, Fennel. If these two knuckleheads," he indicated Loyola and Sullivan, "don't have any hard feelings over you and DeMarco leaving their unit high and dry for greener pastures, I'm not gonna throw a fit over you being out sick and missing a temp assignment you volunteered for. We're cool." He held out his fist for my partner to bump. "Jeez, when did you become this rigid? Is DeMarco riding you too hard?"

"It's not my fault," I said. "I'm a delight. Right, Brad, or do I have to hurt you again?"

Loyola laughed. "Good one, Liv."

Brad rolled his eyes. "Just ignore them. That's what I do."

The conversation shifted back to Red Rabbit's latest victim. Gwynn didn't have a record, but he had a reputation on campus as a party boy. He was an English major, who worked on the school paper and had an online blog and podcast, both of which focused on parties and raves held on and off campus.

"Maybe he mentioned something or someone in one of his entries that might have compromised this new dealer or his supplier. Maybe Red Rabbit's supplier wanted Gwynn dead," I said, "and this was intentional."

"Since you're homicide, you and Fennel should explore that angle. Actually, why don't you run that down for all the previous victims while intelligence and narcotics see what else we can dig up? So far, we've tracked tainted product to several clubs in this neighborhood. Let me show you what we think." Ashmore tapped on the tablet in his hand. The screen filled with a city map. Before he could say anything else, my phone rang.

I read the display. *ADA Logan Winters.* "Sorry, I have to take this."

FOURTEEN

"Wilson Matthews is out," Winters said as soon as I answered. "I thought you'd want to know. His bail's been posted, and the hospital released him earlier this afternoon. There's nothing we can do, unless he violates the terms of his bail."

"Which are?" I hoped the judge slapped him with an ankle monitor and limited his travel radius.

"To show up to court."

"That's bullshit."

"I know, Liv. Don't shoot the messenger."

"Do you realize what time it is, counselor?"

"Yeah, I'm sorry to call so late. I thought you were still working graveyard. Did I wake you?"

"No, but you should be asleep."

"I'm on my way home now. I just finished going through my messages and stumbled upon that. I promised I'd let you know. So that's what I'm doing." The smile crept into his voice. "I'm a man of my word."

"Good. Now go home and get some sleep."

"Are you okay?"

"Fine." But the news made me want to put my fist through a wall. There wasn't a single doubt in my mind that Wilson Matthews was a deranged serial killer. Letting him walk around until his trial put targets on the backs of every sex worker who happened to remind him of his mother. Luckily, his computer and cell phones had been confiscated as evidence. That would make it harder for Matthews to troll escort sites to find his next victim. "I'm just wondering about the legality of monitoring his financials, phone records, and having a few unis tail him."

"I can inquire, but unless you have cause, I doubt it'll fly. Instead, we'll get hit with harassment charges."

"No wonder they say justice is blind, but we can monitor his movements in public. There's no expectation of privacy under those conditions."

"It's a fine line, Liv. But you have a valid point."

"Night, Logan."

"Good night."

Taking a deep breath, I blew it out and went back to the cluster of detectives. I caught the tail-end of Ashmore's plan to monitor the nightclubs and bars in the area to see what we could learn about Red Rabbit and how to procure some of the hottest new drug.

"What about the college campus?" I asked. "Three of the victims had some sort of tie to the university. Most of the bars and clubs you pointed out are close enough to be regular hangouts for the students."

"We've spoken to a lot of students and put the university on notice, but nothing's shaken loose yet," Ashmore said. "It looks like a dead end."

"College kids aren't going to talk to us or any of their administrators. More than likely, they wouldn't go into details even if they ended up at the health clinic on campus because of some recreational drug they took. Drug use is grounds for suspension or expulsion, not to mention loss of scholarships, campus housing," Sullivan puffed out his cheeks, "and lord knows what else. At least that's how it was back in the day. And that was twenty years ago. It's probably worse now." He looked at me. "Is it?"

"I don't know."

"You're the youngest one here. What was it like for you?"

"My dad's a cop. I never did any of those things or affiliated with people who did."

Ashmore narrowed his eyes at me. "How old are you, DeMarco?"

"Twenty-eight."

His eyes grew a little wider. "Damn, you moved up the ranks fast."

I swallowed, wondering if he was going to blame nepotism on it, but he didn't. "Undercover has a few perks."

"So you graduated when? Six years ago?

"It's closer to seven. This May will be seven."

Ashmore rubbed his chin. "We'll run that idea by Captain Grayson when he gets in and see what he thinks. In the meantime, our best bet is to focus our efforts on the clubs and bars where our nine victims partied."

"Only eight," Brad said. "We found Macy Lowan in her apartment."

"We tracked her car using DOT footage. We know she was at Crystal earlier that evening, before she got into the accident." Ashmore tapped on the screen, moving the map outward. He drew an x over a club that was eight blocks from our current location. "Sullivan and Loyola, finish interviewing the staff and see if the uniforms found anything useful during their canvass. We need to ID the woman Gwynn met. She might have given him the drugs, or she might have sampled some herself. Either way, we need to find her. Fennel and DeMarco, head back to the precinct and start digging through the intel we've gathered on our nine vics. Find me some overlap. I'll wait for the ME to arrive and gather whatever additional security footage I can find. We'll reconvene in Captain Grayson's office at eight a.m."

Loyola and Sullivan went to speak to the remaining club staff, who looked tired and annoyed by the delay. I wondered how Lt. Winston would take the news that Brad and I would be working past shift change. According to Sullivan, Grayson already cleared this with our unit commander, but since Winston had a perpetual stick up his ass, I had a feeling this wouldn't end well for us.

"Who was on the phone?" Brad asked as we made our way across the parking lot.

"Logan Winters."

Brad gave me a strange look. "Booty call?"

"How many times do I have to tell you I have no interest in dating Winters?"

"Who said anything about dating?"

I slapped his arm. "Behave or I'll hurt you."

"Just so you know, Loyola's the only one who believes that."

I gave him my death stare.

"Okay, so if Winters didn't call you in the middle of the night for some action, what did he want?"

"Wilson Matthews is roaming around free, at least until his trial date. But something tells me he won't stick around that long."

"With five million dollars on his head, I'm not sure he has a choice. The bondsman will be incredibly motivated to make sure Matthews doesn't skip town."

"Do you think the bondsman is motivated to make sure Matthews doesn't start killing while he's on the outside?"

Brad sighed. "Let's deal with one problem at a time."

"What did I miss?"

"Nothing, really. Ashmore caught me up to speed on what the task force has been doing for the last few weeks. Ever since intelligence stepped in, they've been mapping out the territories where they suspect Red Rabbit is being dealt and keeping watch on the clubs. But with so many possibilities, we have no way of knowing what's slipping through the cracks."

"Everything," I said. "We're spread too thin. I'm sure the Cap knows that too. Frankly, I think that's the only reason narcotics let the intelligence unit take over their op."

"Narco's case wasn't going anywhere. Ashmore's been digging into it way too long. Elswin has grown impatient. The unit already has too many other ops in play to worry about this. They probably planned to stick it on the backburner, but since the bodies keep turning up, they had to do something to address it. They've got their CIs putting feelers out everywhere, but no one's come forward with any intel. Valuable or otherwise."

"Not even dead ends?"

"Nope."

"That doesn't make any sense. We've seen the baggies at too many crime scenes. Red Rabbit isn't some top secret thing. It's circulating. Someone must know something."

"Informants aren't always the most reliable, Liv."

"True, but the hungry ones like getting paid. For them to keep their mouths shut, there has to be a reason. More than likely, they've been threatened."

"Unless whoever's supplying Red Rabbit has separated everything from production to distribution so perfectly that no one knows where it's originating or who's behind it. Any informant who's been at this for a while will know they're not going to make much on intel that doesn't lead to a major bust."

"Also possible."

"For the time being, we'll let Ashmore worry about that. Right now, we're supposed to dig up whatever we can on the vics and see what's what. We should start with Paul Gwynn and work our way backward."

"Sounds like a plan." I slid into the passenger seat and closed my door. "How are you?"

"Fine. Why the sudden concern?"

"I heard what you said about going back to work for intelligence."

"I was joking."

But I didn't believe him. "How about your side? When Sullivan poked you with his pen, I felt it. He didn't reopen your wound, did he?"

Brad chuckled. "It's been over a month. I'm fine. You don't have to worry so much." He eyed my outstretched hand which had wandered past the gearshift, as if wanting to press against his ribs. "Do you want to compare battle scars, or is this just a ploy to get me to take my shirt off? Y'know, if Winters doesn't want a four a.m. booty call, I'm sure I can think of a few other guys who'd be happy to help you out."

"Do you want to get slapped again?"

"Some people pay good money for that."

"Are you one of them?"

He continued to snicker as he pulled away from the nightclub. "Man, you're feisty tonight."

"Sorry. I'm just worried. Why didn't anyone tell us we were earmarked to join the task force?"

"We're grunts, Liv. We go where they tell us and do what they tell us. That's just how it is. Did you really think the LT was going to give us the heads-up after we didn't keep him looped in? It's called payback. Plain and simple."

"What exactly did Winston say to you the other morning?"

"Not much. I already told you not to worry about it."

"But I am."

"Regardless, there's nothing we can do about it. Winston knows I went undercover to bust Gallagher. He also knows that I shot him."

"Do you think he wants revenge?"

"No." Brad scratched the stubble on his cheek, another physical manifestation that everything was not right with my partner. "He thought I should have come to him with my suspicions and looped him in on the investigation and the progress I was making."

"Did you explain why you didn't?"

"More or less. He didn't like it. He said he doesn't want any more secrets in his unit."

"But he kept us in the dark instead of telling us that we just got traded back to our old unit like a couple of baseball cards."

"It's temporary. We didn't get traded. We got subbed in for one game."

"Does Grayson know that Winston knows?"

"Liv, calm down. You're going to work yourself into a lather. If it makes you feel any better, you can talk to Cap about this after our task force meeting." He bumped his knuckles against the outer part of my thigh. "Don't worry. I won't let anything happen to you."

"That's not what I'm worried about." I was terrified for him, of word getting out and having other cops turn on him. We'd made some progress since the Serpico days, but we weren't as far as we should be. Still, I'd never met a cop who didn't love and respect my partner. I just didn't know if they'd still feel that way after they found out. "I'm worried about what this will do to your friendships, your career," I swallowed, "and your physical well-being."

"And I worry about you." He gripped the wheel in both hands, adjusting in his seat to shake out the tension in his shoulders. "That's why we're the perfect team."

"Better than Loyola and Sullivan?"

"Like you have to ask."

FIFTEEN

While Brad spoke to Paul Gwynn's friends, I dug into our latest victim's background. Thankfully, Ashmore said he'd handle the notification, but more than likely, I'd have to speak to Paul's parents at some point. Just not tonight.

I looked at the clock. It was morning. By now, most people were waking up to start their day. I didn't want to think about the devastating news Mr. and Mrs. Gwynn would be receiving and how their lives would be forever changed. Instead, I had to concentrate on tracking down the drug that killed their son.

Paul had over a hundred videos posted online for his podcast. From the listed dates, he must have started chronicling his partying and barhopping when he went to college. Given the nature of his podcast, I wondered if he'd reported his own illegal activities. But the kid hadn't been stupid enough to post himself drinking or doing drugs online.

I bypassed the earlier entries and scrolled down to the most recent. Paul had posted his last video three nights ago. I scribbled down the name of the club he'd gone to, checked to see if I spotted any women on screen who fit the description his friends had provided, and moved on to the next video. I only went back three months. Anything before that was irrelevant. Then I moved on to Carla Doucette's social media pages.

The photos she posted made her look like a fun kid. Already, her pages had been changed to memorialize her life. I had to scroll through hundreds of comments friends and acquaintances left, saying how much they loved her and how much she'd be missed. I read the comments, my heart breaking.

Brad came around the side of my desk, opened the bottom drawer, took out one of the chocolate bars, and placed it beside me. Then he took his seat, scooting the tissue box he kept in the corner a little closer to me.

"I'm okay." I unwrapped the chocolate bar, broke off a piece, and offered him some. "Did you learn anything else?"

"Not really. Paul's friends didn't see much. They were on the prowl. They didn't care one of their herd broke off. They just figured Paul was off somewhere getting lucky."

"We need to get a look at his phone. Given the number of videos and photos he has posted online, I wouldn't be surprised if the kid recorded everything."

Brad shot a text to Ashmore, Loyola, and Sullivan, asking if any of them had checked the victim's phone. "The screen's cracked. They had trouble getting into it. The techs can probably pull everything we need," Brad read.

"Does Ashmore think Paul has his drug dealer on speed dial?" I asked.

"I think so."

"It wouldn't hurt to cross reference the call logs from all of the vics either. Maybe we'll get lucky and figure out who's dealing tainted Red Rabbit the easy way."

"You mean you haven't already done that?" Brad asked.

"I was distracted."

"I'll pull records and see what's what. Are you still tracking down the bars and clubs they visited?"

"Yep." I pointed to a stack of files that contained the financial information for seven of the victims. "Carla didn't have a credit card in her name, per se. From what I found in Ashmore's interview notes, her parents gave her a prepaid card each semester. They thought it would teach her to be responsible with her money."

"Did she have a part-time job?"

"In addition to a work study. The checks from the part-time job got cashed, and her work study money got deposited into her campus account."

"Wow, I didn't know college kids still used paper money."

I leafed through the files. Most of the charges didn't match. The victims didn't have much in common, but one place kept popping up. I highlighted it. "Maybe they needed the cash. You can't exactly pay your dealer or tip strippers with plastic."

"Unless they have card readers hidden between their ass cheeks."

I laughed, despite the circumstances. "What titty bars have you been going to?"

He raised his palms. "I'm just saying." He leaned closer, breaking another piece of chocolate off the forgotten bar and popping it into his mouth. "Did each of the victims visit strip joints?"

"Possibly. Have you ever heard of Milk and Honey? It looks like a popular hangout." I opened an internet search window and typed in the name.

"That's not a strip joint."

"It sounds like one."

"It's a tea shop." He frowned. "Tea house?" But that still didn't sound right. "I don't know what you call it. It's like a coffee shop, but they specialize in tea. I guess it's a tearoom."

I read the online listing. My partner was right. "How did you know that?"

"I know things. Do you remember Elizabeth? We dated for a few weeks last February."

"Did I meet Elizabeth?"

"Blonde. British."

"They're all blonde, Brad. I don't remember her."

"We always went to Milk and Honey for breakfast. It was the only place that served tea the proper English way, or so she said."

"What is the proper English way?"

"In a cup with your pinky lifted."

"Do they sell anything else besides tea?"

"Biscuits, which look and taste a lot like cookies and flat muffins that can be smeared with jams and butter."

"English muffins?"

"I try not to stereotype."

I stifled a snort. "You need some sleep." But I knew he was doing this to cheer me up. Death always drained us. "I wasn't asking about their breakfast selection. I was curious if you thought they were dealing on the side."

"I never got that vibe. But it's possible. We always went during peak hours. The place was packed. It was a fight to get a table. From what I remember, they did an excellent business. They have the tea market cornered. It's not one of those rigid, prim and proper tearooms. Milk and Honey is just a cozy café right next to campus. Tea and academia go hand in hand. I'm sure there are just as many professors who frequent the café as there are students."

"According to this, Milk and Honey's been in business for two years. More than likely, every student has gone there at least once."

"Macy Lowan might have gone while she was still a student, or maybe she had friends who hadn't graduated that she met up with at the café more recently."

"Possibly."

I flipped through her financial statements. Sure enough, they'd all gone to Milk and Honey. "This is the only commonality I've discovered. But based on these charges, our nine victims never went to the café at the same time or even on the same day. Still, they could be meeting a dealer there."

Brad reached for the nearest file. "Kevin Harrison, twenty-seven, doctoral candidate. He died just outside Club Nova three weeks ago. His financial statement shows he'd gone to Milk and Honey that morning." He grabbed another file. "Reba Morgenstein, twenty-one, she worked full-time as a waitress in a sports bar. She has no obvious connection to the college, but she went to Milk and Honey twenty-nine days ago. She died the day before Macy

Lowan." He eyed me. "Do you really think she bought drugs and held on to them for two weeks before taking them?"

"They're recreational. Maybe she didn't have time to recreate until then."

"Do you think people who want to party have the kind of self-control to wait? That doesn't make a lot of sense."

"We still need to check out Milk and Honey. Are you trying to avoid it because you don't want to run into Elizabeth?"

"Not really. Last I heard, she went home to London."

"Is that why you broke up?"

"More or less." He wrote the name and address down. "We'll run it by the task force. Still, I don't think this is the connection we're looking for." He pushed the files back toward me. "I think the college is our connection."

"You just said one of the victims had no ties to the college."

"She waitressed at a sports bar and grill that caters to the college crowd. They have the place decorated in the school's colors and have tons of photos and gear from the school on display. It's one of the more famous college hangouts. She must have crossed paths with other students." His fingers flew over his keyboard. A smug smile tugged at his lips. "She was dating a college junior. She probably went to campus parties with him."

"You think Red Rabbit's getting dealt on campus?"

The look on his face said he had a theory. "Actually, I think it's getting dealt exclusively on campus and nowhere else. That's why we haven't been able to get a lead on it."

"That doesn't make any sense. How would Macy Lowan have gotten her hands on it? And what would a doctoral candidate be doing fraternizing with underclassmen? That's not how the college scene works."

"No, but there are certain services on campus and areas that everyone uses, things like the parking garage, library, coffee shops, the book store. You know, places like that."

"I hate to argue with your logic, but none of the deaths occurred on school grounds. Every one of the victims, with one exception, dropped at or near a club. If someone was dealing Red Rabbit on campus, that's where we'd find the victims." I did a quick check, but no 9-1-1 calls had been made from campus and no reports had come in. The college didn't report any criminal activity or medical emergencies either.

"It makes about as much sense as saying the dealer's working out of Milk and Honey. None of the reports originated from there either."

"We're still missing something." I skimmed the files again. "What aren't we seeing?"

"Whatever it is, at least three other detectives failed to notice it too." Brad pointed to the clock. "We should go."

"We have another ten minutes until the eight o'clock meeting."

He pushed his chair beneath his desk. "C'mon, Liv, we don't want the rest of the team to have to wait for us."

But I knew the real reason behind his eagerness. He didn't want to ask permission from Winston. "Go on ahead. I'll be there in a minute."

"Fine. I'll save you a seat. If the Cap's still springing for those fruit deliveries, I'll grab you an orange."

"Thanks."

I closed the tabs on my computer, put in a request for Mac to see what she could find on Paul Gwynn's phone, and grabbed everything off my desk. Just then, Lt. Winston entered the bullpen. His tie swung free from his jacket, but he didn't notice.

"Sir, do you a have a minute?" I asked.

"What is it, DeMarco?"

"Fennel and I were asked to join the Red Rabbit task force. I just wanted to make sure we didn't get any more wires crossed."

"Nope. You're good to go." His eyes narrowed at the phone on my desk. "Did you catch any homicides last night?"

"Just another Red Rabbit call. Nothing else."

"Okay, good. You got nothing on your plate to worry about." Winston squinted, the lines deepening around his eyes. "What's a matter, DeMarco? Afraid you're gonna get transferred back to intelligence?"

"Is that a possibility?"

He barked out a laugh. "The reason you and Fennel got to join my team was because we were short-staffed. I have no intention of losing another detective, not because of a transfer or any other reason." He stared into my eyes. "Make sure your partner knows that."

Before I could reply, he went into his office and shut the door. Shaking it off, I headed for the stairwell. I nearly collided with Voletek as I pushed my way through the double doors.

"Where's the fire?" Voletek asked.

"Which one?" I shook my head. "I'm guessing you didn't get the four a.m. call from ADA Winters. Wilson Matthews is out on bail."

"Shit." Voletek ran a hand through his hair. "Are we maintaining eyes on him?"

"No."

"We should."

"I agree, but we're not in charge of these things."

"Let me see what I can do. Do you want a detail to keep an eye on you?"

"Why?"

"In case you've forgotten, you have the same physical characteristics as his victims, and he threatened you. I can get a patrol car to shadow you and make sure you're safe."

"Jake, no. I'm fine. I don't want special treatment. Every cop who's ever made an arrest has received the same threats I have. It's no big deal."

"It better not be."

SIXTEEN

Our first official task force meeting didn't go well. Brad and I shared our findings and theories with the group. Loyola and Sullivan hadn't gotten anything useful from the club staff. They'd gone back over every note and conversation officers had with the clubgoers they questioned, but no one remembered seeing the girl with whom Paul Gwynn had disappeared.

"Surveillance footage doesn't show us much. I handed it over to the techs. They'll try to clean it up, but from what I've seen, the girl never showed her face to the camera," Ashmore concluded.

"What about exterior cameras?" Captain Grayson asked.

"They're spotty at best. With the foot traffic around the club, she could have easily blended into the crowd."

"What does she look like?" I asked.

"Short, about five foot three, spiky red hair, thin. She wore a grey camo skirt with a black mesh top over a red tank top. Paul's friends remember she had extensive ink on one of her arms. They just don't remember which," Ashmore said.

I glanced at Brad, who nodded. At least the frat brothers had stuck to the same story, which meant it was unlikely they were lying. "We should let them sit with a sketch artist."

"After which, we should get them to look at some mug shots. If this young woman gave Gwynn the drugs that killed him, it's possible she's been brought in before." Captain Grayson flipped through our reports. "How much cash was on the body?"

All eyes turned to Detective Ashmore. "Forty-three dollars."

"How much did he normally carry?" Grayson asked.

"Roughly that. His friends said he kept enough on hand to afford a ride home."

"That doesn't tell us how much," Brad said. "He might have had more, bought the pills, and made sure to have enough left over for a cab. Did his friends know how much he had when they went out that night?"

I looked at my partner. "You didn't ask them?"

"Twenty-twenty hindsight."

Loyola grinned. "Well, I thought to ask. It seemed like an intelligent question."

The captain cleared his throat. "What did they say?"

"They didn't know," Loyola admitted.

"All right." Grayson pulled Paul's ID photo from the file and pasted it on the whiteboard beside Carla Doucette's photo. "Nine people are already dead. The woman Paul met probably supplied him with the drugs. If not, she may turn up as number ten or she can point us to the dealer. That means locating her is our priority."

"Agreed, Cap," Ashmore said.

"Once we get a sketch, get that copied and passed around. Hopefully someone in narcotics will recognize her or knows someone on the street who will recognize her. Loyola and Sullivan, stay on top of the ME. As soon as they get the tox report back, I want to know what Paul Gwynn took and what the precise cause of death is. At the very least, we need to figure out how this drug is killing people. Once we know, we can warn them, and maybe get a few people to think twice before taking it."

"Yes, sir," Sullivan said.

Brad's phone buzzed, and he pulled it out. He read the

text message and slid it across the table for me to see. Captain Grayson stared at us, like a teacher who caught his students passing notes. "Fennel and DeMarco, since you think Red Rabbit's being dealt on the college campus or somewhere nearby, I'm gonna let you run that down. We've already explored that option, but Milk and Honey might be worth looking into. Check out the café and see if there's anything you can learn about their operation or the people who hang out there. If that's the headquarters for Red Rabbit distribution, I want to know about it."

My phone buzzed a moment after Brad's did. But I didn't bother to pull it out. Something told me I'd just received the same message he did. FBI Agent Anderson had more questions concerning the Gallagher investigation. Since Winters had reached out to him concerning Gallagher's connection to Wilson Matthews, I had to assume that's why he wanted to speak to us again.

"DeMarco, are you listening?" Grayson asked.

"Of course, Captain."

"All right, everyone, get out of here. It's been a long night. Go home and get some sleep. We'll start back fresh tomorrow." He saw the look on Ashmore's face. "If you want to put in more time, go ahead. But we might get better results from our witnesses once they get some sleep."

"Yes, sir." Ashmore grabbed his reports and nodded to the rest of us. "We'll reconvene at start of next shift. Gentlemen." He nodded. "DeMarco." He left the conference room and headed straight to the stairs.

"Why does he think he's in charge?" I asked.

"It was originally his case," Loyola said.

"His unit's case. He was assigned to work on it," Sullivan corrected.

"It's fine," Grayson said. "I don't mind. Narcotics asked us to assist. Frankly, I was surprised when they turned the whole damn thing over."

"They have a lot on their plates," Brad said. "The cartels and gangs are in the midst of some major power plays. Unless Red Rabbit is part of that, they don't have the resources necessary to devote to pulling this crap off the street."

I slid out of my chair and gathered my things, carefully folding my orange peel into my napkin before picking it up and tossing it into the waste bin. Sullivan and Loyola headed out. I was about to follow them when I remembered to check my messages. As I suspected, Agent Anderson had a few more questions for me. And he wanted them answered this morning.

"Hey, Cap," I made sure the door to the conference room had closed, "we have a problem."

"Agent Anderson," Grayson said. "I know. He called me first thing this morning." He turned to my partner. "I owe you an apology. When you went under, it wasn't supposed to get this twisted and complicated."

"Twisted and complicated is what we do around here," Brad said.

"Lieutenant Winston knows," I blurted out. "Did you tell him?

"No, Liv." Grayson rubbed his temples. "He might have spoken to someone in IA. Then again, with Voletek working homicide, Winston could have used that as a means to gain access to the commissioner's office and find out the details concerning how a cop who used to be under his command ended up dead. Don't jump to any conclusions yet. We don't have any reason to think Winston's a bad seed."

"Is this why Anderson wants to meet with us?" Brad asked.

"I'm not sure. The FBI doesn't readily share internal intel, especially when it involves their investigation into allegations of police corruption."

"At this point, it's more than allegations," Brad said. "They have all the proof they need. They have the recordings I gave them, access to Gallagher's financial records and phone logs, and my account and Liv's of the night Gallagher tried to kill me." He glanced at me. "Us."

"I don't think the FBI wants to talk about Lieutenant Winston. I think they have a few questions concerning Wilson Matthews' connection to Detective Gallagher," I said.

"Why?" Brad asked. "Because of ADA Winters?"

"That and Matthews is roaming free."

Grayson's brow creased. "What does any of this have to do with Winters?"

"The district attorney's office is looking for ways to have Matthews' bail revoked. Winters went to the FBI to ask if their investigation into Gallagher turned up any additional evidence against Matthews. More than likely, that's why Anderson wants to speak to us this morning," I said.

"That would explain why he didn't want to speak to me," Grayson said. "He just gave me the heads-up that details of the investigation might leak. Apparently, they already have."

"Winters won't say anything," I said.

"He might not have a choice, Liv." Brad looked at me. "But it doesn't matter. Winston already knows."

"We still don't know how he found out." A cold, clamminess settled in the pit of my stomach. "The FBI's still trying to identify all the cops and civilian personnel who helped Gallagher steal evidence and destroy cases. Do we think Winston's in on it?"

Grayson cleared his throat. "Detective, you know how dangerous rumors can be. Unless you have absolute proof, it's unwise to speculate."

"But Cap," Brad began.

Grayson held up his hand to silence my partner. "I've known Winston a long time. Until we learned Gallagher was the leak in the department, I never thought about it. Now, I'm not sure how all the things Gallagher did while working in homicide went by unnoticed. Then again, Winston forced him to transfer out. Maybe he had suspicions and no proof. I don't know. But we can't jump to conclusions."

I turned my gaze to my partner. "We should be prepared to run damage control, just in case." I glanced back at Captain Grayson. "In the event Winston was involved, do you think he'd retaliate against us?"

"No." Grayson's conviction eased some of my fears.

"You should get going, Liv. Anderson's expecting you at ten o'clock, and it's already after nine," Brad said.

"What about you?"

"I'll meet you there."

I nodded goodbye to Captain Grayson and went out the door. Brad wanted to hang back so they could speak in private.

By the time I arrived at the federal building, I was ready to do whatever Agent Anderson wanted. A strong sense of justice had been instilled in me ever since I was a baby. That had never changed, from standing up for classmates who got bullied on the playground to supporting Emma through all of her trials and tribulations, to following in my father's footsteps to help make the city safe for everyone.

Before stepping through the metal detector, I held out my badge. Building security waved me around to a desk, where they checked my ID and copied down my badge number. "I have a meeting with Agent Anderson."

"He's waiting in his office."

I went up the stairs and down the hall. I'd been here a few times in the last month. Gently, I knocked on the doorjamb. Agent Anderson looked up. "Close the door, Detective DeMarco."

"What's going on?"

"I just wanted to go over a couple of things again." He gave me that practiced professional smile. It was the same look accountants have when they sit a client down to go over taxes. "Tell me about the night of the shooting." He didn't have a folder or notepad in front of him. Instead, he focused entirely on me, his hands folded neatly on the desk in front of him. "Walk me through what happened."

"Detective Fennel was asleep on the couch in my living room. I had gone into the kitchen to get some water. Gallagher was already inside, but I didn't know that."

"How did he get in?"

"At the time, I didn't know, but techs said he bumped my deadbolt and picked the lock on the handle." I paused, wondering if Anderson would pose another question, but he didn't. "Gallagher jumped me from behind. He put his hand over my mouth to keep me quiet, but when he realized that wouldn't work, he held a gun to my head."

"Did he tell you what he wanted?"

"He said he wanted to make Detective Fennel pay for his betrayal."

"Did he mention anything else?"

I exhaled, trying to recall every detail, but when it happened, I'd been too focused on neutralizing the threat that Gallagher's words were meaningless. "He was pleased to find us together. He intended to harm or kill me because he hoped that would make the case against Wilson Matthews disappear."

"Then what happened?"

"I fought with him, but I couldn't overpower him. He was armed, and I wasn't. Our fighting woke Fennel. He intervened. They were both on the ground." I swallowed, hearing the sounds of their struggle play through my head. "Brad screamed." I cringed because I recalled that sound so vividly and also because I'd referred to my partner in more familiar terms. But Anderson didn't let on that he'd noticed. "Fennel had been beaten earlier that evening on Gallagher's orders. Going into the fight, Gallagher knew how badly injured my partner was and exactly how to hurt him. If Fennel hadn't shot Gallagher, my partner would be dead right now. More than likely, so would I."

"Don't worry, DeMarco. It was a good shoot." He chewed on his lip for a moment. "I'm curious what your partner was doing at your place that night. He was undercover. Did he tell you about his assignment?"

"I didn't know anything about it until I got home that evening and found him bleeding in my bathroom. He only came to me because he didn't have any other place to go. Gallagher had eyes and ears everywhere. Fennel said he was afraid to go to the hospital because that would lead to an investigation. He couldn't reach out to Captain Grayson because Gallagher might have gotten wind of it."

"Still, it was a risk."

"Fennel needed help. He was bleeding and on the verge of collapse. He didn't have a choice."

"As far as I know, you're not a doctor."

"No, but my friend Emma's an ER nurse."

"That's why you called her that night."

"Yes."

"Tell me more about your interactions with Gallagher prior to that night. Did you have any reason to want him dead?"

"No. Like I said before, Gallagher admitted to working for Wilson Matthews, which was the serial killer case I was working. Matthews was my prime suspect, and earlier that night, I arrested him. Before that, Gallagher had tried to get me to drop the case and stop my investigation."

"But you refused."

"Of course. Detective Voletek and I had two crime scenes. The similarities led us to dig up several old cases. Seven of those had been investigated by Gallagher when he was working homicide. When I confronted him, he dismissed the possibility all the murders had been committed by one man and told me to focus on my current cases and not cold ones."

"Did you think that was odd?"

"I thought he was a prick, but I didn't know just how much of a prick. I didn't know enough to want him dead." I cleared my throat. "I thought you said it was a clean shoot."

"It was."

"So what is this about?"

"The district attorney's office asked me to look into the possibility Wilson Matthews might have sent Gallagher to your apartment to kill you. I figured if we went over everything again, I might have a better grasp of what went down that night."

"I never had many interactions with Gallagher, aside from that one confrontation at the precinct."

"But he spent a great deal of time with your partner."

"You'll have to ask Fennel what they talked about." I thought about my few encounters with Brad during that time when everyone in the department had been convinced he'd lost his shit and walked off the job. Even I didn't know what was going on, but Brad had done what he could to protect me. "Fennel volunteered for that undercover assignment because we'd just recovered from a close call after a string of close calls and leaked intel. According to Detective Shaw in IA, every compromised case we worked was due to Gallagher pulling strings in the background."

"Do you believe Gallagher targeted you specifically?"

"No. It wasn't just our cases that were compromised. Plenty of other cases got thrown out for insufficient evidence due to Gallagher's interference. Do you know how he made that happen?"

"The FBI has a list of his accomplices, everyone from decorated police lieutenants to civilian personnel. The problem is figuring out who knowingly aided and abetted, compared to fulfilling their duties by answering the requests made by a detective. That's where it gets tricky." He held out his hand. "Thanks for your time." We shook, and I stood up. "One final question, Detective. Wilson Matthews was arrested with a bag full of money inside a hotel where he had just met with Gallagher. Are you certain he didn't try to hire Gallagher to kill you?"

"I don't know. Maybe you should ask Matthews about it."

SEVENTEEN

By the time I'd gotten out of the interview, Brad was on his way in. We passed each other in the hallway. His expression asked a million questions, but all I could do was shrug. I had no idea what Agent Anderson thought or who else on the force might be dirty. I wasn't even convinced that was still one of Anderson's priorities. Maybe the FBI was helping the DA with its case against Wilson Matthews. Even though Matthews' crimes didn't fall under their jurisdiction, he was a serial killer. That gave the Bureau some leeway to explore the matter further, especially since it overlapped with their ongoing corruption investigation.

My head spun as I entered the lobby. The sky was overcast, but the morning light still brightened the entrance. I blinked against it, waiting for my eyes to adjust. Once they did, I was sure I was seeing things.

"Have a seat, Mr. Kincaid. An agent will be with you shortly."

"Axel?" I asked, as he cleared the metal detectors and headed for the row of chairs against the wall.

He cocked his head to the side, amused to see me. "Liv."

"What are you doing here?" Maybe Anderson had called him too.

Axel looked like the cat that swallowed the canary. "Official business. Why?" He held the sly smile. "Were you hoping to find me in cuffs?"

"No, I..." A million questions went through my head. "Are you here because of Fennel's investigation?"

"Not at all." Kincaid looked intrigued. "I think I've already done more than my fair share. I allowed your partner to place recording devices inside my club to gather evidence. Did something happen to the recordings?"

"Not that I know of."

His brow furrowed. "Why do you look so troubled?"

"Mr. Kincaid, this way, please." An FBI agent stood in the corridor, gesturing for Axel to join him.

Axel held up his pointer finger. "Just a sec." He continued to stare at me.

"Go. It's no big deal. I'm fine. I'll see you later." I tried to move past him, but Axel grabbed my arm.

"We can finish this conversation as soon as I get out. This shouldn't take long. Unless you have to run back to the precinct."

"I'm free. I just came off shift."

I wondered if talking to Axel was a good idea. As a self-proclaimed former car thief and current nightclub owner, Axel had finagled himself a sweetheart deal as a federal informant. He had his finger on the pulse of the crime world. He was willing to provide intel in exchange for law enforcement looking the other way on several of his indiscretions. He might know more about Gallagher's operation. If not, I could quiz him on Red Rabbit. He had a strict anti-drug policy inside his club, but I knew that didn't apply to the other events he hosted. He had to know something. I'd bet my afternoon on it.

He jerked his chin toward the double doors. "I'll meet you outside."

I exited the federal building. A bright blue Bugatti was parked in a visitor space. That had to be Axel's car. The cop in me wondered if he'd stolen it or won it in a bet. Spark was notorious for its gambling and illegal car races.

I chuckled. Axel Kincaid—a walking contradiction. He kept drugs and prostitutes out of his club because he didn't want to risk getting busted. He didn't want to lose everything, but at the same time, he catered to a very specific clientele. He offered the club's members what he liked to call the Vegas experience. He claimed he could get anyone anything they wanted at any time. And just like the Las Vegas slogan, what happens at Spark, stays at Spark.

Moving closer, I peered through the tinted windows, but I couldn't see any obvious contraband inside. A part of me wanted to run the plates to find out if they matched the vehicle or if they'd been reported stolen, but since I intended to ask the man for a favor, that wouldn't be a good way to start the morning.

Still, I couldn't help but look for obvious signs of forced entry on the vehicle. Yet, Axel was skilled enough to never leave a mark on any of the cars he stole. And he hadn't been arrested for boosting a car in more than a decade.

"Wanna go for a ride?" he asked. "She tops out around 230."

I jumped, surprised that he'd snuck up on me. "You're done?"

"I told you it wouldn't take long." He clicked a button on the fob to unlock the doors. "What do you think? I usually have a thing for Italians, but I couldn't pass this up. She's sexy as sin." He wasn't wrong.

"Don't refer to it as a she."

"Why not?" His lip quirked playfully. "It's only fitting since I rather enjoying being inside of her."

"Goodbye, Axel." This was a mistake. I turned to walk away.

He chuckled. "Lighten up, Detective. I thought you could use a laugh. Apparently, you're not in the mood for jokes."

"Not really." I stopped a few feet away. "How'd you get the car?"

"Is that really what you want to ask me?"

"No."

He opened the passenger's side door. "Get in, so we can talk in private."

Reluctantly, I slid inside. The soft leather seats had just the right amount of give. Axel climbed in on his side, removed an envelope from his jacket pocket, slipped it into one of the compartments, and turned to face me.

The last time I sat inside one of Axel's cars was the day he took me to an illegal street race and told me he knew I was a cop. This didn't bring back good memories. In fact, my chest felt tight. "Did you provide the FBI with any other information regarding my partner's investigation besides the recordings?"

"No. That's what Detective Fennel and I agreed to."

"That's it? The Feds didn't question you?"

"They tried, but I didn't have anything to say. When Detective Fennel came to me for a favor, I set the terms. You know how I feel about cops inside my club. Spark doesn't have surveillance inside. My members' privacy is of the utmost importance. Letting your partner use my club as part of his sting operation went against every cell in my body, but I let him." He stared at me. "You know why."

"We both know you have security cameras inside."

"First, you need to prove it. Second, get a fucking court order."

"I don't want a court order. I want to know if you have any other footage of Ian Gallagher or Wilson Matthews."

"Gallagher only gained admittance to Spark because Fennel was with him. I wasn't letting that asshole inside without a damn good reason."

"What about Matthews?"

Axel licked his lip. "What do you want me to say?"

"The truth."

His lips twitched from side to side. "Are you sure?"

"For god's sake, I know he was inside the club the night we had dinner. He was downstairs while we were upstairs. Brad showed up that same night. You knew he was on his way. That's why you begged me to go to dinner with you. You lied to me, and you swore you'd never do that."

"I never made such a promise. I simply said I wasn't a liar. And I didn't lie. You asked me if Fennel was downstairs. I said he wasn't. That was true. He arrived after you left."

"But Wilson Matthews was there."

Axel gave me a blank stare. "Is that supposed to mean

something? Fennel never mentioned anything about him to me."

Arguing with Axel was like trying to stop a charging rhino. "Wilson Matthews," I repeated.

"What about him?"

"You know what he's accused of. He's out on bail. The Feds called me in to ask about his connection to Gallagher. If more evidence surfaces or if additional charges can be made for crimes we don't yet know about, his bail might be revoked. Do you know anything or have anything you're willing to share? He's going to kill again. I can feel it."

"Once he does, arrest him. Maybe this time it'll stick."

"It stuck the first time, until some moronic judge let him out until trial."

"Next time, maybe he'll land in front of a rationally-minded judge who will do what you want."

"At the cost of another woman's life?" I knew Kincaid's darkest secret and weak spot. "He kills sex workers. He slices them open and bleeds them dry. I don't want that to happen to anyone else."

"I don't have anything for you. Everything I had was turned over. I'm sorry, Liv. Truly."

"Are you sure?"

"You asked me about this when that woman was killed a few blocks from my club. I looked into it then. If I had found anything, I would have given it to you." His eyes showed nothing but sincerity. "I'm sorry. Monsters like him have no place in this world."

"What about his application to Spark? He became a member when Gallagher requested they meet there. You run checks on your members. Maybe you found something we missed."

"Are you saying my private background checks are more thorough than the police department's?"

"I'm saying it wouldn't hurt to double-check my work with yours."

"I didn't put much work into it. It would have been a waste of time. Matthews got a temporary membership. One night only. He sure as shit isn't welcome at my club ever again. I never wasted my time running him when he isn't

Spark material."

"Can I see his application?" Spark kept records on its members. I always thought it was so Axel could blackmail them, if necessary. But I'd never been able to prove it.

He hit another button on the fob, and the engine purred to life. "Buckle up."

Before I had time to tell him my car was parked a few spots away, he zipped out of the space and into traffic. Instead of protesting, I white-knuckled the bar while Axel sped around the slower moving vehicles.

"You do remember I'm a cop, right?"

"Do you have your badge?"

"Of course." What kind of question was that?

"Great. If I get pulled over, I'll need you to show that to the traffic cops." He eyed me. "That is, if they can catch me. And to date, you're the only one who's even come close to catching me."

He made a sharp turn into the alleyway beside Spark, cut the engine, and opened the door. At this time of morning, the place was shut down. He unlocked the side door and held it open for me to enter. The clean-up crew had already finished for the day, probably three or four hours earlier.

"Would you like a drink?" Axel asked.

"It's not even eleven a.m."

"How about coffee?"

"I need to sleep at some point."

"That's right. You're on graveyard this week."

"How do you know that?"

"You told me you just got off shift. What else could that mean?" He tapped his temple twice. "Someone's not thinking clearly, Detective."

I followed Axel into the manager's office. He pushed the chair aside and went to the filing cabinet. He unlocked the bottom drawer, leafed through the folders, making sure I couldn't read the labels from where I stood, and pulled out an application. It was marked "destroy" in red letters. But something told me he'd held onto this for a reason. Maybe he was psychic, or he'd found out what Matthews was capable of doing and planned to take care of it himself.

"Due to privacy concerns, I can't let you keep my copy," he said.

"Not a problem." I took out my phone and photographed each page. "Thanks."

"Do you think there's something in there that might help?"

"I don't know. But I have to try." I eyed him curiously. "Why did you hand it over so easily? You always make me work for favors."

"This is different. Matthews needs to be locked away." He slid the application back into the drawer.

"That being said, I was hoping you might be able to help me with another matter."

"You and your favors. I am not a genie, Detective DeMarco. I don't grant wishes."

"Red Rabbit, have you heard of it?"

"I don't allow drugs inside my club."

"I know, but you've heard of it."

"Maybe. Why are you asking about it?"

"I need to find the supplier. The shit's laced with rat poison. It's already killed nine people."

"Do you expect me to fix the world's problems?"

"No, Axel. But I hoped you'd help."

He rubbed a hand over his face, regretting having picked me up from the federal building. "Nine people."

"Yeah, the ninth one dropped in the middle of a club last night." I told him where each of the victims had died.

"Those aren't mob or cartel controlled clubs." His eyes narrowed. "And the locations are too spread out. None of the local gangs have control of that much real estate. Most of them aren't even in gang territory."

Narcotics had reached the same conclusion. "The victims vary, but they're all in that eighteen to thirty-five age range."

"Not surprising, given that they died inside clubs. You don't see as many established adults playing around at those places. By then, they have more defined tastes."

"So they'd come to Spark instead?"

"And they wouldn't be looking to buy a cocktail of MDMA and date rape drugs."

"That's what Red Rabbit is?" We suspected, but I hoped by playing stupid Axel might provide me with additional information that we didn't possess. "How does that even work?"

"The majority of the high comes from the MDMA. It gives users that warm, tingly feeling, like they want to fuck like a rabbit. The rest of the mix is supposed to be micro-doses of a bunch of shit, Special K, GHB, rohypynol, et cetera. That's to counteract the stimulant effects of the MDMA and relax and mellow out the user so it's a smoother, more enjoyable high. It seems like a waste to me, but what do I know. I was never one for depressants, aside from some finely aged spirits. Normally, I prefer as much stimulation as I can get."

"Just another thing you and my partner have in common."

"What?"

"Never mind. Why is it called Red Rabbit?"

"It's a branding thing. The pills are bright red." He realized his mistake a moment too late. "Surely, you knew that."

"Not until just now. We haven't been able to get our hands on any. That's why we're in such a bind trying to find the supplier or even some low level dealer. Anyone who can lead us to the cook." I glanced around the room. "You can get anything for anybody, right?"

"That's entrapment, Detective. I'm not that stupid."

"Do you know how to get your hands on some? Maybe you could inquire and point me in the direction of your source."

"I'm not a snitch."

"We both know that's not true."

He glared at me. "That's not what I call the service I supply to the law enforcement community. My clients know they can trust me. They know Spark is sacred ground, unless they break the rules, and those violations are often dealt with in-house."

"That's a fine line. Look, I'm telling you this as someone who cares. You don't want any of your members to drop a few tabs of Red Rabbit before they arrive at Spark or once they get here because it doesn't take very long before they're dead on the floor. And you don't want to have that kind of mess to clean up."

"Thanks for your concern, but no one's dropping dead inside my club without my permission."

EIGHTEEN

Despite being back at home, Wilson Matthews didn't sleep well. Perhaps the pain in his head played a factor, but he didn't think so. He hadn't realized just how violated he felt until he returned to his apartment. His computer and cell phones had been confiscated as evidence. Even the clothes in his drawers had been picked through and searched. Thankfully, he'd moved every item of importance to a secure location before the police raid.

"You want to make this more complicated, don't you?" he mumbled. The detective had messed with him. It was only fair he return the favor.

The police would be monitoring his internet activity, so he'd have to use public wi-fi or borrow from one of his unsuspecting neighbors. His attorney had gotten him a throwaway phone and a cheap netbook that would allow him to search the internet. That's all he needed to conduct his research.

He plugged in the netbook, searched for nearby networks, and selected the only one that wasn't password protected. As soon as he got online, he enabled a VPN to further mask his movements. That wouldn't keep the cops from discovering what he was doing, if they came looking.

But he didn't expect them to have the pull or wherewithal to monitor all possible wi-fi networks he might access. And since the netbook was given to him by his attorney, they would have no way of tracing its purchase back to him.

Convinced he was safe, he got started. But where to start? He recalled so many details about her, but the way she looked and smelled, how she moved and sounded, those weren't helpful for his internet search. He took a moment to rein in his thoughts. Then he began to type.

Detective Olive DeMarco. He'd memorized her badge number. Her name had been on a lot of official documents that had crossed his attorney's desk. Since she was the lead detective, he hoped he had everything necessary to find her.

He found himself desperate to scratch that familiar itch. Scoping out the local escort sites was a waste of time. He already knew who his next target would be, but he couldn't help himself. He was curious to see if the fake profiles she'd created still existed. But they'd been deleted.

Instead, he found himself searching for another way to see her. The desire to study every line of her face and curve of her body was nearly overwhelming. She didn't have any social media profiles that he could find. Then again, most cops wouldn't take that kind of risk. That meant she was smart and careful.

Exhaling slowly, he performed a general internet search. He found a few dated news articles which only mentioned the DeMarco name in passing. But it wasn't Liv. These articles were written about a police captain.

He blinked against the constant headache. The concussion was keeping him from thinking clearly. Until he was back at full capacity, he'd have to stick to research and planning. This time, he was chasing deadly prey. He'd have to be at the top of his game. More than any of his other victims, Liv DeMarco deserved to die.

As a last ditch effort, he searched people listings and the white pages. The city didn't have a shortage of DeMarcos. But they only had one Olive. He copied down the address and phone number. Not even the police could completely protect their privacy when it came to public records.

Imminent Threat

He smiled down at the information he'd written. The intermittent dizziness and headache told him he should wait before performing any recon, but he'd been locked up for too long. The desire to explore and hunt was undeniable.

The phone number beckoned to him. He had to find out if that was her private number. He wanted to hear her voice. Would she sound anxious at receiving his call, or would she taunt him?

*   *   *

The ringing phone startled me out of my nightmare. I woke up covered in a cold sweat. The phone continued to let out short, shrill rings. Without looking, I hit answer.

"Hello," I grunted.

"Hi."

I didn't recognize the caller's voice. "Who is this?"

"Have you already forgotten me, Liv?"

A shiver traveled through me. "Who is this?" I repeated more forcefully.

"Don't worry about it. I'll be seeing you soon. That's a nice apartment you have." Abruptly, the call ended.

I pulled the device away from my ear and stared at the number. I didn't recognize it. But I'd worry about that later. Right now, the last words he said were far more disturbing.

The curtains gently swayed in front of the window, causing the shadows cast by the late afternoon sun to dance along my walls. Another shiver traveled through me. Was I alone? Had he made the call from inside my apartment?

Stop it, Liv. This isn't a slasher movie, I chided. But it felt like one.

Climbing out of bed, I reached into my nightstand drawer for my service piece. I knew this was ridiculous. But my pounding heart told me otherwise. Between my nightmare and the phone call, I couldn't shake the feeling someone was watching me, and the swaying curtains did nothing to assuage my fears.

I moved methodically through my apartment, clearing one room at a time. No one was hiding in the closets, behind the shower curtain, or under the bed. There were no bodies, just the permanent bloodstains on my carpet.

I examined the locks on my front door and each of the windows. None of them appeared to have been manipulated or tampered with. I was alone.

Once I was convinced it was safe, I went back to my room. It was still early. I didn't have to report to the precinct for several more hours. I thought about trying to go back to sleep since I hadn't been sleeping well. But after that, I knew it would never happen.

The only thing I wanted to do was get the hell out of here. I pushed the curtains aside and cracked the blinds. I didn't see anyone suspicious on the street below. It was broad daylight. No one would be stupid enough to make a move on a cop in broad daylight.

But I'd been on the job long enough to know that wasn't true. Instead, I threw on some clothes, packed a bag for work, and an overnight bag, just in case, and locked up my apartment. The caller's voice continued to repeat through my head. I had no proof, but every cell in my body knew Wilson Matthews made that call.

I kept my head on a swivel as I made my way to the car. But I didn't see anyone. I didn't relax until I made it inside the precinct. As far as I could tell, no one had followed me.

"DeMarco, what's wrong?" Detective Lisco asked when I entered the bullpen. "You're white as a sheet."

I looked around. "Where's Voletek?"

"He's on a call. Is there something I can do?"

I handed her my cell phone. "I got a call from an unrecognized number. I need to know who called."

"What did the caller say?"

"He said I have a nice apartment."

"You don't know who this is?"

"Run it for me?"

"Sure." She took the phone and checked the call log. She entered the number and waited. "It's an unregistered burner."

"I'm not surprised."

"Did the caller threaten you besides the apartment thing?"

"No, that was more than enough." I took back my phone. "When Voletek gets in, tell him I need to see him. I'm gonna hunt down Mac and see what she's up to, and then I'll be in the gym."

"All right."

I found Mac in one of the tech labs. Four monitors were angled around her as she sorted and analyzed video footage. At the sound of my footsteps, she glanced up. A huge smile erupted on her face. "Hey, I didn't expect to see you. Aren't you early for graveyard, or did time get away from me again? I hate it when that happens."

"You're fine. I'm early." I put my phone on the desk beside her and tucked my hands into my pockets.

"I've been doing my best to fulfill your request, but I didn't find any new videos on Paul Gwynn's phone. Everything he had saved was already uploaded to his blog. I looked into the security footage from the club, and actually, several other clubs too. I can't seem to narrow in on the tattooed redhead, but she's got one rockin' hairstyle. It's like a pixie cut, but the dye job is awesome. She's like some badass anime chick. Do you want to hear the weird thing?"

I didn't have the heart to cut her off when she was in the middle of one of her rambling reveals. "Sure."

She gave me a sideways glance before hitting the keys and bringing up the footage on several different monitors. "It's hard to tell, but I think she was at all three of these clubs the night someone died. This one," she pointed to the monitor on the far left, "is from Club Nova the night Kevin Harrison died. These two," she pointed to the two middle monitors, "are the best shots I can get of her from the Gwynn crime scene. And this one," she pointed to the monitor on the right, "probably looks familiar."

"That's the bar where Carla Doucette died."

"You can see the sign for the band. I can't be certain it's her. But the hairstyle's the same. I'm still working on finding common reference points to determine if the woman on all these screens is the same one, but I think so."

She beamed. "It looks like you might have a suspect."

"Yeah, we figured that last night. Do you know if anyone has made any progress IDing her?"

"I don't think so." She stopped for a moment to scrutinize me. "Why do you look like you're wearing pajamas?"

"Am I?" I looked down to make sure I'd changed. "These aren't pajamas. These are my workout clothes."

"You look too tired to work out. What's up?"

"I got a creepy call. Detective Lisco ran the number for me, but it's an unregistered burner."

"Let me see what I can do." She shifted to another computer terminal, entered the number, and waited. "I can ping it."

"Do that."

"I can't get an exact address without digging deeper. Do you want me to?"

"No," I said. "This is off the books for now. If I need more, I'm gonna need to obtain it legally." I examined the red circle on the screen. "Can you pull up Wilson Matthews' home address?"

She looked up at me for a moment, a look of concern and disbelief etching her otherwise youthful expression. "Yeah, I can do that." She pulled his address and had the computer place it on the map. It fit perfectly inside the red circle.

"I knew it." A million curses went through my head. Voletek wanted to put a detail on Matthews to keep an eye on him. Now, I wanted that too. More than anything.

"How did he get your number?"

"I don't know."

"What did he say?"

"He said he'd see me soon and that I have a nice apartment."

Mac swallowed, the color draining from her face. "Do you need somewhere to stay? Somewhere safe? You could stay with me. I'm sure Brad or Jake would let you stay with them too. Not that you'd want to stay with them. But you probably could. I mean, not like that. Well, unless you wanted. I'm sure they want. Actually, I'm not sure, but I bet they would. Y'know...never mind. I just want you somewhere safe, somewhere some psycho knife fetish lunatic can't find you."

"Mac, breathe." I took a seat beside her. "What did I tell you about caffeine?"

She reached over and gave me a big bear hug. "It'll be okay."

I squeezed her back. "Yeah, I know." But I wasn't so sure.

NINETEEN

Twenty minutes later, Jake Voletek found me in the gym. I planned to take out some of this inner turmoil on the punching bags, but I was too exhausted from working all night. Instead, I did a relaxing yoga flow and had been in Savasana for the last five minutes. If I stayed here much longer, I might actually reach inner peace and fall asleep.

"Hey," he offered me a hand up, "patrol's been monitoring Matthews' movements all day. The only time the bastard left his house was to go to the grocery store. They followed him there and back. He didn't go anywhere near your apartment."

"Are you sure?"

"Yes." Jake hauled me to my feet. "The LT wants to know if you changed your mind about the protection detail."

"I haven't."

"Maybe you should reconsider."

"Are you going to let a patrol unit follow you around all day and night?"

"No."

"Why should I?"

"Matthews called you. You're his type. As far as we

know, he's never killed a man."

"He's never killed a cop either."

Jake sighed. "Have you told Brad about the phone call?"

"Not yet."

"You should call him."

"Do you think he's in danger?" Flashes of my morning at the federal building came to mind. Wilson Matthews had just as much reason to target Brad as he did Jake.

"No, but I'm hoping he can talk some sense into you."

"I appreciate what you're trying to do. To be honest, I am tired and scared. But I have a job to do. As long as I'm doing my job, other cops have my back. The department doesn't need to divert additional resources to tail me. It's going to make my work that much harder. You understand that, right? Do you think I'm making the wrong call?"

He let out a frustrated sigh and ran a hand through his hair. "Not when you put it that way, but what about when you go home?" He glanced around and lowered his voice. "Do you want me to stay with you?"

I pressed my lips together, trying not to laugh. "Mac already volunteered you, but I don't think that's a good idea. You're on days. I'm on nights."

"We need to get you off nights," Jake said.

"What we need is to get Wilson Matthews back inside a jail cell. If he's going to call and threaten me, eventually he'll screw up. But right now, I don't have any proof it's him. I tried calling the number back, but he turned his phone off or chucked it. I hoped maybe I could spook him or get him to say something else threatening that the court would take seriously. But that didn't work. I already spoke to ADA Winters. Matthews didn't actually threaten me, even though I took it that way. And we can't prove he's the one who called. Until that changes, we can't do anything to him."

"Every cop in this building would take that as a threat."

"Yeah, well, normal people might think it was a compliment."

"Only a dumbass would think that."

I chuckled. "We know he didn't come near my apartment, so it was just something for him to say to screw with me. Unfortunately, it worked." I eyed the entrance to the locker room. "I'm going to shower and get something to eat now that I know we've got eyes on Matthews and he isn't lurking in the shadows. Thanks for looking out."

"Always." He picked a piece of lint off the sleeve of my hoodie. "If you change your mind on the protection detail or you decide you want some company when you get home, let me know."

"Won't you be working?"

"I'm off tomorrow." Voletek's eyes darkened. "Maybe I'll perform some recon."

"Don't get in trouble, and don't make this worse than it is. The last thing we need is Matthews claiming we're harassing him."

"But he's harassing you. That's not fair."

"That's the job." I ducked into the locker room. Before grabbing my shower caddy, I tried calling Brad, but it went straight to voicemail. He'd been so tired lately; I didn't blame him for putting his phone on do not disturb or turning it off. But the tiny voice at the back of my head wasn't convinced that's why he didn't answer. I shushed her and went into one of the stalls.

The hot water eased the tension in my shoulders and back. I held myself under the spray for longer than I normally would. When I heard voices in the locker room, I decided I better get moving. So I dried off and changed into my work clothes.

Since I wouldn't be able to make much progress on the Red Rabbit case without Mac or the rest of the task force, I decided it might be best to get out of the precinct for a little while. Somehow, I ended up near Wilson Matthews' apartment. Since I was just a few blocks away, I figured I should pass by just to make sure the bastard wasn't up to anything.

The first thing I spotted was his silver sports car. It was parked a few blocks from his apartment. His attorney must have gotten it out of impound once CSU finished going over it. But with a head injury, Matthews wasn't in any condition to drive.

The patrol unit watching him said he walked to a nearby

market and then back. But just in case, I made a mental note of the exact space where it was parked. I'd check back later to see if it had moved.

I continued toward his apartment, but I didn't see a patrol car or any unmarked vehicles idling nearby. The blinds were closed, so I couldn't see in. With any luck, Matthews was holed up inside. Without a computer or tablet, gaining access to escorts would be a lot harder. But nothing was impossible, especially with a burner phone.

When I stopped at the next light, I called Jake. "We need to make sure a warning gets issued to all local escort services. Wilson Matthews is out on bond and might try to book a date. The list of his previous aliases is circulating, but we need to make sure the services are aware."

"It's already been taken care of. The department actually offered to run background checks on every new client they book. I'm not sure they'll take us up on it, but they're aware of the danger. The sooner we put Matthews back behind bars, the sooner the escort services can get back to business as usual. With that logic, they might just let us help."

"What about the patrol unit you assigned to sit on him?" I asked. "I didn't see anyone outside the apartment."

"Hang on." Voletek put me on hold while he checked on a few things. I thought about circling back around to make sure I hadn't missed something, but I knew that wasn't the case. I shouldn't even be here. I wasn't supposed to let this lunatic get inside my head. But there he was.

He'd been the star of my most recent nightmares. The two most gruesome crime scenes I had ever visited had been courtesy of the serial killer.

"Liv, you still there?" Voletek asked.

"Yeah."

"Okay, it turns out Matthews went for a walk. He stopped at an ATM, got a sandwich from a food truck, and now he's eating dinner on a park bench. Would you like to get hourly updates on what I've dubbed Wilson Watch? I can have them text you whenever he moves."

"I only want updates if he leaves his neighborhood."

"I'll make sure that happens." Voletek made a note. "At least now he knows we're watching. That should encourage him to behave and leave you alone."

"Or he'll take it as a challenge."

"There's always the nuclear option. One call to the media outlets, and reporters will swarm him like a bunch of angry hornets. After that, he won't be able to go anywhere without all eyes on him."

"Don't do it. We don't need this to leak. Even more crazies will come out of the woodwork. It'll be a PR nightmare for us. Just imagine how that could sway a jury or compromise our evidence, especially if some other whack-a-doo kills someone in a similar fashion. It will confuse everything."

"Wow, Liv, I never realized you immediately jump to the worst case scenario. How did we work together for over a month without me realizing that?"

"You must have forgotten, or you just weren't paying attention. Anyway, we're taking precautions. I'm not sure there's much else we can do."

"You could take a few more."

"We'll see. If he starts venturing out or the unit gets pulled, I'll consider it."

"Okay. In the meantime, we'll do our best to make sure he doesn't hurt anyone else while he's on this little furlough. Once that trial date rolls around, he'll be locked away for good. Maybe they'll even reinstate the death penalty just for him."

"Wouldn't that be ex post facto?"

"I'm not sure, but there are exceptions to every rule, right?"

I rolled my eyes. "Goodbye, Jake. Watch your back."

"You too, princess."

By the time I hung up, I realized I was almost at my parents' house. Mom had invited me for dinner, but with everything that had happened today, I'd forgotten to get back to her. Hopefully, she wouldn't mind the intrusion.

I pulled into the driveway and called Brad again. But like before, it went straight to voicemail. I hated when he was unreachable. My mind always went to bad places. Dammit, Jake was right; I couldn't help but jump to conclusions.

I left Brad a message, telling him he could join us for dinner whenever he got this. If not, I'd see him at work. Then I peered into my side and rear view mirrors, watching the neighbors walk their dogs or pull in their trash cans. Even as I made my way to the front door, I couldn't shake the feeling someone was watching me. But I knew officers had eyes on Matthews. Whatever I was feeling was nothing more than paranoia.

"Liv?" I jumped, my hand moving to my holster. "What are you doing here?" my mother asked. She had been trimming the rose bush at the far end of the porch. The side of the house had concealed her from my view.

"I'm sorry, Mom. I thought I'd come by. Maybe have dinner before I go to work." I stepped backward. "But you're clearly busy. I can leave. It's no big deal."

"Olive, don't be ridiculous." She pulled off her gardening gloves and picked up the clippers. "I'd give you a hug, but I have to get washed up first." She offered me her cheek, and I gave her a kiss. "Is your partner joining us?"

"I don't think so."

"Emma should be here. Is that why you didn't bother to RSVP to my text?"

"I haven't talked to Emma in a few days. We're working opposite shifts, but we're supposed to go to yoga together on Saturday."

"I'm making her favorite. You like that, right?"

"What is Emma's favorite?" She'd probably had over a hundred favorites in the last ten years.

"BLAST salads with a few CCs. I came up with that name since she's a nurse. Isn't it cute?"

"What is it? It sounds like an astronaut's medical procedure."

"You're silly." My mom put the gloves and trimmers back into the bucket she used for gardening and tucked it neatly away in the hall closet. Then she went into the kitchen to wash her hands while Gunnie charged at us, barking excitedly. The puppy jumped up on me, and I scratched him behind the ears. "Gunnie, down," Mom said in the same tone she used to use whenever she scolded me.

The puppy dropped back to all fours, but he didn't leave

my side. He could sense my anxiety. I knelt down so I could continue fluffing his ears. "What is a BLAST salad?"

"It's like a BLT, but in salad form with shrimp and avocado. And since Emma loves veggies, I added a few others that start with C."

My stomach growled, which made Gunnie's ears prick up. "It sounds great. What can I do to help?"

"Can you make the marinade for the shrimp?"

I mixed the ingredients and poured it into a bowl, covered it, and turned to find my father watching me from the living room.

"Hey, Dad. Can I talk to you for a sec?"

He always knew when I wanted to talk about work. He led me down the stairs to show me something in the basement, that way Mom wouldn't overhear us. "You can always talk to me, honey. What's going on?"

I told him about the phone call and what was being done. "Am I being stubborn?"

"You're a DeMarco. You're always stubborn. But a patrol car following your every move will make your job more dangerous. That's why you'll be behind your desk while at work, and the patrol unit will follow you home and remain stationed outside until you leave the next day. It's basically escort service to and from work."

"We're in the middle of a major case involving three units. They even set up a task force."

"Ooh, a task force," Dad mocked.

"You know what I mean."

"What does Fennel think?"

"I haven't been able to reach him. We had an eventful night and morning." I filled him in on the details. "I'm hoping he's just passed out asleep." And not drunk.

"Don't you dare tell your mother I said this." He glanced toward the stairs. "But as long as someone is watching Matthews, they don't need to watch you too. If that changes, if they get called away or have to respond to a crime in progress, he could slip away, but the timing would have to be perfect and he'd have to get lucky."

"So you don't think I need to agree to the protection detail?"

He sighed, afraid to say one way or the other. "Tell your partner what's going on. He'll be at risk just by being with you, and given everything Fennel's gone through to make sure you're protected, he should have some say in the matter. The two of you decide what's best, and go from there. But Liv, I'd prefer if while you're working nights, you come home to sleep during the day. I'll be here. Between the security system, Gunnie, and the artillery I keep in the closet, no one's gonna get near you or anyone in this family."

"Gunnie, really, Dad? He's not much of a guard dog."

"You're wrong. He alerts us to everything, falling leaves, birds, other dogs, people walking. No stranger or creature can step foot on this property without him barking."

"Okay. I'll get my bag out of the car."

TWENTY

I was the first one to arrive to the task force meeting. Brad was the last. We went over everything Mac had found, which wasn't much. The tattooed woman had been spotted on surveillance footage from three different clubs. So finding her was the priority. None of the surveillance footage ever got a good enough glimpse of her face, so facial recognition was out. Paul Gwynn's friends had sat with the sketch artist. They each provided details on her appearance. Right now, we had five different versions of what the woman looked like. They'd been combined to extrapolate the most likely version. That's what we'd use to try to ID her.

"Are you all right, DeMarco?" Ashmore asked.

"I'm fine." I stifled a yawn. "Milk and Honey's only open from seven a.m. to eleven p.m. We'll run by there tonight to see if anything's going on after hours, but we'll have to go back during normal business hours in order to question the staff."

"Tell Captain Grayson. He'll get your schedules fixed. Until then, do what you can." Ashmore glanced from me to Brad. "You were only at two of the crime scenes, right?"

"Yeah," Brad said.

"That means no one at the six other clubs knows you're cops. We should try to keep it that way in case we need you to go in undercover." Ashmore turned to Loyola and Sullivan. "The same's true for the two of you at the other two scenes. Let's keep that in mind and try not to burn potential covers in the event we need them." Ashmore waited to see if anyone had any questions or ideas, but no one spoke. "All right, dismissed." He left the room without another word.

Sullivan turned to me. "What's tonight's game plan?"

"I'm not sure." I looked uncertainly at my partner.

"We'll continue researching and see what we find, unless you need us for something," Brad said.

"We'll probably be doing the same." Sullivan sighed. "Let's just hope we don't get another call."

"From your lips to god's ears." I backed toward the door, desperate to speak to my partner alone. "We'll be downstairs if you need us."

Brad stopped me once we made it to the stairwell. "Hey, I'm sorry I missed your calls. My battery died. What's going on?" My partner smelled strongly of aftershave, which meant he had a date or he was masking the scent of alcohol.

"How was your meeting at the federal building?"

"No problems. Anderson wanted to go over the details of my interactions with Wilson Matthews and how that relates to your case." He leaned over the railing and peered up and down the stairs, but no one else was in the stairwell. "I told him everything I could, but I didn't know much at the time, and even with twenty-twenty hindsight, I'm not sure I was able to give him anything helpful."

"It's okay. That wasn't your job."

"Hey," he tilted my chin up so he could see my eyes, "what's going on with you?"

"Wilson Matthews called." I unloaded everything. "My dad's right. You're my partner. You should have a say in this."

"You've had a detail assigned to you before. You know how it works."

"Not when I'm on the job." I licked my lips. "Dad said they'll put me at a desk until it's resolved. Wilson Matthews' trial date is months away. I don't think I can do that."

"You shouldn't. It sets a bad precedent and sends the wrong message. That being said, I'm gonna make absolutely certain there is always someone watching your back."

"Thanks."

He nodded and tugged on the door handle. We went through the doors marked *Homicide* and made our way to our desks. "The reason I was late to the meeting is I came here first. I was actually waiting for you. We normally don't get our signals crossed."

"It's been an off day." I picked up the cup he'd placed on my desk. "What's this?"

"Coffee."

"And yours?" I jerked my chin toward the cup on his desk.

"Coffee."

I held out my mug. "Switch."

"Mine has sugar."

"It's that kind of day."

"I already drank out of it."

"So? You eat off my plate all the time. I'm pretty sure you don't have cooties."

"There's plenty coconut sugar left in the bag I stashed in the break room. Go nuts and sweeten away." He picked up his cup to take a sip but paused mid-raise at my inscrutable stare. Annoyed, he lowered the cup, suspecting the real reason for my insane request. "Fine." He pushed his cup toward me, and I took a sip, relieved it didn't contain any hair of the dog. "Do you want to give that back now?"

"Nope. It's delicious." I took another gulp and smiled.

He snatched the untouched coffee cup off my desk and pointed a finger at me. "I'm on to you, DeMarco."

While Brad was in the break room fixing his newly acquired cup of coffee, I went back to the research I'd been doing at the end of last shift. We now had two possible commonalities among the victims. They visited the same café and might have interacted with the same red-haired, tattooed woman. Could she work at the café?

I dug deeper into Milk and Honey. Their website only listed the menu, the history of tea, their humble beginnings, and allergen information. In my tired state, I had gotten distracted by their gluten-free options.

"Detective DeMarco, this just came for you. Special delivery."

I looked up at the desk sergeant who stood beside my desk, holding out a small bubble mailer. "Who brought it?"

"I don't know. I saw your name on the outside and thought it might be important."

I took it from her outstretched hand. The envelope didn't provide me with any clues.

Brad looked at me. "Fan mail?"

"Must be."

My partner didn't like it. "Is there a return address?"

I held it up for him to see. "Nothing."

"Since when do we let strangers leave unattended packages at the front desk?" Brad asked.

The desk sergeant gave him a bewildered look. "I'm sure that's not what happened."

"Liv, careful. It could be a bomb or poison."

Gently, I felt around the front of the package. "It's kind of flat for a bomb." I slit the top of the envelope. Brad eyed it like it might explode or release anthrax. Slowly, I squeezed the sides and peered inside.

"What is it?" Brad asked.

I turned the envelope upside down and let the baggie drop to my desk. "Red Rabbit."

Brad grabbed a latex glove and an evidence bag from his drawer. "Forensics might be able to pull prints or find additional evidence on the packaging." He lifted the baggie with the tiny rabbit logo up to the light. "How would someone know we've been trying to get our hands on this?" He glanced at me. "Do you have a source I don't know about?"

I thanked the sergeant and waited for her to walk away. "I think Axel sent it."

Brad dropped the baggie into the larger evidence bag

and reached for the bubble mailer. "Kincaid? I can't believe you went to him for another favor, and you didn't tell me. Why didn't you tell me?"

"I didn't go to him. He bumped into me." I shook my head. The logistics didn't matter. "Anyway, there was nothing to tell. I asked if he could hook us up with some Red Rabbit, and he said no. He must have changed his mind. I'm sure he took every precaution to ensure this doesn't link back to him."

Brad tucked the bubble mailer into the evidence bag. "The lab needs to analyze this. They're going to want to know where you got it."

"I can't say for certain. Can you? The desk sergeant doesn't know. We should check the precinct's footage. Maybe we'll see who dropped it off."

"Liv, if Kincaid sent this, he has access to the dealer. He might have gotten it directly from the supplier. We need to know who his source is. We can shut this whole thing down and save lives. Why are you protecting him?"

"I'm not, but he'll deny everything. We can't go at him hot. He'll never talk to us. You know that as well as I do. There's also a third possibility."

"Which is?"

"He confiscated it from someone at his club."

"You can't honestly believe that."

"I told Kincaid this shit was killing people. Based on his reaction, I don't think he knew about it. None of the deaths have been publicized. We both know he's careful about letting drugs inside Spark. I told him he needed to be extra careful because he wouldn't want someone to drop dead in his club. More than likely, he took this off someone at the door."

"We need to talk to him."

"And we will. You and me. Agreed?"

"Fine." He climbed out of his chair. "Let's get this to the lab to analyze. Then we'll tell the team someone sent you a sample."

The lab wasn't able to pull any prints off the bubble mailer except the sergeant's and mine. The baggie containing the two pills was just like the others we'd found at the various crime scenes. At least we finally had access to the pills. Now we could determine what was in them.

"The analysis should be done by morning," the tech said.

"Thanks, Benny." Brad led the way out of the lab. "What are you going to tell the rest of the team?"

"The truth."

After updating them on the anonymous delivery, Brad and I returned to our desks and got back to work. We'd swing by Spark a few minutes before closing time when Kincaid would be more willing to speak to us. Spark's members might include judges and city officials, but when they were at the club, the last thing they wanted to see were a couple of on-duty detectives showing up with questions.

"Hey, Liv."

I blinked a few times, wondering how long my eyes had been closed. "What?"

"You said you were checking into Milk and Honey. Did you notice anything strange on their social media pages?"

"No." I shook my mouse to get the screensaver to go away, but the lapse in time had caused the computer to automatically log me out. "What did I miss?"

He spun his monitor around. "This is a shot of their grand opening. The woman in the middle has a lot of ink on her left arm."

She looked to be nineteen or twenty. She had medium-length blonde hair with dark, streaky roots that looked intentional. "When was that taken?"

"Two years ago."

"I'm guessing that would put her in her early twenties." I reached for one of the printed sketches. "It could be her. Then again, this photo is dated and the sketch isn't necessarily reliable." I read the caption, but none of the employees' names were listed. "Do they have any other photos? Anything more recent?"

"Not that I found." He turned the screen back and scrolled up. "She might not work there anymore."

"Print out that photo. We'll find out in the morning."

TWENTY-ONE

"Business or pleasure, Detectives?" Axel Kincaid asked when he met us at the front door to Spark. He glanced down at the badges clipped to our belts. "Never mind. Asked and answered."

"Can we come in?"

Kincaid glanced over his shoulder. "Meet me at the side door in five minutes." The door shut in our faces.

Brad snorted. "Does that seem ominous or overly cryptic to you?"

"Nah, not at all," I said sarcastically.

"Good, so it's just me." We made our way around the side of the building. Brad insisted on remaining some place he could keep tabs on those exiting from the front. That was a good call, considering how Kincaid liked to sneak around. But no one of any particular interest came or went while we waited. "Do you remember the last time we were in this alley?"

"Bad memories," I said.

"Mostly."

I glanced at my partner. "Mostly?"

He grinned. "It could have been worse."

The door creaked open. Axel waited on the other side.

"All right. Everyone's gone home. You can come in." He didn't wait to see if we would follow before heading down the hallway, past the locker room, and back to the bar. The cleaning crew and staff were tidying up while Axel mixed himself a Manhattan. "What would you like?" He focused on me. "You look like you could use an espresso martini."

"We're working," I said.

"An espresso then?" Axel didn't wait for me to answer before starting up the machine. "What would you like, Detective Fennel?" He lifted a bottle of spiced rum. "High ball? Low ball?"

"Like Liv said, we're working." Brad gazed longingly at the bottle of tequila. "Did you stop by the precinct earlier tonight?"

"I've been here and haven't left." Kincaid slid the tiny mug of espresso toward me and set to work making another one. "Why? Did something happen?"

"Stop playing games."

"Brad, easy." I nudged him gently with my arm. "I got this."

Axel finished with the espresso machine and put a cup down beside my partner. "Got what?"

"A few hours ago, someone dropped off two tabs of Red Rabbit. I'm sure you don't know anything about that." I kept my voice down so it wouldn't carry.

"How would I? I've been at the club all night. Hundreds of people can vouch for me."

"We spoke about this earlier in the afternoon."

"I told you I couldn't help. Nothing's changed." Axel picked up his cocktail and took a long sip while staring at my partner. "This sure is tasty. How about just a nip? I won't tell."

"We need to know how you got your hands on the drugs," Brad hissed. "Lives are at stake. We have to shut this thing down. People are dying. Don't you understand that?"

"I understand plenty. This is my club. Do you know what happens after a drug bust? Everything gets confiscated. Money, property, cars, whatever was paid for with drug money gets taken. I would never risk anything like that happening here. My assets are mine. This club is mine. I control what goes on inside. I don't let dealers in here, so no, Detective Fennel, I don't know who's dealing that shit. I don't know where it's originating. I don't know a damn thing about it."

"We understand that," I said, hoping Brad wouldn't let his temper get the better of him. Most of the time, my partner was the most level-headed guy I knew, but when it came to Axel Kincaid, all bets were off. "But that doesn't mean some Red Rabbit wouldn't hop into someone's pocket and get into your club that way, right?"

"I don't know where it came from." Kincaid eyed my partner, a smug challenge on his face.

"Axel," I stepped between them, "please."

Finally, he looked at me. "I told you earlier, I don't have access, and if I did, giving drugs to a cop is asking for trouble. It would lead to a lot of questions that I can't answer. Questions just like the ones you're asking right now. Whoever sent you the tabs must be doing you a favor, but it wasn't me."

"Do you believe him?" Brad asked when we got back to the car. "You didn't push. Normally, you push."

"I don't know. He has every reason to deny it, but why would he go out on a limb to help us and then refuse to cooperate?"

"Isn't that his MO? He does this all the time." Brad rubbed a hand over his mouth, fighting to keep from saying what was on his mind. "He wants you to think he's a good guy. That he's one of *the* good guys. Like I've told you before, he's in love with you, Liv."

"Yeah, right."

"Fine, he's infatuated."

"You mean he wants to fuck me."

"I wasn't going to put it that way. But yeah, and he enjoys fucking with me while he's making googly eyes at you. This is fun for him."

"You're right, at least about that part. But Kincaid wasn't lying about the drugs either. He's obsessed with that club and his exotic sports cars. Those are his babies. He'd never do anything to jeopardize them. The entire time I was undercover at Spark, I never witnessed a single drug deal. No powder in the bathroom. No discarded needles. No one doing lines on the tables. Nothing. That wasn't because he was being careful. That's because he won't let it happen at his club. The events he holds at other locations are a different story. Anything goes, but not inside the hallowed halls of Spark."

"Which means he knows plenty of dealers. He might even have cartel connections. This is Axel Kincaid we're talking about."

"Sure, but you heard Ashmore. Red Rabbit's not being moved on that scale. It's designer, probably local."

"Still, Kincaid knows how to get his hands on it."

"Maybe, but he won't talk. We came here tonight to reason with him. It didn't work. He didn't even offer to trade in favors. I don't know how else to persuade him. We have no reason to arrest him. So what do we do?"

"We could make his life miserable."

"Except he's helped us both out recently. Just this afternoon, he gave me a copy of Wilson Matthews' membership application. We don't want to burn any bridges, not when we can benefit from maintaining a cordial relationship with him." With everything that had been going on today, I'd forgotten to delve deeper into the info on Matthews' application. I'd do that as soon as I had a few free minutes.

"You could sleep with him. That might loosen his lips."

"Okay. Turn the car around."

Brad gave me an exasperated look. "I know you're joking, but no."

"It was your idea."

"It was a joke. A bad one. Like the kind of jokes you make."

"Hardy har."

"All right, so Kincaid's a bust. What do you want to do now?"

"I guess we should see if anything's going on at Milk and Honey." But no one was around.

Brad circled the block a few times. A few drunk college kids were on their way back to the dorms from other parts of the city. We saw them walking together in small clusters. They didn't appear to be in any distress or looking to score. We didn't spot any unsavory types skulking in alleyways or on street corners.

When we got tired of cruising up and down the same few streets, Brad headed for the nearest bar. It was after four, so every place had shut down for the night. But that didn't always mean the party was over.

"Do you remember what Vincent told us?" Brad asked. "He followed a specific route to collect the bottles and cans. We should question him again if we don't get any leads on the tattooed woman. The kid might have seen her while he was making one of his stops."

"Possibly."

He parked outside the bar, and we got out. No one appeared to be inside. We looked around back, but no one was there.

"We're looking for a needle in a haystack. Do you have any idea how many bars and clubs are in this city? We can't possibly stop at each one to see if someone's dealing Red Rabbit in some alleyway," I said.

"What else are we going to do?" My partner had never sounded quite so desperate.

"We need a better plan than that."

"I'm out of ideas. We can't do anything until Milk and Honey opens. At least if we're driving around, I feel like we're actively doing something. I don't want to wait for the phone to ring so we can get another report of a body found." He looked at me, his eyes pleading. "I need to be doing something."

"Okay, we'll drive around."

After we scoped out the previous crime scenes, I asked Brad to take the scenic route through Wilson Matthews' neighborhood. The silver sports car hadn't moved from its previous spot, which eased my nerves. Brad double-parked beside the squad car and rolled down his window.

"Slow night?" he asked.

"Just the way we like them," the officer inside said. "The guy hasn't gone anywhere since we got here. Last shift, said he went for a walk. That's about the most excitement they saw from him."

"Let's hope it stays that way," I said.

"Night, fellas." Brad waved and resumed patrolling. When we stopped at a traffic light, he turned to look at me. "Do you want to talk about it? I know you haven't slept. I also know Wilson Matthews is the reason."

"We already talked about it."

"We talked about a unit parked outside your house when you're at home. We didn't talk about how you're feeling or what you're thinking."

I sighed. "I can't get those two murders out of my head. He sliced them open and let them bleed out. It reminds me of what happened in the liquor store. I don't want him to do that to anyone else. I just don't know how to stop him. Arresting him should have been enough, but now's he out. It's only temporary, and I hope I'm jumping to conclusions, thinking he'd use this chance to strike, but..."

"He called to taunt you."

"Yeah." I stared out the windshield. "Voletek thinks Matthews might make a move on me."

"Because you arrested him?"

"Because we lured him in by making me his ideal victim. He didn't get to carry through with his plans, and until he does, that obsession is going to eat at him."

"Do you believe that?"

"It doesn't matter what I think. The only thing that matters is we keep Matthews from hurting anyone else."

"So far, so good."

"I guess." I took out my phone and found the photos I'd taken of Matthews' application. He listed his home address, but the phone number was different. The rest of the information appeared to be the same as what we had in our files, but I'd have to do a side-by-side comparison to make sure. "I'm so tired of playing whack-a-mole with a bunch of lunatics."

"Me too." Brad adjusted the thermostat. "You should get some shuteye while we wait for Milk and Honey to open. The staff must get there early to bake. With any luck, we'll spot our girl."

"Aren't you tired?"

"I'm good."

I adjusted my seat and closed my eyes. "Only if you're sure."

"I am."

TWENTY-TWO

"Why didn't you wake me?" I rubbed my eyes, wondering what time it was. When I closed them, it was dark. Now it wasn't.

"I didn't see any reason."

"What did you do all night?"

"I watched your back."

I couldn't help but smile. "That's why I slept so well."

He grinned. "I'm glad." He pointed to the front door. "I haven't spotted anyone who fits the description Gwynn's friends gave us. I've been trying to remember if I've ever seen her here before, but I don't recall. You would think I should."

"How many times did you come here?"

"Ten or twelve. Probably not more than that. Elizabeth and I only dated for about a month."

I straightened, combing my hair out of my face with my fingers. "How did Elizabeth hear about this place?"

Brad shrugged.

"Please tell me she wasn't in undergrad."

"She was a doctoral candidate in linguistics."

I blinked. "How did you meet?"

"I ran into her at my therapist's office."

"Ah," I nodded sagely, "so she was crazy."

He laughed, that velvety, melodic sound I loved. "Absolutely."

"How is that going, by the way?"

He stared out the windshield. "One step forward, two steps back." He didn't want to talk about how his last assignment had triggered his PTSD or PTSS or whatever it was called. "Finally." He pointed to the man flipping the sign on the door from closed to open. "We should get in there before the crowd arrives."

Almost like clockwork, a group of seven entered the café. I scrambled after Brad as he crossed the street. Once inside, we waited at the end of the line. We'd just made it to the counter when another group entered.

Brad ordered a bag of gluten-free croissants and a cherry almond tea. "Liv?" I grabbed two containers of fruit salad from the cooler beside the register and ordered a breakfast blend.

"That'll be $22.50," the man behind the counter said.

Brad put the money down before showing the guy his badge. "I also have a couple of questions."

"Okay," the guy said uncertainly.

"Do you recognize this woman?" Brad showed him the compilation sketch.

The guy at the counter peered at it for a moment. "I don't think so."

"No problem." Brad reached for his phone and showed the guy the photo from the café's social media page. "What about her?"

"That's Darcy."

"Last name?" I asked.

"Kolado. Darcy Kolado."

"Is she here?" Brad asked.

"She quit last month. She said it was getting to be too much with her class schedule. She still comes by a lot." He looked around at the growing line. "Honestly, I haven't seen her in a couple of weeks, but I've been on vacation."

"Is this photo up-to-date?" Brad asked.

"No, her hair's short and this deep, dark red. I don't know how to describe it."

"Can you describe the tattoos on her arm?" I asked.

"She has a full sleeve on her left arm. It's a bunch of flowers with vines and thorns. I don't know. There might be a bird, I think. Maybe some butterflies." He looked down at his forearms. "This is all I got. Nothing major, but it's good enough. I can't imagine sitting under the needle that long." He had a small infinity symbol on the inside of his arm. Another worker placed the bag of croissants on the counter. "Is there anything else I can get you?"

"That's it. Thanks for your help." Brad picked up the bag. I grabbed the two cups with the dangling tea bags and filled them with hot water from the dispenser. Afterward, I snagged a few packets of honey and took a seat beside Brad at one of the tables. He took out one of the croissants and bit into it.

The entire café smelled like fresh-baked bread.

"Emma won't approve," I said.

Brad chewed thoughtfully. "Oh well." He glanced at me. "Do you want one? I won't tell."

"I'd regret it later." Instead, I opened my container of fruit and put the other one in front of him. "Aren't you worried about preservatives, stabilizers, and other weird chemical things?"

"They actually sell the mix to make these." He pointed to a row of little cloth sacks labeled *Croissant Mix* on a nearby display case. "It's the exact same blend they use to bake them fresh daily. I've read the ingredients. Amazingly, they don't use any of that stuff."

"No wonder you came here so often." I gave the croissants a sideways look. "Still, grains."

He laughed. "That's your thing, not mine. When I used to come here with Elizabeth, they didn't have fruit cups, and Elizabeth wasn't exactly into the primal, natural foods lifestyle. But relationships are about compromise. It just helps when the compromise is delicious."

"The food or Elizabeth?"

"I don't kiss and tell." He jerked his chin toward the door. "Did you know tea's big with the entire fraternity?"

Two of Gwynn's friends, Ryan and Nathan, entered the café. They wore their backpacks over one shoulder. Ryan carried a notebook in one hand with a pen behind his ear. We waited for them to sit down before we approached.

"Morning, gentlemen," Brad said. "How are you?"

"Okay," Nathan said.

Ryan stared at the table. "Have you learned anything else about Paul's death? Do you know what happened?"

"We're still investigating," Brad said. "Do either of you remember any other details from that night?"

"No, sorry." Ryan rubbed his hands up and down the cup.

Nathan shook his head.

"What about the woman? Do you remember anything else about her?"

"No, nothing." Ryan checked his phone. "I need to get to class. Am I free to go?"

"Sure, but if something comes to mind, give me a call."

"Will do." Ryan grabbed his tea and chocolate chip muffin and headed for the door.

"Do you know Darcy Kolado?" I asked.

"I don't think so. Who is she?" Nathan asked.

"I was just curious."

"Did you and Paul come here often?" Brad asked.

"Paul came a lot. This was one of his favorite places. In the afternoons, it's a lot more chill. He used to come here to work on his newspaper articles. The coffee shops get super crowded. He liked this better."

"Was he seeing anyone?" I asked.

"Yeah, several people, but no one serious."

"Did you ever see him with her?" Brad showed him the photo of Darcy.

Nathan cocked his head from side to side like a spaniel. "I'm not sure. A lot of girls come and go."

"You live in the frat house?" I asked.

"Yeah. You can come by some time and check it out."

I smiled. "Maybe I'll do that."

"I better get going too. Chem lab's starting in an hour, and I'm supposed to meet with my lab partner so we can finish our report." Nathan collected his things and pushed in his chair. "I'll see you guys around."

We waited for Nathan to cross over to the campus

before we returned to our car. "They don't seem that affected by their fraternity brother's death," I said.

"That doesn't mean they aren't." Brad put the bag of croissants on the floor beside my seat, making sure the bag was folded over and secure before heading back to the precinct.

When we arrived, the task force meeting was already underway. Brad put the bag of baked goods on the table. Sullivan reached for it and pulled out a croissant before passing it around.

"How was your night?" Ashmore asked.

"We may have a few leads." I updated the team on what happened.

Ashmore made some notes. "I already searched Paul's room in the fraternity house. He didn't have any pills. I found a small stash of marijuana and beer, but that was it."

"Did you notice any signs he has a girlfriend?" I asked.

"Not really, but my guess is he saw plenty of action." Ashmore eyed me. "His parents said he wasn't seeing anyone. Take that for what it's worth."

Captain Grayson reached for the tablet, entered Darcy's name, and showed us her ID photo. In it, she had long, straight brown hair. She didn't wear any makeup. "Obviously, she likes to change her looks. Mac believes Darcy is the woman from the club surveillance footage, but facial rec couldn't verify it."

That was good enough for me. "Darcy has to be the girl last seen with Paul Gwynn. We know he frequents Milk and Honey where she used to work. The manager we spoke to this morning said she still hangs out there a lot, and according to Nathan, Paul's friend, he also hung out there a lot. That can't be a coincidence."

"His credit card receipts don't show that many transactions," Loyola said.

"Maybe he just hung out there. Buying a beverage or snack isn't required, and unless we gain access to the café's surveillance footage, we won't know how often he visited. He might have paid with cash."

"I already put in the request for a court order," Grayson said. "This is our connection, so we're going to work it hard." He slid the lab report over to me. "Any idea who sent you the pills?"

"No, sir."

Grayson gave me a second look. "As you can see, the lab only found trace amounts of anticoagulant rodenticide in the pills. This is nowhere near enough to cause death."

I scanned the chemical breakdown. "This appears to be made up mostly of MDMA."

"We think it was intended to be an alternative to E or molly," Ashmore said. "The chemical composition has been slightly altered, but it still falls into the illegal category, so even though it's designer, it wasn't designed to avoid punishment and prosecution."

"Have we compared the samples we received to the toxicology reports the ME gave us?" Brad asked.

"That's the first thing we did," Grayson said. "It's possible each victim happened to get a hold of a bad batch, like we suspect. It could also be the result of an intentional poisoning."

"How many pills would it take for these levels to match what we saw in any of our victims?"

"At least twenty pills. The ME would have found remnants in the victims' stomach contents if they'd taken that many, but he never did."

"Could the poison have built up over time?"

"Possibly, but the coroner said the victims would have exhibited other symptoms prior to just dropping. They would have been sick enough to seek help. None of them did."

"Something else is going on here." I just didn't know what.

TWENTY-THREE

Captain Grayson gave Brad and me the morning off, but we had to get moving on this. Every day that passed was another chance for an unsuspecting user to die from poison. Since my partner let me sleep for a good portion of our shift, I wasn't particularly tired.

After a short nap, I had breakfast with my parents, took a shower, and got dressed. The hot water and clean clothes did wonders to make me feel like a new person. Then I went back to work.

While I waited for the background check to run on Darcy Kolado, I pulled up the Wilson Matthews file. The phone number was the only thing we didn't have on record. Curious, I dialed the number. But it was disconnected.

I looked up the information. The number had been deactivated. It was never registered to Wilson Matthews. The man must have bought stock in burner phones.

I reread his application twice more. He left most of the more personal information blank. He listed the job he'd left as current employment and put a hefty six figure number in for yearly income. For vehicle info, he listed his sports car. By all accounts, Wilson Matthews would have been an ideal candidate for Spark.

Of course, Matthews had no intention of joining the elite nightclub. That wasn't his scene. He preferred taking escorts to hotel rooms to do the deed. And Axel immediately nixed the application once he realized Matthews only went to the club to meet with Detective Gallagher. That connection automatically meant Matthews was trouble, and at least one cop knew it.

Still, I couldn't help but wonder what would happen if Axel reached out and offered Matthews entry to the exclusive club. Now that Matthews was being watched so closely, he might want to have a hangout that had a strict anti-police, anti-surveillance policy. While I debated the merits of asking Axel for another favor in the hopes of catching Matthews partaking in illegal activities, the background check completed.

Darcy Kolado was a junior at the same college as Paul Gwynn. Like most of the students, she lived on campus. The background check didn't turn up her address, but it did give me a telephone number.

I tried calling, but the recorded message said the user had exceeded her limit. Great. How was I supposed to find our mystery woman or her look-alike when she couldn't even be bothered to pay her phone bill?

"That's why they call it legwork," I mumbled. Brad wouldn't be in for another two hours. But I could make plenty of headway without him.

When I arrived at the registrar's office, the woman at the reception desk made me wait for the dean of admissions. I paced back and forth. The polished mahogany furniture, thick area rugs, and oversized doors and high ceilings screamed academia. No wonder colleges charged so much for tuition. They had to keep up appearances. Meanwhile, I'd bet most of the classrooms had press wood podiums and uncomfortable chairs.

"Detective, how may I help you?"

I turned away from the oversized door. "I'm looking for Darcy Kolado. She's a junior."

The dean quirked an eyebrow. "What is this in regards to?"

"Her name has popped up in the course of an ongoing

investigation. I can't disclose the details of the case, but it's possible she might be a suspect or in danger. I need to find her."

"What kind of danger? Should I alert campus security?"

"No, ma'am. This isn't a violent matter."

"Okay." The dean stood in front of a computer and typed in the name. "She's not in class right now. I can print her schedule for you, but according to attendance records, she hasn't been to class at all this week." She scrolled down farther. "She resides on campus. Let me give you her dorm assignment." She wrote it down. "Campus security will take you there."

"Thank you."

But she didn't immediately hand me the paper. "Detective, I run a tight ship. This school has a reputation to protect. Is there something I should know?"

"Not yet."

"When there is, you'll tell me."

"You have my word."

She nodded and handed me the building assignment. "I appreciate it."

A man dressed in a pale blue uniform came up behind me. He took the slip from my hand. "That's just across the quad." He led me down the path. "I applied for the police academy a couple of times but never got in."

"I'm sorry to hear that."

"That's when they were doing the big recruitment campaign. Everyone was applying for civil service jobs then. I ended up as a mailman for a short while, but I never lost that itch to do some good. So I became a campus cop. These kids need someone watching out for them."

"Yes, sir," I said.

"What are we looking at here? Rape? Drugs? Something like that?"

"Are those common problems you deal with?" We'd already checked the reports, but maybe the school was more interested in protecting its reputation than its students.

"We do what we can. My team and I keep our ear to the ground on college parties. We offer rides back to the dorms and walk the female students to their cars. Still, these kids drink too much and don't always realize someone's looking to take advantage. It doesn't happen much, but when it does, it breaks my heart."

"Are drugs a factor?"

"Like date rape drugs?"

"Or party drugs."

"The school has a zero tolerance policy. If we find that stuff on campus, the student gets suspended or expelled, depending on the severity."

"What about marijuana?"

"They get a pass on that. Alcohol too, as long as they're twenty-one. But we know it gets passed around to the underclassmen. Like I said, we do what we can."

"You ever see any red pills getting passed around?"

"No." He laughed. "Though, I do remember seeing plenty of blue pills making the rounds. Some idiot thought taking ED meds would improve performance a couple of years back. The clinic saw a bunch of young men coming in with some very interesting side effects."

"I bet." We entered the building and made our way up the steps. "How about in the last month or so?"

"Nothing I can think of."

"Are you sure? It'd really help my investigation. Most of my department's stumped." Appealing to his ego and previous desire to carry a badge might get him to open up.

"What are we talking about exactly? It's been quiet lately. I always worry when things get too quiet. It's like the calm before the storm or the eye of a hurricane."

I stopped walking and lowered my voice. "You have to keep this between us. Okay?"

His eyes lit up. "Yeah, no problem."

"Red Rabbit, have you heard anyone talking about it?"

"What is it?"

"It's basically MDMA."

"They do that from time to time, but the last time we caught anyone with a stash was, gosh," he scratched his head, "eight months ago. It was during summer semester."

"What about drug dealers? You ever see anyone suspicious lurking around on campus or engaging in sketchy behavior?"

He laughed again. "You're talking about college kids. Every single one of them lurks and looks sketchy, but we don't have problems like that on this campus. We monitor everyone who comes in and out. You passed the security station when you arrived. We're right out front, that way no one gets any funny ideas."

Those weren't the answers I hoped for, but maybe the campus really was relatively safe and secure. "I'm glad you're on the job."

"Thank you, ma'am." He saluted, even though he was twice my age.

We continued our trek to Darcy's room. When we arrived, I saw two names written on the hanging chalkboard. The security guard knocked. The dull hum of the stereo turned off, and a young woman opened the door.

"Campus security," he did his best to sound official, "is Darcy Kolado here?"

"Darcy, no." The girl eyed my badge.

"I'm Detective Liv DeMarco."

"She's with the city," the security officer said.

I turned to him. "I think it'd be best if you let us speak privately."

He backed away, holding up his palms. "Right. Right. I'll meet you downstairs."

"No need," I said. "I can find my way back."

"All right." He looked at the woman at the door. "It'd be in your best interest to answer her questions truthfully."

The woman looked even more bewildered. I rolled my eyes and let out a sigh. She watched the security guard retreat before speaking again. "Are you really a cop?"

"Yes, is Darcy here?"

"No."

"When do you expect her?"

"I'm not sure." She stepped away from the door, allowing me to enter. "Is Darcy in trouble?"

"Honestly, I'm not sure." I looked around the small, cramped room. It wasn't much larger than a prison cell. The room was divided in half. Each side had one twin bed, a closet, a desk, and a shelf over the top of it. The middle of the room was the common area. A microwave sat atop a dorm fridge. They had a sink and a small cabinet they used as a pantry. "When's the last time you saw Darcy?"

"It was sometime last week." She sat on her bed. "Is she okay?"

"I don't know that either. How long have you known her?"

"Since freshman year."

I spotted a few photos of the girls on a corkboard. "Do you have a recent photo of Darcy?"

She leaned back and plucked one from the center. Darcy was sporting a spiky, red hairstyle.

"Do you know where Darcy was a few nights ago?" I consulted my notebook, giving the exact date and approximate time Paul Gwynn encountered the mystery woman.

"She went to a club. I'm not sure which one. That's not my scene. I'm more of a homebody."

"Has she ever mentioned Paul Gwynn?"

Her expression said it all. "Only a million times. He was one of those pricks who made her life miserable. When she worked at M&H, he'd drive her crazy. He asked her out all the time, but she always refused. He didn't get that it's not cool to pursue a girl after she says no."

"Did she ever report him?"

"She didn't see the point. He never actually did anything. He'd just ask."

"How often did she see him?"

"He'd go to M&H almost every afternoon. He never tipped. He'd leave his cup and plate on the table, expecting her to clean up after him. One time, she said he'd gotten bored and decided to write her a message in honey. She spent an hour trying to scrub it off the table and chairs."

"Why didn't the manager ever say anything or ban him from returning?"

"No one cares. Paul wasn't the only one who did shit like that. She had tons of obnoxious regulars who'd treated her like dirt. Food service jobs are the worst, except for maybe retail, and honestly, it might be a toss-up."

"Does Darcy work retail?"

"No, I do."

"I'm sorry."

She pulled her hair into a ponytail. "Thanks."

So Darcy knew Paul. "Did she ever mention any of his fraternity brothers?"

"Not by name, but they probably stopped by to get muffins and biscuits and stuff. Everyone around here does. That place is amazing."

My partner seemed to think so too. "Do you remember if Darcy ever complained about any other customers by name?"

"Um...there was a professor or a TA she used to bitch about. I can't remember who."

"Let me read you some names." I listed the other victims, but Darcy's roommate didn't recognize any of them. "Does Darcy usually disappear for days or weeks at a time?"

"Kind of. It's gotten worse lately. She's dating this older guy. He's a real loser. He lives some place off campus. I think she's been staying with him."

"Do you know his name or where he lives?"

"Sorry."

"According to the registrar, she's missed class the last three days. Is that normal?"

"I'm not sure what normal is anymore. Darcy used to be serious about school, but after she flunked one of her classes and had to retake it, things changed. I think she's having a quarter-life crisis. She had this whole plan, but it kind of fell apart. Now all she does is party."

"What's her major?"

"Um...it was chemistry. Then she changed to accounting. Now I think it's marketing or business."

"Those are all hard majors." I glanced at the walls behind me. "Do you mind if I look around while we talk?"

"Help yourself."

I crossed to the other side and leafed through the notebooks on her desk. Her class notes had random doodles and sketches in the margins. "Does she have a computer?"

"A laptop, but she takes that with her everywhere."

"What about a number where you can reach her?"

"I've tried calling, but she didn't pay her bill this month, or she went over her plan again. The damn thing is turned off."

"And you don't have any other way to reach her?"

"No."

I was running out of ideas. A flattened paper wristband caught my eye, and I picked it up. Printed on it was the name of the bar and the band that played live the night Brad and I found Carla Doucette dead in the bathroom. I held it up. "Do you know if Darcy went to this bar?" Mac had shown me footage of someone matching Darcy's description entering the bar earlier that night, but we had yet to prove the mystery woman was Darcy.

Her roommate laughed. "That's all I heard about for like a month. She loves that band. She couldn't wait for the show. She bought tickets the minute they went on sale."

"Did you go with her?"

"I had an exam the next day."

"Did she go alone?"

"No, she went with her loser boyfriend."

I had a sneaking suspicion who Darcy's boyfriend might be. But I must be wrong. It wouldn't make any sense. "Is his name Jimmy?"

She scrunched up her nose as she thought. "Now that you said it, that sounds right. I don't think she ever told me his last name."

"Did you meet him?"

"Once, I think. He wasn't anything special. He wore a bandana to cover this greasy hair that flopped down near his ears. He looks kind of scrubby. I don't know what she's doing with him. He's like six years older than she is, and he doesn't even have a real job. I accused him of living in his mom's basement and smoking pot all day because that's how he looks." She stared at me. "You know the type, right?"

"I'm familiar."

"So you get it. But Darcy got all defensive. She said he has his own apartment and a job. He's like a food delivery guy. After that, we kind of stopped talking about him and what she does with him. That's when she started disappearing for days at a time. I figured it was better if I didn't know." She stared at me with sad eyes. "Is Darcy okay? She's my best friend."

"I hope so."

I finished searching Darcy's desk and shelf, but I didn't see anything that would lead me to her location or tell me what her future plans were. Carefully, I opened her closet door. Crammed inside were several towers of free-standing plastic storage drawers. Kneeling down, I went through each drawer, then all of her bags and purses.

"What are you looking for?"

"Do you know if Darcy ever experimented with drugs?"

The roommate blinked a few times.

"It's okay, but there's a bad batch of a new party drug circulating. Several people have died from taking it."

"Is that what happened to Paul Gwynn?"

I nodded.

She exhaled slowly. "I don't know. Darcy's always had a wild streak, but she tries to mitigate the risks. Do you think she's dead?"

"Have you ever seen her with red pills? Did she ever mention Red Rabbit?"

"Is that bad?"

"Tell me what you know."

"Not much. Honest. I saw her with a baggie. She said it was a party favor. She wouldn't tell me where she got it. I told her to be careful, but she said it was no big deal. The pills were red, about the size of baby aspirin. Is that what you're talking about?"

"Possibly. Did you see a rabbit logo on the bag?"

"I didn't look that closely. I didn't really want to know."

"Did Darcy get pills or party favors often?"

"No."

"When she did, where did she usually get them?"

"I dunno."

That didn't help me any. "When was this?"

"It was before the concert. Actually, I think it was the day of the concert." She bit her lip, her eyes becoming unfocused as she thought back. "That's right. It was right before she left to go to the bar. She had pulled them out of her purse and tucked them into her pocket."

"How many pills did she have?"

"I'm not sure."

"What was she wearing that night?"

Her roommate crossed to the closet and pulled out a pair of skinny black jeans and a shimmering, asymmetrical black and red top. "These."

I checked the pockets again but didn't find anything. "Do you mind if I take a few photos? It'll make IDing her on surveillance footage easier." And it would prove beyond a doubt the woman on the footage was Darcy.

"Go ahead."

"Just to clarify, you've seen Darcy since then, right?"

"Yeah, she came home late that night super pissed. I asked her what was wrong. She said she got into a fight with her boyfriend. But he called two days later, and they made up. Do you think he hurt her?"

"I shouldn't speculate without investigating further. Are you sure you don't know anything else about her boyfriend or where she might go?"

"That's everything."

"What about her parents? Would they know anything?"

"She never talks to them. They got so annoyed when she switched majors. They stopped speaking after that. They'd be even more annoyed to think she can't even bother to pay her phone bill."

"When's the last time you saw or spoke to her?"

The roommate looked lost. "I'm not sure. I've lost track."

"All right." I wrote my cell number on the back of my card and handed it to her. "If you see Darcy or remember anything else, call me. And if you happen to overhear anyone else on campus talking about Red Rabbit or taking red pills, please let me know. Nine people have already died because of them."

TWENTY-FOUR

As soon as I stepped out of the girl's dorm, the tiny hairs on the back of my neck stood at attention. Someone was watching; I could feel it. I went down the front steps, searching the grounds in front of me. Several students and faculty were hurrying to class. Others were casually strolling while chatting or staring at their devices. Small groups were having heated debates on benches, and a few students were sprawled out on the grass.

My eyes continued to scan my surroundings. I'd learned to survive on my cop instincts, and right now, every cell in my body warned me of danger. A man leaned against a tree on the far side of the quad. He wore sunglasses and a cap. But even from fifty yards away, I could feel the intensity of his stare. I'd felt that once before. Wilson Matthews.

When he realized I was watching him, he turned and headed up the sidewalk. Breaking into a run, I hoped to catch him. I wasn't sure what I'd do once I did, but I'd worry about that when the time came. As the distance between us decreased, he ducked into the humanities building. I darted around the students and pushed my way inside.

Where was he? A staircase circled up to my left. Bathrooms were to the right, and classrooms and lecture halls lined the corridor in front of me.

I glanced up the stairs, but I didn't spot anyone dressed like that. More than likely, he went into one of the rooms. Moving as swiftly as possible, I peered into each room I passed, bouncing from one side of the hallway to the other like a pinball. The second door on the right led to a lecture hall with auditorium-like seating. There I spotted the cap and jacket moving down the rows of stairs.

"Stop." I flung myself forward and grabbed him by the shoulder. Every person entering the room turned to stare at me.

The guy turned his head. "What's your problem?" It wasn't Wilson Matthews.

Releasing him, I held up my palms. "Sorry. I thought you were someone else."

He gave me a bewildered look and headed for his seat. A couple of students in the corner pointed at my badge. Two of them grabbed their phones. The last thing I needed was this to get posted all over the internet. Ducking my face away, I hurried back up the stairs and out of the room.

Had I really hallucinated seeing Matthews here? Unsure what to do, I called Brad. He answered on the first ring.

"Where are you?" he asked.

"The college campus. I spoke to Darcy Kolado's roommate. She pretty much said Darcy's our mystery woman. Apparently, Darcy and Paul had a history, but that's not why I called. Something weird just happened. I thought I saw Wilson Matthews. I followed him into one of the buildings, but I lost sight of him. At least, I thought I saw him. I don't know."

"Call dispatch and find out if Matthews is on the move. I'm on my way to you now."

"Don't bother. I'm almost finished. I just want to ask Darcy's former boss a couple more questions."

"Great, so do I. I'll meet you there."

After we hung up, I phoned dispatch and had them redirect me to the unit sitting on Matthews.

"We got called off a little while ago due to an attempted carjacking six blocks from here. When we got back, Matthews' car was gone. We don't know where he is."

"How long has he been gone?"

"We got the call ninety minutes ago."

So the man I'd seen could have been Wilson Matthews, but how would he know where I'd be? Since I couldn't shake the thought, I stopped by the security office and spoke to the overly helpful guard from earlier. According to him, I was the only visitor who arrived on campus in the last two hours.

"Are you certain?" I described Matthews to a T.

"I haven't seen him." He stopped me before I could leave. "Did you get everything you needed?"

"I'm not sure. Has anyone ever complained about Paul Gwynn?"

"Let me check my records." The guard entered the name. "I'm not seeing anything. Did Darcy's roommate say something?"

"She said Paul harassed her at work."

"Frat guys," he mumbled. "If there's anything else, I'll be happy to follow up on something for you, just give me a holler."

Leaving my car in the parking lot, I walked across the street to Milk and Honey. By now, the morning rush had died down. Several students were camped out at tables with their laptops open and their earbuds in. The manager we spoke to earlier was refilling the pastries in the display counter. At the sound of the door chime, he looked up.

"Welcome back."

I looked around the room, fighting against the unease that continued to nag at me ever since I left Darcy's dorm. But no one posed a threat. "I have a few questions about some of your customers. Is there some place we can talk in private?"

He called to one of the workers to finish with the display case. "This way." He lifted a flap near the counter and led me through a swinging door and into the kitchen. The smell of freshly baked treats grew stronger.

"Why didn't you mention Darcy had problems with several customers?"

"What problems?"

I summarized a few of the issues Darcy's roommate had

told me about. "It sounds like Paul Gwynn was particularly difficult."

"Eh, kids. I was just as stupid at that age."

By the looks of him, that hadn't been that long ago. "Why didn't you ever say anything to him?"

"M&H doesn't want bad reviews. People complain for all kinds of reasons. But we have a pretty good rating. So we put up with people's crap and abuse. That's just part of the job. This isn't a hostile work environment. Darcy was never in any harm. No one here is."

"You said she still hangs around a lot."

"Yeah, so?"

That didn't make any sense if she hated this job so much. "When's the last time you saw her?"

"I don't know. Didn't your partner ask me this earlier?"

I didn't remember. "Just give me your best guess."

"I've been on vacation the last two weeks. I saw her maybe three or four days before that."

"Have you met her boyfriend?"

"Yeah, um..." he exhaled loudly, "Justin or James. Wait, no. Maybe it was Ben."

"Would anyone here know for sure?"

"I don't know. Tonya and Darcy were close. She also used to take breaks with Chuck, but that was about it."

"Okay, I'll talk to them in a sec. In the meantime, describe this Ben to me."

"Was it Ben?" His face scrunched up. "Maybe it was Dean. I don't know."

"Jimmy?" I asked.

"Was that it? That doesn't sound right."

"It doesn't matter. Just tell me what he looked like."

"He has dark hair that falls to his chin."

"Anything else?"

"Um, no."

"Did he buy anything?"

"He had a muffin."

"Did he use a credit card?"

"Darcy paid for it. I always gave her a discount since she had been such a wonderful employee."

Annoyed, I left the kitchen and spoke to Tonya and

Chuck, her former coworkers. But they weren't particularly helpful either. From the looks they gave me, they shared Darcy's opinion about the job, but like most struggling college students, they took what they could get and put up with a lot of crap. That training would probably make them great cops, I thought ironically.

While I was speaking to Chuck, Brad came in and stood beside me. Once I was finished asking questions, he led me back to the main counter where he presented the manager with a court order for the café's surveillance footage. We already had the receipts. But this was better.

"The hard drive only holds data for a month," the manager said.

"That's more than enough." Brad went with him to get it while I waited out front.

The streets and sidewalks were crowded with mid-day traffic. Despite all the hustle and bustle, one man stuck out like a sore thumb. He stood across the street, half a block away. While the rest of the world continued to spin, he remained motionless, staring straight at me from behind his mirrored shades.

My blood ran cold. Should I chase him? Should I wait and see what he'd do next? I had no grounds to arrest him. Honestly, I had no idea what to do. And I didn't like it.

The faint sound of the chime sounded behind me. I turned, only for a second, to make sure Brad was behind me, and when I turned back around, the man across the street had vanished.

A city bus had passed, but it didn't stop. He couldn't have just dematerialized. Was I losing my mind?

"Liv, what's wrong?"

I pointed. "I swear he was right there."

"Matthews?"

"Yeah."

"Okay." He tucked the hard drive into his pocket. "Stay close." He shifted beside me, moving more like a human shield than my partner. "What is he wearing?"

I stopped suddenly. Matthews had crossed the street and was heading straight for us. A huge smile was plastered on his face. Brad pushed me to the side, making sure Matthews couldn't get close enough to touch me. His hand rested on the butt of his gun.

"Good afternoon, Detective DeMarco. Funny running into you here." He glanced up at the café sign. "I thought cops only went to donut shops. I must have been misinformed."

"What are you doing here?" I asked.

Matthews removed his sunglasses, giving me a glimpse of the extensive bruises on his face. "Isn't it obvious?"

Brad tensed. "Stalking's a crime."

Matthews snorted. "That would require establishing a pattern of behavior. I've exhibited no such pattern." He winked at me. "Yet."

"You have no business here," I warned.

"This is a public place. I have every right to be here."

"Move along," Brad said.

Matthews stared at him. "I have your number too."

"What's that supposed to mean?"

Matthews held that sickening grin. The fingers on his right hand began to rub small circles against the hem of his shirt. When he looked at me again, his eyes were slightly dilated. "I told you I'd see you again. Have a good day." He pulled on the door handle to the café. "I know I will."

TWENTY-FIVE

Wilson Matthews' entire body tingled. His pulse quickened every time he looked out the window. She had been so close. In fact, she was still close. He could see her sitting beside the man with the brown hair as they watched him from inside a dark blue sedan.

What was his name? Matthews wondered. He'd seen Brown Hair at least three times prior to being arrested. Brown Hair had been working for Gallagher. Matthews bit his lip, trying to recall. Brad. That was it.

He sipped his tea before placing the cup back on the table. He liked this. She was watching him while he watched her. It was perfect, like a goldfish and a housecat. He was the cat, and she was the fish. No matter how fast she swam, he wouldn't lose sight of her.

"You look happy," someone said from a nearby table. "Is the tea really that good?"

"It's incredible," Matthews said. "Warm. Seductive. I just had to get some."

No matter how hard he tried, he couldn't shake the smile from his lips. Liv DeMarco was scared. He liked that. Wanted that. He never imagined he'd be able to get under her skin this quickly. All it took was one phone call and a chance meeting to put that level of fear in her eyes.

When he trailed her onto the college campus, he had planned to keep his distance. But the desire for more had overwhelmed him. After all, he'd gone through a lot to get here. He couldn't walk away empty-handed. He wanted something to show for it. He hoped to sneak up on her, smell her hair, feel her clothes, or have some other kind of sensory experience that he could focus on until he moved on to the next phase of his plan.

But she'd spotted him and gave chase. Ducking into the men's room made him feel like a coward. But there was nothing else he could do. Her desperation to get to him made her actions unpredictable.

He could only imagine she wanted him as badly as he wanted her. Again, a pleasant shiver shot through him. Ooh, he liked that. He liked that a lot.

However, he was unsure what she would have done if she caught him. Would she have arrested him? He didn't think she had grounds, but that wouldn't stop her from slapping on the handcuffs and dragging him into the police station. Once there, he didn't want to risk having to explain why he was on a college campus to her fellow officers or a judge. He had no reason to be there. However, no one could fault him for going to a café.

After his narrow escape inside the humanities building, he realized the smart thing to do was leave. But fate had intervened again. He'd spotted her entering the café just as he was getting into his car. Clearly, their paths were meant to cross. So he took advantage.

A part of him wanted to lure her somewhere secluded, slice her open, and watch the life drain from her. The anticipation had been building ever since he first laid eyes on her, and it had gotten nearly unbearable while he was imprisoned. But he didn't want it to end that quickly. She would be his masterpiece, possibly his last, at least for a while. He wanted to take his time. He wanted it to be unforgettable.

He'd spent the last twenty-four hours figuring out where she lived and ways to get to her so he could observe and learn from her behavior. The biggest obstacle had been figuring out how to lose the police officers parked outside his house. But for whatever the reason, they just drove away.

At first, he'd been convinced it was a trap. They'd followed him everywhere yesterday, in the car and on foot. He hadn't been able to lose them. So he figured they must have upped their game. Maybe the PD had decided an unmarked car would be better suited to keep tabs on him. So when he got in his car and drove to the precinct, he fully expected to be followed. Once he was sure, he'd go inside and launch a complaint. He didn't expect it to do much, but none of that happened. For the first time since getting released on bail, he was truly free.

He figured he'd ditch his car, visit his secret hideaway, stock up on supplies, and settle in, but then she strutted out of the precinct. It's almost as if she sensed he was close. And their dance began.

She hadn't taken her eyes off of him for the last twenty minutes. He lifted his cup and toasted in her direction. That made her look away, but Brad's scowl only deepened.

Gallagher had said Brad was Liv's partner. But from the way he behaved on the sidewalk, Wilson Matthews realized they were partners in every sense of the word. Men like Brad didn't act that protective over any woman. Brad thought she was special.

That thought made the smile waver on Matthews' face. *She's just another lying, cheating whore intent on hurting and destroying.* And that's when Matthews decided he'd make sure Brad discovered what a deceptive bitch his partner really was.

* * *

Once the patrol car arrived to keep tabs on Matthews, Brad drove me back to my car. "I don't like this, Liv. How did he know you'd be here?"

"I don't know. The only thing I can think of is the department still has a leak."

"That's the same conclusion I reached."

"We don't know for sure," I said.

"No," he exhaled, glancing in the direction of the café as he double-parked behind me, "but what else could it be?"

"I'll have Mac check my phone to make sure there isn't any malware or tracking software installed that I don't know about."

He got out of the car and felt around my bumper. "Why don't you drive my car back? I'll take yours. I'll have the guys in the garage check it for trackers."

"I'm okay."

His brown eyes searched mine. "I know, but I'm not. Take my car. I'll follow you back."

"I love that you want to, but I don't need you to protect me."

"I protect you. You protect me. That's how this works. We keep each other safe."

I tossed him the keys. "I'll see you back at work."

"Yep."

On the way back, I called Ashmore. "Whatever happened with Jimmy Stark? Did he or Marietta ever give you anything useful?"

"He described several suspicious people he saw that night. I went back through the footage and spoke to the bar staff, but I wasn't able to ID any of them."

"I'm guessing he was lying." I told Ashmore my suspicion that Jimmy had gone to the bar that night to see his side piece, Darcy Kolado. "Darcy's roommate said Darcy had pills with her."

"Do you think she's our dealer?"

"I think Jimmy is, but she could be involved. Brad just picked up surveillance footage from Milk and Honey."

"Do you have evidence?"

"Darcy was at the bar that night. I found her wristband, and Mac IDed her on the security camera from outside the bar."

"Was she with Jimmy?"

"They arrived separately."

"The bartender never said anything about another woman."

"We didn't ask."

"All right, I'll go talk to him. Was the show a closed

performance?" Ashmore asked.

"They sold tickets, so probably. Is there any problem with bringing Jimmy back in for questioning?"

"None that I can see," he said. I resisted the urge to point out how much closer we'd be to the truth if narcotics hadn't cut Stark loose after I arrested him. "I'll get a couple of unis to bring him in. He'll be waiting for you."

"I appreciate it." I hung up, spotting Brad in my rear view. He rubbed his cheek with one hand while he clenched the wheel with the other. He always did that when he was nervous.

How could we have so many problems at once? Brad nearly sacrificed his life and his career to plug the leak in the department, but Matthews' appearance at Milk and Honey signified we still had a problem. Agent Anderson said the FBI was looking into it, but telling a suspected serial killer with a vendetta where I'd be went far beyond a corrupt cop taking a bribe, making evidence go away, or letting it slip where a witness was being held. This was a total betrayal. And it felt personal.

I couldn't stop the question from coming to mind. *Who wanted me dead?* Maybe my prior close calls hadn't been close calls. Brad had suspected someone was out to get us. And after what just happened, I feared he might be right. Was I the target?

My entire career had been plagued with snide comments and thinly veiled insults. Being a woman in uniform was hard. Being the daughter of a police captain made it harder. A lot of guys on the force resented me. But I worked hard and made sure I earned everything I got. No matter what I accomplished, not everyone saw it that way. Most did, but there were always a few who didn't. Could one of them be so deluded and jealous to actually set me up to be killed?

That sounded crazy. But was it? *Shake it off, DeMarco. You are not that egocentric.* I'd have to explore every other option before considering this one again. Perhaps, it was just a coincidence. But Brad would never see it that way. He was convinced we were under attack. That I was under attack. And that usually brought out the worst in him.

By the time he met me upstairs, he looked ready to kill. He put my keys down and took a seat. Gripping the edge of his desk, he inhaled, held it for a count of four, then exhaled for a count of six.

"Make a list of everyone who knew where you were going. Agent Anderson will want that information."

"Did you speak to him?"

"I called him on the way here."

"Brad—"

"I know, but I'm not waiting for someone to make another attempt on your life before we look into it. We need to be proactive."

"All right." I picked up the pen and held it over the paper. Not a single name came to mind. "We discussed this at the morning briefing."

"Right."

"But I didn't know I was going to the college or back to Milk and Honey. I didn't know anything about Darcy until I ran her name through the database."

"Are you sure you didn't mention it to anyone?"

"I don't remember."

Brad worked his jaw from side to side. "That complicates things." He looked in the direction of Lt. Winston's office. "Did you ask the LT for permission?"

"No. In fact, I haven't seen him at all today." Even now, the lieutenant's office was dark.

"All right."

"Do you really think Winston would do that? You heard what Captain Grayson said."

"Winston knows more than he should, and Anderson pointed out that even decorated lieutenants were on the list of potential accomplices."

I knew better than to argue with Brad when he got like this, particularly when he had such valid points. "We have to table this for now."

He agreed. "I gave the hard drive from Milk and Honey to Mac. Did you give her your phone to check?"

"That's the first thing I did when I got here."

"Good."

I pulled up Jimmy Stark's interview transcripts and

read them. He hadn't provided Ashmore with anything except the descriptions of a few shady people he noticed hanging around Carla Doucette. But those never panned out. I wasn't even sure if Ashmore had found anyone else he could bring in to question. Was narcotics really that desperate to find a dealer that they'd let the obvious choice slip through their fingers?

I rocked in my chair. "I have a theory."

Brad folded his hands together and leaned closer. "Go on."

"Darcy Kolado had at least two red pills in her possession before she went to the concert, the same concert at the bar where Jimmy Stark was. According to Darcy's roommate, Darcy's dating some loser named Jimmy who delivers food for a living. She described him as having greasy hair that falls to his chin. Jimmy had his hair slicked back the night we arrested him, but it was about that long. And we know he delivers food."

"That was his alibi."

"Plus, you saw how Marietta acted or reacted. While it's possible she's just jealous and insecure, it's also possible Jimmy gave her a reason to feel that way."

"All right. I'll bite. But that doesn't explain how Darcy figures in to Kara," he winced, "I mean Carla's death?" The light bulb clicked before I could open my mouth. "Every victim had a connection to Milk and Honey, which is where Darcy used to work and now hangs out. Do you think she's dealing?"

"Possibly. It gets worse. Paul used to harass Darcy." I told Brad everything the roommate had said. "I didn't find any drugs in Darcy's dorm room." I ran a quick check on her roommate. "Her roommate struck me as a good kid, not much for partying. She wouldn't have wanted to room with someone like that."

"Okay, so, what are you thinking?"

"I think Jimmy's dealing, and he pulled Darcy into it. She could easily hook him up with dozens of people looking to party."

"Very possible, but Darcy hated Paul Gwynn. Why would she go off alone with him if she despised him?

Shouldn't his friends have recognized her from Milk and Honey?"

"From the way the roommate made it sound, the frat guys and the other troublemaker customers treated the employees like shit. I doubt they saw them as people, which means they probably didn't see them at all."

"Oh, I get it. The help's invisible."

"Something like that. You heard Paul's buddies. They had no idea who he was seeing."

"Revolving door," Brad muttered. "The women become interchangeable."

"It's possible. It's also possible they were too dumb and drunk to recognize her as the server without the apron on."

Brad jotted down a list of points. As usual, he crossed off the ones he found invalid or improbable. "You still didn't answer my question. Why would Darcy go off with Paul if she hated him?"

I pressed my lips together and waited, hoping Brad wouldn't make me say it.

"She wanted revenge. That could mean she knew the pills were tainted, making at least one of the ODs premeditated murder." He sucked in a breath. "If that's true, it might be true for all of them."

"It's also possible she took Paul to meet Jimmy. Maybe she figured Jimmy would rip him off, or she thought Jimmy would scare him into leaving her alone. We know Jimmy has a history of violence."

"We need to have another chat with Jimmy and see what's what."

TWENTY-SIX

The security cameras inside Milk and Honey had caught all sorts of things. But with a month's worth of footage, Brad and I didn't have time to watch all of it. Instead, we only watched the footage of Darcy. As far as we could tell, she never made any handoffs.

"She's not dealing from Milk and Honey," Mac said.

"Keep going," I said.

Mac scanned the footage, moving it forward a few days until we spotted Darcy's next appearance. She entered the café alone and talked to Chuck and Tonya for a while until the place got busy. That's when she took a cookie and sat down at one of the tables near the door.

"That's a bad angle," Brad said. The table was right next to the door, and since the surveillance camera was above the door, it made it difficult to see the other side of the table. On the previous footage we watched, Darcy had always sat in the back corner, close to the counter, so she could talk to her friends and help herself to whatever she wanted. But for some reason, this particular day was different. "Is she talking to someone?"

Mac zoomed in and tried to clear up the pixelation, but that didn't work. Instead, she returned to the normal magnification and sent it to the larger monitor. "Her lips are moving. She could be talking or maybe she's singing to herself. I do that sometimes, especially if the radio in a store is playing a song I like."

All three of us leaned in closer. "No, she's talking," Brad said. "The breaks and pauses don't follow much of a rhythm to be a song."

"Fast forward," I said. Three minutes later, a man leaned in for a kiss.

"Freeze it," Brad and I said at the same time.

Mac laughed. "Man, I missed you guys so much. I love this."

"Me too." I pointed to the printer. "We need a copy of that."

"On it." Mac moved the footage forward and back, frame by frame, until she found the best still and handed me the printout. "What are you going to do with that?"

"I'm going to see if the man waiting inside interrogation room two would like to provide a caption." I smiled. "This should be fun."

Armed with the photo, I went down the hall to the interrogation room and stepped inside. Jimmy Stark looked up, a smug grin on his face. "Hey, maybe you didn't get the memo, but I'm not supposed to be here, babe."

"Detective DeMarco, not babe." I put the photo on the table in front of him. "Feel free to walk out anytime you want, but if you do, I'm gonna have to ask Marietta about this." I tapped the printout. "Are you sure you want to play it this way?"

The grin evaporated from his face. "What's this supposed to be?"

"You know what it is." Brad entered the room and pulled the door closed. "That's your other girlfriend, Darcy. The one you met at the bar the night we arrested you." Brad sat down. "Where is she?"

"How should I know?"

"Where is she?" Brad repeated.

Jimmy stared down at the photo. "That's not from the bar. For all I know, you doctored this photo."

"Don't sell yourself short, Jimmy," I said. "I understand

why you'd think we'd have to perform computer magic to get a woman to kiss you. It is hard to believe anyone would do so willingly, let alone two women."

"No, nuh-uh." He shook his head emphatically. "I'm never gonna admit to that."

"Marietta's got your nuts in a vise, huh?" Brad asked knowingly. "I see how it is. She wears the pants in your relationship. She tells you what to do, and given the way she reacted the night she found you at that bar, I'm guessing she's not going to be too happy about this. I'll tell you what. You give me the heads-up before you go home, and I'll have EMTs on standby. If it's a clean cut, they might be able to reattach your penis after Marietta castrates you."

"First off, no one tells me what to do." Brad's comment had lit a fire beneath our suspect. "Second, I'll screw whoever the hell I want and do whatever the hell I want. Marietta doesn't control me."

"That's not what you said last time. You said you'd never step out on her. It turns out you lied to more than just us." I pulled my phone from my pocket. "I wonder how Marietta's gonna take the news."

"No, no way. You got it wrong. My relationships are my business. They got nothing to do with you."

"Does Marietta know about Darcy?" Brad asked.

"No." Jimmy tapped anxiously against his thighs, his left leg jiggling up and down. "Darcy and I aren't even like that. There's nothing for Marietta to know about."

"It looks sexual to me." Brad held up the photo, so I could see it. "Liv, do you meet your friends for coffee and kiss them on the mouth before you leave?"

"No." I looked at my partner. "Is that a guy thing?"

Brad made a show of scratching his head as he contemplated the question. "If it is, no one told me. Maybe it's a French thing." He held up the photo again to examine. "That looks a little French to me." He turned the photo to Jimmy. "Did you use tongue? It looks like you had some tongue action going on there."

"I'm not sleeping with Darcy, and even if I am, that's not a fucking crime. She's over eighteen." He blinked rapidly a few times. "She's like twenty-one. She had to be to get into the bar."

"Carla Doucette wasn't twenty-one," I said. "She was nineteen years old. And she's dead because someone sold her bad dope. Do you want to tell us about that?"

Jimmy swallowed, his leg creating mini-earthquakes inside the room. "I don't know her either. You gonna say I was sleeping with her too?"

"Where's Darcy?" I asked.

Jimmy appeared to be suffering from whiplash. "I don't know."

"Call her," Brad said.

"I can't."

"Why not?"

"I don't have her number."

I eyed him. "You expect us to believe that the woman you're tonguing in this photo, who you met at a concert, didn't give you her phone number?"

"No."

"Darcy's roommate says you've been dating for months. Stop lying to us, Jimmy."

Brad put the photo back on the table, went around, and laid his hand on top of Jimmy's knee to stop the jittering. "Come clean, and none of this gets back to Marietta."

"Why should I believe you?"

"Believe me or not, it's your call," Brad said. "But Darcy Kolado's missing. No one's seen her in days. The last time anyone saw her, she was with a guy who died of an overdose an hour later. Right now, we have every reason to believe Darcy could be dead or her life could be in danger. If you care at all, you'll tell us where she is."

Jimmy took a breath. "Am I under arrest?"

"Not yet," I said.

"Then I don't have to stay here and listen to this. Call Marietta and tell her whatever you want. It's not my problem. I didn't do anything wrong. That girl, Darcy or whatever you said her name is, we met at that coffee place a few times. She used to work there, and she'd flirt with me whenever I made pick-ups for my job. One day, I stopped in for lunch, and she gave me a discount, so I kept going back. I'm not exactly flush. Every little bit helps. Maybe she got the wrong idea." He glared at me. "Hell, she probably went home and told her roommate how great I am. I don't know. I don't really care. That," he pointed to the photo, "was the one and only time we ever kissed. She came on to me. Not the other way around. She was sweet, but nothing special. I don't know. Maybe she mentioned the concert to me one of the times I was at that café. I can't remember. But that might have been how I heard about it. We didn't go together. I don't even remember seeing her at the bar that night. I didn't go there to see anyone. I went to drink and listen to some music. That was it." He got out of the chair. "The girl was wild. I hope when you find her, she's okay, but a girl like that is trouble. So," he shrugged, "whatever happens, happens, y'know."

"It's not a coffee place," Brad said. "It's a tea place. They don't sell coffee."

"Whatever it is."

Brad watched him head for the door. We weren't in any position to arrest him yet. We had no proof he'd done anything wrong, but my gut said the first thing he'd do once he was free was contact Darcy. Luckily, an unmarked unit was ready to follow him as soon as he left the building. "Jimmy, hold up. I want to offer you a word of advice."

Jimmy turned at the door. "What?"

"The next time you lie, make it less complicated, and make sure the details you provide are accurate. It'll help sell your story."

"Eat me."

Brad winked at him. "I'll be sure to pass that along to your future cellmate."

"Fuck off."

Jimmy walked out of the room, holding up his hands as he maneuvered around the officer outside. The officer looked at us.

"Let him go," I said. "We don't have grounds to hold him." But we had enough circumstantial evidence to continue investigating. I exhaled and pushed Jimmy's chair under the table. "That went better than I thought. At least he didn't spit on me this time."

"I'd like to teach him some manners," Brad mumbled.

"Marietta will take care of him when she gets a whiff of this." I peered into the hallway to make sure Jimmy was gone. "I'm still not convinced she didn't play a part in Carla's death."

"She didn't help, which means whatever she did hurt. But we don't know exactly what happened. Without surveillance footage, an eyewitness, or a confession, we'll never know."

"Let's just hope Jimmy leads us to Darcy."

TWENTY-SEVEN

We met the surveillance team outside a bar. One of the cops pointed to Jimmy's car. "He went inside twenty minutes ago. My partner's keeping an eye on him."

"Has anyone approached?" Brad asked.

"No. He's been sitting alone at the bar."

"All right, once we get inside, tell your partner he can walk away. We'll take it from here." Brad fist-bumped the officer, who returned to his car.

I popped the trunk and handed Brad a hoodie and cap. He put them on while I tied my hair up and put on a short, blonde wig and stripped out of my button-up blouse, leaving just my tank top on. I stepped into a skirt, pulled it up around my waist, and slid out of my pants.

Brad watched me from the corner of his eye. "One of these days, you're gonna get arrested for indecent exposure."

"Did I expose anything?"

"I don't know. I wasn't looking."

I smiled. "The hell you weren't."

After tucking my gun, cuffs, and badge into an oversized purse, I slung it over my shoulder and put on a pair of lightly tinted glasses. Brad put his hood up, pulled the sweatshirt down over his gun, and wrapped his arm around my waist.

When we entered the bar, Jimmy didn't bother giving us a second glance. Brad found a table near the back where we could keep an eye on him and a good deal of the room. He slung his arm around the back of my chair, so he could lean in close for us to whisper back and forth.

"Do you see Darcy?" Brad asked.

I turned in my chair, looking over his shoulder for anyone who fit her description. "I don't see her, and with that red hair, she'd be hard to miss."

"That's assuming she hasn't changed her appearance since the last time we spotted her on surveillance footage."

"Good point." From the photos I'd seen, Darcy was a chameleon.

When a server came to ask for our drink orders, we got two club sodas with lime. Brad kept his focus on Jimmy, glancing every now and again at the bottles behind the bar.

"What is he drinking?" I asked.

"Rum and coke." Brad stared for a moment longer. "He's on his third."

"We've only been here forty minutes. He's been here an hour. He might have had more than that."

"I'm guessing his game plan involves getting drunk."

Jimmy's phone buzzed, and he glanced down at it. Shaking his head, he drained his glass and got up from the barstool. He remained still for a moment, as if wanting to make sure he was balanced before heading in the direction of the men's room.

After Jimmy walked past our table, Brad got up and followed him. Jimmy didn't appear to notice, but I didn't trust him. I shifted to the edge of my seat, ready to assist my partner, but I didn't hear any sounds coming from the bathrooms.

The bell above the front door caught my attention, and I turned to see a woman entering. She wore a baseball cap and sunglasses, but she was short and small in stature. The sleeves of her shirt ended just above her elbows. Intricately detailed vines ran down her left arm. Darcy.

I remained in my seat, not wanting to spook her. She

was across the bar. If I announced, she'd run out the door and disappear before I could catch her. I had to be smart. Patient. I had to wait.

She stood in the doorway, carefully scanning every inch of the room. I returned my gaze to the glass on the table in front of me, hoping she hadn't noticed the intensity of my stare. Ever so slowly, she approached the bar.

Swallowing the remainder of the sparkling water, I picked up my glass and made my way toward her. The bartender had his back to us while he filled a pitcher of beer. Darcy didn't take a seat. Instead, she made her way to the spot where Jimmy had been drinking. She picked up his napkin and studied it.

"Darcy?" I was less than three feet away.

Reflexively, she looked up. "How do you know who I am?"

"Jimmy mentioned you. I just want to talk."

She waited for me to get a step closer before shoving the barstool into my stomach and bolting for the door. The sudden impact knocked the wind out of me. As soon as I got my breath back, I burst out of the bar after her.

"Stop. Police," I shouted.

The soles of her shoes slid on the asphalt when she took the corner too fast. She cut across the street and turned down the first driveway. Luckily, I hadn't changed shoes when I changed clothes.

"Darcy, stop. I don't want to hurt you."

She didn't even turn. She just kept running, like her life depended on it. She slowed when she saw the end of the driveway had been partitioned off by a tall wooden fence. I charged forward and got a hold of the back of her shirt.

She tried to yank free, but with the grip I had, the momentum made her move sideways. She kicked off the side of the wall, launching backward toward me. The sudden shift in direction made me lose my balance.

My arms pinwheeled, trying to keep my body from falling over. But it was too late. At the last second, I pushed my head up, so I didn't crack my skull on the pavement. Darcy landed on her side, rolled, and jumped to her feet. With the agility of a cat, she climbed the stack of cardboard boxes which were piled beside the fence, clung to the top and kicked the boxes away before hauling herself over.

"Dammit." I raced back down the driveway and onto the street. By the time I found another opening and made it across to the other side, Darcy was gone. I called it in, hoping a patrol car was in the area. But no such luck.

"We'll keep an eye out, DeMarco."

I put my hands on my knees, hoping to catch my breath before heading back to the bar. On the ground near where Darcy scaled the fence, I spotted the napkin she'd taken from the bar. Someone had written a list of addresses on the inside.

Afraid of what it might mean, I trudged back to the bar. When I walked in, Jimmy was on the barstool. Brad looked up, relief on his face. "You okay?" he mouthed.

Anger boiled inside of me. Jimmy was nothing but a liar and a cheat. No wonder Marietta behaved the way she did. Before I could confront Jimmy for the second time today, Brad intercepted.

"What happened? Where'd you go?" he whispered.

"Darcy." I showed him the napkin. "Let's bring Jimmy back in."

"Liv, wait." Brad scanned the details again. "These are all bars and clubs."

"How do you know that?"

"These are the same addresses Ashmore wanted investigated. They cater to the college crowd and fall within our estimated radius."

"Great, let's ask Jimmy about it."

Brad bit his lip, glancing over my shoulder at Jimmy who was helping himself to a bowl of nuts while he waited for the bartender to refill his drink. "Let's think about this for a minute."

"I hate it when you say that. What's to think about?"

"Jimmy doesn't know we have this. Darcy doesn't know we have this. She came all the way here to get it. Her appearance seconds after Jimmy got a text and got up to go to the bathroom isn't a coincidence."

"Right, so let's ask Jimmy about it."

"We have a napkin with addresses. We can't hold him

on this. What would the charge be? Vandalism?" Brad pushed me into one of the booths when Jimmy looked up from his bowl of peanuts and played with the strands of my wig. Again, Jimmy looked right past us and went back to minding his own business. "He didn't write this."

"How do you know?"

"We haven't seen him write anything the entire time we've been here. If the surveillance team had noticed, they would have told us."

"Where did he get it?"

"I don't know."

"Well, let's go ask him."

Brad chuckled. "Liv, I want this guy too. And I want Darcy, and I want people to stop dying, but this is our first real lead. We have to be patient."

"How do you know it's a lead?"

"Why else would this be important enough to pass along using a dead drop of sorts?"

I rested my head in my hands. "I don't like this. This doesn't seem like the right move."

Brad pulled out his phone and handed it to me. "Call Grayson. He's in charge. We do what he says."

TWENTY-EIGHT

Captain Grayson agreed with Brad's assessment. It'd be better to keep this quiet so we could put eyes on every single one of the addresses without compromising our operation. If Darcy showed up at any of the clubs, we'd be waiting. However, if this fell through, we could always drag Jimmy back in.

"You really don't think Jimmy wrote the list?" I asked, while we continued to watch him down drink after drink.

"No."

"Where did he get it?"

Brad eyed the bartender. "Jimmy picked this bar for a reason. I'm guessing those are delivery locations where he's supposed to move more product. He must have realized we'd be keeping tabs on him, so he found some way to get a message to Darcy to pick up the list and make the deliveries."

"You think they're working together?"

"That's the best explanation we have."

"You think whoever works here is involved in moving Red Rabbit?"

"Could be." Brad glanced back toward the bathrooms. "I noticed a lot of top-of-the-line security features around the rear storeroom, way more than a dive like this would need." He shot a text to Ashmore. "Vice might have to raid the place. I haven't seen the bartender ID anyone who's come inside. Have you?"

"No, I have not."

Brad smiled. "They're going to hold off until after we leave. They don't want to spook Jimmy."

"Do you think he has any intention of leaving? It looks like he's settled in for the long haul. If this is where he picks up product, he might be hanging out until after close to get more pills to distribute."

"In which case, we bust him and the supplier."

"But Darcy's still in the wind."

"One problem at a time."

"How did she know to come here?"

"He must have called her or texted. She must have said she was coming inside, and that's why he went to hit the head. He knows it's not safe for them to be seen together."

"Why didn't he text her the list of locations?"

"You ask a lot of questions." Brad squeezed the lime into his glass of melting ice.

"That's what we get paid to do."

"When we get a warrant for his phone records, which is already in the works, we'll know everything he sent and to whom. He might look stupid, but I don't think he is."

Another hour dragged on. Brad's upbeat attitude had started to wane. The waiting was painfully boring.

"Do you think he's looking for liquid courage in order to come clean to Marietta?" Brad asked.

"I don't know."

"Maybe I should call dispatch and tell them to put a bus on standby. He's bound to black out at any moment."

"Maybe we should question him now. He might be more forthcoming, and there's a good chance he won't even remember."

"I'm guessing the DA would frown on that."

"What do you think Marietta will do if she finds out Jimmy's doing shady things and he's doing them with another woman?"

"I don't want to know." He sighed. "Here's another

thought. What if she already knows about Darcy?"

I mulled it over for a while. She might, but based on Jimmy's reaction when we threatened to tell her, I suspected she probably didn't know.

We hadn't gotten a look at Darcy's phone records or financial statements yet. Those would be telling, but we only IDed her this morning. We had to wait for her records to come in. In the meantime, maybe we'd get Jimmy's records.

"If narcotics didn't interfere, we might have been able to do something. Paul Gwynn might still be alive."

Brad put his arm around me, but this time it wasn't to sell our cover. He gave me a squeeze. "Man, wouldn't it be nice to have a drink right about now?"

I laughed, despite sensing some truth to his words.

Based on the background check I ran, Darcy didn't have any priors, and she didn't have a car. With her phone out of service, we couldn't use that to track her. Her social media presence was sparse. We couldn't use it to locate her either. She must have another phone. That's the only thing that would explain the text Jimmy received.

I sent a quick text to Mac, asking if we got access to Jimmy's phone records yet. She said we should have them within the hour.

Brad and I remained at that bar for another forty-five minutes, watching Jimmy drink himself into a stupor. Eventually, the bartender cut him off, took his keys, and put him in a cab. We followed it back to Jimmy's apartment.

He stumbled out of the car, tossing dollar bills at the driver. Most of them landed on the sidewalk, and the cabbie shouted profanities at Jimmy's back.

While the cabbie got out to collect the rest of his fare from where it had fallen, Brad found a metered space nearby. "Do you think Marietta's home?" Brad asked.

"I don't know, but given Jimmy's condition, I'm not sure he made it all the way upstairs before passing out."

"I'll check. Keep an eye out, and this time, call me before you try to run down a suspect on your own."

"Will do."

Two minutes later, Brad returned. "Jimmy's not passed out in the hallway, so I think we're okay. How about you change back into you and we'll knock on a few doors and see if any of his neighbors remember seeing Darcy hanging around here?"

"What's wrong with what I'm wearing?"

"Absolutely nothing. But I thought you'd be more comfortable in your work clothes."

"Yeah, yeah." I rolled my eyes. "You better be careful. The more time you spend with my mom, the more you sound like her."

TWENTY-NINE

After an hour of banging on doors, I came to the conclusion Darcy Kolado had never been to Jimmy's apartment. For her safety, that was probably a good thing. Brad met me at the car.

"Anything?" he asked

"No. How about you?"

"No one's seen Darcy. The neighbors I spoke to know next to nothing about Jimmy. I even asked if any of them had heard of Red Rabbit or seen pills circulating."

I'd just stuck to the basics, flashing photos and inquiring as to Jimmy's comings and goings. "How did that go?"

"Not a single person would cop to knowing anything about drugs."

"In this neighborhood?"

He shrugged. "We've done what we can to put the screws to Jimmy. I guess we should settle in for the night. Marietta's not home, so maybe Darcy will show."

"After what happened earlier, I doubt it."

"Don't kick yourself. Sometimes suspects get away. It happens."

"I should have been faster."

His eyes twinkled. "That's right, Liv. You should have."

I laughed. "Screw you."

Brad bumped his knuckles against my thigh. I'd forgotten how his teasing usually made me feel better. Before he could say anything else, his phone rang. He looked at the screen. "It's Cap." He pressed the speaker button.

"Units entered that bar, checked everyone's ID, and cited the management for serving alcohol to one person underage. They didn't uncover anything else, but we didn't have a search warrant. We couldn't get into the locked rooms. I've assigned a surveillance van to keep watch. At the rate I've been assigning units at your request, the department's going to run out of vans soon," Grayson teased.

"Sorry, Cap," Brad said.

"Don't worry about it. That's not important. What's important is figuring out where these pills are coming from. After what you said, I got a look at Jimmy's phone history and credit card statements. He goes there a lot. I wouldn't be surprised if that's where he picks up the drugs."

"That's what I was thinking," Brad said.

"Yeah, well, it's a nice thought. But we need evidence."

"What about the text message he received?" I asked.

"The message came from Jimmy's other line. It looks like he texted himself."

"He must have given his other phone to Darcy. Maybe that's how they are staying in touch since her phone is out of service."

"That's what it looks like. The next time she uses that phone to contact Jimmy, we should be able to pinpoint her location."

"Great." A weight lifted from my chest. We finally had a way to find her.

"I'm sending an unmarked to take over Jimmy watch," Grayson said. "Loyola and Sullivan are already scoping out the bars and clubs on that list. But they need your help. No one wants to talk to cops. You think you can handle that?"

"We've been doing this all day," Brad said.

Once our relief arrived, we headed back to the precinct for further instructions and updated the rest of the task force. I changed into a different outfit, this time sporting dark skinny jeans and a shimmery, backless ruched top. I applied some heavy eye makeup and a bit of gloss, put a stylish leather jacket on to conceal my cuffs and gun, and met Brad at the car.

Since we figured Jimmy would be sleeping off the rum for the rest of the night, we didn't have to worry about running into him, so I ditched the wig. I didn't want Darcy to see me before I saw her. Brad had changed into dark wash jeans and a black dress shirt with the top two buttons open.

"While you were in the locker room, I called Sullivan. He and Loyola have started canvassing the bars and clubs on the list in the hopes of finding someone who recognizes Darcy or knows a thing or two about Red Rabbit," Brad said. "They want us to meet them."

"Have they made any progress?"

"Not yet. But they think they might be on to something. They need us to go in and pose as a couple of tourists looking to party."

I nodded a few times. "That might work." I gave Brad the quick once-over. "But you're dressed too neatly for someone looking to score."

"It depends on where we're partying." He scrubbed a hand through his hair. "Better?"

I tugged on his collar. "Perfect."

He smiled at me. "I should have realized you like messy. Your desk says it all."

"My desk isn't messy."

"You're right. Messy is too generous."

"I have my own system of organization."

"You're right. You do." We got into the car and headed for the bar. "I believe others would refer to it as total chaos." His gaze kept flicking to the mirrors.

"Is something wrong?"

"No, just making sure." He let out a breath. "Have you given any more thought to how Wilson Matthews found you this afternoon?"

"I can't come up with anything. My phone's clean."

"So was your car, but the department has GPS trackers on all the vehicles. Someone could have accessed that." Brad switched lanes, and I turned in my seat to see if anyone was tailing us. "I spoke to Agent Anderson briefly while you were getting changed."

"Does he have any insights to share?"

"He didn't say anything that sounded particularly promising, just the usual 'I'll look into it.' He thinks it could be a coincidence."

"Milk and Honey isn't close to Matthews' apartment. It's not near his work either, so it's unlikely it'd be one of his usual haunts."

"Were any of his victims college students?"

"A couple, but they didn't go to Darcy's school."

Brad switched lanes again as we got closer to our destination. "He went there for you, Liv. It's the only thing that makes sense. Walk me through your morning."

"I left my parents' place and went straight to the precinct. After I found out Darcy was a student, I went to the college. I didn't tell anyone what I was doing."

"Did you leave the information on your computer screen?"

"I usually log out."

"IT can pull up our searches and see what we've accessed." Brad reached into his pocket and pulled out his phone. "Do you think we can trust Mac?"

"Do you hear yourself?"

"I'm not paranoid. This is happening. This is still fucking happening. I did everything I could think of to stop it, and we're right back where we started."

"You don't know that."

He gave me a look. "I can't do optimism right now, DeMarco. I just can't."

"You sounded awfully optimistic earlier, when we were watching Jimmy."

"I guess I used it all up."

"Why the sudden shift?" I asked.

"For a second, I thought we were being followed. This is what came to mind." He looked at me. "Do you trust her?"

"Yes. Do you?"

He parked the car, his eyes never leaving the traffic as it continued to move behind us. "I used to trust everyone in the department to have our backs, now..." his shoulders hitched, "things are different. Everything is different." Without telling me what he was planning, he dialed Mac's personal line and put it on speaker.

"You rang?" Mac said in a Lurch voice.

"Can you do me a huge favor?" Brad asked. "I want to know if anyone accessed Liv's search history or her car's GPS."

"Um...okay. Gimme a sec." Mac came back a moment later. "No one's pulled anything up. What's going on?"

"Nothing."

"Oh-kay." I could hear the uncertainty in Mac's voice.

"We have a bet," I said. "The task force made a bet to see which unit would crack the case first. Brad wondered if anyone was trying to cheat by looking at our research before we get a chance to bring it to them."

Mac laughed. "Can I get in on that bet?"

"Do you want to have to wash Loyola's car in a bikini?" I asked.

"Never mind," she said.

"Thanks, Mac." Brad ended the call. "Obviously, homicide hasn't dulled your improv abilities."

"That answers your question, though."

"It puts us back at square one." He stared at the neon open sign hanging from the front door.

"Tracking down whoever's dealing Red Rabbit has to be our priority tonight. We have to focus. Hopefully, someone here can lead us to the supplier and Darcy. We'll deal with the Wilson Matthews issue tomorrow." Brad opened his mouth to protest, but I shook my head. "We don't have a choice. People are dying, and I let Darcy escape. I can't let anyone else die because I screwed up."

"I'm with you, Liv. I got your back."

We entered the bar. It had a Western theme. The walls were decorated with saddles and spurs. Most of the people looked like they were dressed to go line dancing. The dress code appeared to be plaid, denim, and cowboy boots.

Without missing a beat, my partner snagged a cowboy hat from where it hung on the wall and put it on his head. "What do you think?"

Strangely enough, my partner looked like he belonged at a country music award show. "You need cowboy boots."

"There's not much I can do about that. Someone should have given us the heads-up."

We spotted Loyola and Sullivan almost immediately. They stuck out like sore thumbs. The off-the-rack suits they wore screamed law enforcement. Loyola was questioning the bartender while Sullivan flashed around a few photos to anyone who happened to look in his direction.

Several people clustered around the pool tables in the back. Loyola glanced in our direction as we made our way to the bar. He flicked his eyes to a man near the pool tables. That's all it took for us to get the message.

Brad slid onto one of the stools and patted the one beside him. I sat, watching everyone from the mirrored reflection behind the bar. I didn't spot Darcy or any familiar faces.

"Hang on." The bartender ambled toward us. "What'll it be?"

"Can we get a couple of shots of whiskey at a table?" Brad pointed to one of the bottles.

"How many do you want?"

Brad glanced at me. "Six."

"Give me a sec." The bartender grabbed a tray and started to pour.

When the bartender was finished, Brad took the tray to one of the tables. Besides the scuffed hardwood dance floor, the only other draw to this place seemed to be the pool tables in the back. I checked the vantage points and sat down. Brad sat beside me, his arm draped over my shoulders.

"I don't think this looks promising," I whispered. "None of these people look much like the party drug type."

"I'll approach the guy in the denim shirt. That's who Loyola's interested in. He's carrying a lot of money, and I haven't seen him sink a single ball yet."

I followed my partner's gaze. The man he was talking

about looked more like he might sling crack or meth. "I doubt he's dealing Red Rabbit."

"The address was on the list, so who knows?"

Sullivan moved around one of the pool tables, keeping his badge visible while he spoke to the people playing at the center table. He held up his phone, showing them photos. The guy in the denim shirt intentionally avoided looking in Sullivan's direction, but his body language told me he was listening to every word. Even though he looked away, he angled toward Sullivan.

A woman at a table nearby reached into her pocket and took out her cell phone. She glanced up, looking first at Sullivan and then at Loyola, before rapidly typing out a text message. I nudged Brad, but he'd already noticed her odd behavior.

He leaned in close, tickling my ear with his lips. "She's warning someone."

I giggled in case anyone was watching us. Brad pulled back with a big grin on his face, all for show. We needed to get a look at her phone.

Brad picked up one of the shot glasses. "I call next." He stumbled toward the pool table, just as she got up. He bumped into her, spilling his drink all over her. "I'm so sorry, ma'am." He had picked up a southern twang to go with the hat. "Are you all right? Let me help you clean that up."

"Bradley, now what have you gone and done?" I wasn't sure how convincing my accent was, so I made sure to slur. "I can't let you out of my sight for one minute." I hurried toward the woman. "Let me help you wash that off, ma'am. You don't want it to stain." I gave a dirty look to Sullivan who had stopped to stare at us. "What? You got something to say?" I narrowed my eyes and lowered my voice. "Yeah, that's what I thought."

"It's fine, really," the woman said.

"But your phone's all wet." I picked it up, wiping it with a napkin while I read the text chain. "It's gonna get sticky. At least let me get you a wet nap or something."

"It's fine." She plucked it out of my hand and left the bar.

Brad eyed me, and I gave him a barely perceptible headshake. She hadn't been texting about Red Rabbit. She wanted her friend to pick her up because her tags were expired and she was afraid if the cops were inside asking questions, there might be more outside who would ding her for drunk driving. At least we'd deterred one person from making a bad decision tonight.

When the pool game ended, Brad took the offered cue stick from a guy wearing a plaid shirt. "Have at it," the loser said, walking back toward the bar.

Brad spoke to the current winner, a forty-something guy with a leather vest and a beer belly. He looked like he should be in a biker bar. Sullivan moved away from the tables as Brad played and came over to speak to me. He flashed his phone in my face.

"Do you mind if I ask you a few questions?"

"It's not like I can stop you." I gestured to the empty chair.

"Do you recognize any of these people?"

"Why would I?"

Sullivan gave me a look, as if to say, *Stop being so difficult.* Halfway through his spiel, the music kicked on and the small crowd who had no interest in playing pool stomped onto the dance floor. Loyola darted around them as they began twirling and shimmying, moments away from getting forced to join in.

"This isn't the right location," I said.

"No shit." Loyola watched as the group did some sort of two-step in perfect time. "This is our third stop. They seem to be getting less and less promising as we go."

"We should focus on the more popular clubs. The kinds of places Paul Gwynn and his fraternity brothers would actually go."

Loyola snorted. "This is one of the places they went."

I looked around, but I didn't find anyone who appeared to be in our target demographic. "You're joking."

"His credit card and blog posts verified it."

"None of his fraternity brothers are here tonight. In fact, I don't think a single college student is on the premises."

Sullivan nodded toward a chalkboard hanging on the

wall beside the bar. "Thursday is ladies' night. Women drink half price. That's always when Paul and his friends came here."

"I hate to point this out, but it's not Thursday." I watched my partner sink another ball. When he scratched, he moved closer to the guy in denim. He pointed to me and spoke in hushed tones. The guy shook his head. My partner reached into his pocket, but the guy grabbed his arm, a warning look on his face.

"Take off," I said to Loyola and Sullivan who obediently walked away.

Brad held up his palms, put the cue stick down, and returned to our table. He picked up a shot glass. This time, he downed it. I didn't react, but for him to do that, I knew we were on to something.

"Is everything all right?" I asked.

"He won't sell with cops here."

"Red Rabbit?"

Brad shook his head. "He said we can get a couple of eight balls but not until they're gone. I'm not sure if that's code because he's playing pool or if he means actual eight balls."

"Let's find out." I sent a text to Loyola with the update. Five minutes later, they left the bar.

But the guy in denim decided to play it safe. He hung around for a few more games of pool before excusing himself. He nodded to Brad and headed to the bathroom.

Brad returned a few minutes later. "Come on, Liv. Let's get out of here."

We made our way across the dance floor, where the crowd had only grown in the last thirty minutes. Instead of getting in the car, Brad led me off to the side and pinned me against the wall. I could feel the rise and fall of his chest against mine.

"I want to make sure we're not being followed."

"What happened?" I ran my hands up his biceps and across his shoulders. To any onlooker, we were just a young couple in love.

"He turned me down." Brad pressed his hand against the wall beside my face while he sent a text with the other.

"We could arrest him, but it's a tough sell. I didn't actually see the goods."

"We'll update the rest of the task force and see how they want to handle it."

He tucked his phone away, the wide brim of his hat concealing us from the world. "I said we were on vacation and looking to have a good time. I wondered if he knew where we could score some molly or something that packs a bit more punch."

"That's why he got suspicious."

"Sullivan." Brad nodded. "I know, but I had to try. He told me to check out a club downtown. That it might be more our scene."

"Which club?"

"DaVinci's." He searched my eyes. "What do you think?"

"It's on the list, so it's worth a look." I pulled the black cowboy hat off his head. "Let's hope you don't need this anymore."

THIRTY

"We need a better strategy." My partner bounced to the pulsing rhythms.

"I agree. You've had uniformed officers arrest six different dealers tonight. This is not how we perform undercover operations. You know that."

"What choice did I have? The only other option was to ignore them completely, and I can't do that. Any one of them might have a Red Rabbit hookup. They are all potential leads."

"It's that damn list. Could it have been a plant? A misdirect? Jimmy might have known we were watching him."

"I don't know what I think anymore. All I know is we need a win. I have to believe what we're doing makes a difference, that something positive is going to come out of it." He eyed the group of young women huddled together on a large, round ottoman. They were drinking something bright pink from martini glasses. One of them had a sash that said "Birthday Girl" with a plastic tiara that said "21" in glitter. "Do you want me to try my luck?"

"No." I grabbed the virgin daiquiri off the bar. "I got this one. See if you can find someone selling little red pills. And don't arrest anyone unless they have them."

"I'll do my best."

I took my drink and headed for the group of girls. "Happy Birthday," I yelled over the music.

"Birthday," they all cheered and took another sip of their drinks.

The birthday girl blushed a little. "Anytime anyone says the B-word, we drink." She looked at her friends who appeared just as wasted as she was. "We've been drinking a lot."

"You got a DD?"

"We got a party bus."

"Awesome."

"Scootch over, Mary Beth." The birthday girl patted the seat beside her. "What's your name?"

"Liv."

"I'm Janice." She introduced me to the rest of her group. "You should totally hang out with us." She reached up and ran her fingers through my hair. "I love your hair. It's so silky."

Mary Beth reached over and stroked the other side. I resisted the urge to yank away. I wasn't used to be treated like a pet. Was this how Gunnie always felt?

The birthday girl continued to speak. "I had highlights, but when they grew out, they were just blah. Yours are so cool, they just like fade, like seamlessly. Where'd you get them done?"

"My best friend did them."

"Lucky." She finally pulled her hand away. "Do you want to party with us?"

"Actually, I'm supposed to meet Darcy here. Do any of you know her?"

"Darcy?"

"Yeah." I described her. "She's twenty-one too. I think you guys go to the same school." I tried to look at each of them, but that was impossible from this angle, so I stood up. "I should get back to looking for her."

"Wait," the birthday girl whined, grabbing for my wrist, "I think I know who you're talking about. She works at Honey Milk, right?" She bit her lip. "Money Hilk. Hilk and Money." She blinked a few times. "Switch that."

"Milk and Honey."

She grinned. "That's the one."

"Oh, yeah," Mary Beth said, "she's the weird goth chick."

"She's not goth," one of the other girls said. "She's just weird."

"I think her hair's cool," the birthday girl said. "It's all spiky. I wonder if it's sharp to touch."

"Have you guys seen her tonight?"

The birthday girl laughed so hard she snorted, which made the rest of the girls fall into a fit of uncontrollable giggles. When she looked up, her eyes were tearing. "You could say that." They started laughing again.

"I don't understand."

"She gave me a present." Janice pressed her finger to her lips. "Shhh. No one can know." But considering how loud she said it, despite the music, half the club probably heard her.

I crouched down, noticing how red and glassy her eyes were. On second glance, all the girls had very red eyes. "What did she give you?"

"It's a secret."

"Come on," I tried to smile, "tell me your secret and I'll tell you mine."

"She gave us bunnies," Mary Beth blurted out.

"Bunnies?"

Mary Beth snickered. "Little red ones. They went hippity-hop, hippity-hop right down our throats."

"That was at the other club," Janice said. "So that couldn't have been the same Darcy. Liv said she came here to find Darcy. But Darcy's at the other club."

"Where were you before you came here?" I asked.

"I don't remember the name. It's the one with the columns out front."

I turned, searching for my partner in the crowd, but I didn't see him. Instead, I sent him a 9-1-1 text. "Did Darcy give you red pills?"

"Party favors for my birthday."

The group screamed birthday and drained their glasses.

"Is that what she called them?"

"Yeah."

"Do you have any more party favors?"

"Oh, maybe. Mia's a baby. She only took one." Janice opened the tiny bag hanging from her wrist. Inside were six empty baggies with the familiar rabbit sticker.

"I'm not a baby," Mia said. "I have to go to my parents' house for brunch tomorrow. I don't want to be totally wrecked."

Out of the five girls, Mia appeared to be the most sober. "Mia, do you know Darcy Kolado?" I asked. "Can you tell me where she is?"

"I don't know where she is. I didn't see her. She was in the bathroom."

"But you know her?"

"Not really. We had Western Lit together." Before Mia could say anything else, the other girls started talking about the literature professor.

"Hey," the birthday girl tugged on my wrist to get my attention, "I think one fell out. Oohhh, there it is." She plucked it from the lining of her purse. "You can have it." She pulled out a red pill and held it in her palm. "I'll give this to you only if you promise to party with us the rest of the night."

Using the napkin from beneath my glass, I scooped the pill out of her hand and folded it up. "When did you guys take these?"

The birthday girl stared blankly at me. "Um..."

I turned to Mia. "How long have you been here?"

"Three drinks," she said.

At the rate they were drinking, that was probably an hour or an hour and a half. "How many of you took these?"

"All six of us. But I only took one. They took two." Mia sunk down, looking ashamed.

"Darcy Kolado gave you these pills?"

"Um..."

"Where's Darcy?"

Brad appeared behind me. "Liv, what's going on?"

I handed him the napkin. "They've all ingested Red Rabbit." I crouched down in front of Janice. "Where's your other friend?"

The girls looked around. "I don't know. Did she ever come out of the bathroom?" Janice asked. The rest of the group shrugged, almost in unison.

I realized one of the other girls was pulling my zipper up and down a few inches on my jacket. They weren't just drunk. They were stoned. "We need multiple ambulances. We have to get them to the hospital now." I spoke to the birthday girl. "This is Brad. He wants to get to know you better. I'm going to run to the little girls' room for a minute. Talk to him, okay?" I noticed each of the young ladies had a sash that said *Birthday Squad*. "Who's missing from your group?"

"Sylvia," Janice said. "She can't hold her liquor. The second we got here, she disappeared."

"I'll find her. Does she have brown hair?" I asked.

"That's right." She smiled. "Do you know her?"

"Not yet." I stood up. Brad was still on the phone with dispatch. "I'll look for Sylvia. She's wearing a sash and has brown hair. Stay with them. If you spot her, let me know."

He nodded, too busy communicating the severity of our situation to speak to me directly. I raced through the club, shouting to people as I passed if they saw anyone matching Sylvia's description. Most people ignored me. A few shook their heads.

I elbowed my way through the line at the restroom. "Sylvia?" I pushed open the stall doors. "Sylvia?" I climbed onto the toilet seat so I could see over the top, but no one matching Sylvia's description was passed out.

Dashing out of the bathroom, I moved away from the dance floor to the more secluded areas of the club. The tables and booths along the walls were far enough out of the way that no one would immediately notice an unconscious woman. A few men, around my age, were seated at one of the tables dressed like they'd just spent the day on the trading floor.

"Did you see a young woman?" I described her.

"Yeah," one of them said, "our friend took her outside to get some air. She didn't look so good."

"Which exit?"

The guy pointed to the closest door. I ran for it, bursting out of the noisy club and into the cool, quiet night. Fifteen feet away, Sylvia lay on the ground. The guy knelt beside her, his phone to his ear.

I pulled my badge. "What happened?"

"I don't know. Her nose just started bleeding, and she collapsed. I'm on the phone with 9-1-1. They're sending help." He stared at me. "Did they send you?"

"No." I held out my hand for his phone and told the operator what was going on.

"Several ambulances are already en route, responding to another call we just received."

"That was my partner. This isn't the only victim, but she's the only one who's exhibited symptoms so far." I looked at the guy who had tucked his hands beneath his underarms, practically hugging himself to soothe his anxiety. "How long has she been down?"

"I don't know. Five or ten minutes."

I pressed my fingers against her neck, surprised to find anything. "She's suffering from an overdose of rat poison. She's hemorrhaging. Her pulse is weak, but her heart's racing."

"She's bleeding internally." The operator gave me instructions on what to do until the EMTs arrived. Once they were on-site, they ran a central line and hooked her up to a saline drip before administering other medications.

I stepped back, shaky from the adrenaline. "I'll need a few details from you." After getting the man's contact information and statement on what happened, I went back inside to find the rest of the birthday party being loaded onto stretchers. The EMTs wheeled two of the girls out. Brad was in the midst of questioning the last two while the EMTs checked their vitals and hooked them up to IVs.

"You can continue this at the hospital, Detectives."

Brad and I watched as the ambulances sped off, their lights and sirens leaving just an echo of what had happened in their wake.

THIRTY-ONE

After speaking to the party bus driver and getting a copy of the venues the birthday party had already visited, Brad and I headed to the last club the ladies had visited. The line outside ran down the block. Darcy Kolado had already handed out six party favors. I feared how many more she might have moved in a club this crowded. It was the last address on the list.

Two squad cars pulled up, followed by three unmarked vehicles. This was an all-hands situation. Loyola and Sullivan met us at the door. We flashed our badges. "Police emergency," Sullivan said.

Ashmore and two other narcotics detectives joined us just as the doorman waved us inside. "We've been briefed. I passed around photos of Darcy. Any idea what she's wearing tonight or where she was last seen?"

"She's dealing from somewhere inside this club. At least, that's what five very inebriated young women said." Brad stared into the abyss of strobing lights and blaring music. "They didn't remember what she was wearing. All they said was she was shiny, whatever that means."

"All right." Ashmore nodded to the two other detectives. "Let's find her before more people end up in the ER." He pulled Brad and me aside. "Is she working with anyone?"

"I don't know. The unit outside Jimmy Stark's apartment said he hasn't left," I said.

"None of the ladies could remember if Darcy was alone," Brad said.

"Where did she pass them the drugs?" Ashmore asked.

"I believe she approached Janice in the bathroom," Brad said. "Or at a table. She wasn't quite clear on that. She wished her a happy birthday. From the way it sounded, she didn't accept payment for the pills."

Ashmore nodded. "First one's always free."

But I didn't think that's what this was. However, we didn't have time to debate. Instead, we split up to search inside. Since I was the only female cop on the scene, I started with the ladies' room. Darcy wasn't there.

About ten minutes into our search, more patrol units arrived to shut the club down. We checked IDs, questioned the guests, and searched high and low. We didn't find any red pills or empty baggies. And we didn't find Darcy.

"Are you absolutely certain this is the club the ladies said they encountered her?" Ashmore asked.

"That's what the entire birthday party said," I insisted.

"You have to keep in mind, when we found them, they were highly intoxicated. It could be bad intel," Brad said.

"But you're certain they said Darcy gave this to them?" Ashmore asked.

"Yes." But I was second-guessing myself. I brought Darcy up to them, not the other way around. Still, they provided details.

"All right, I'll update the BOLO. Are you heading to the hospital?" Ashmore asked.

"That's our next stop," I said.

"Okay." He glanced from me to Brad. "You did good tonight. We're gonna find her."

When we got back to the car, the sun had already risen. I pressed the heels of my hands against my eyes. Since the hospital hadn't called with an update, I assumed the best. Normally, they only called with bad news.

"Liv?" Brad sounded just as defeated as I felt. "You still with me?"

"I am so tired of this."

"You're preaching to the choir. What would make some kid with a bright future suddenly decide to get involved in this shit?"

"She didn't think her future was that bright. She failed a class and lost her way. Don't you remember what it was like at that age? Every decision seems irreversible. Every mistake is like the end of the world."

"It's a big jump from waitress to this."

"You heard Janice and her friends. Every one of them insisted they got the drugs from Darcy."

"What they said was Darcy gave them party favors. They didn't pay. She handed them out like candy. Six baggies, two pills each." He worked his jaw for a moment. "They knew Darcy from Milk and Honey, didn't they?"

"Yeah."

"More bad customers?"

"I don't know."

"Maybe I'm wrong, but they seemed like the sorority clique type. Darcy might have gotten wind of their party plans and..."

"You don't think this is about slinging pills. You think this is about getting the ultimate revenge."

"So do you, but you're afraid to say it." He turned to me. "Why? You never used to be this squeamish."

"I don't want to jump to conclusions. She has no priors, no history of mental illness, nothing to indicate she'd ever be violent. I just don't see why she'd knowingly pass out tainted pills that are killing people."

"Someone pushed her to her breaking point."

"Yeah, I guess."

"We still don't know if it's a bad batch or some intentional alteration. The sample Axel sent us contained small amounts of rat poison." He took one hand off the wheel and pointed a finger at me. "Don't say it didn't come from Axel. We both know it damn well did."

"That's not what I was going to say. Based on Sylvia's condition when I found her, she must have gotten some bad pills. I wonder if she was the only one out of the group tonight who did."

"The lab will be able to tell us more based on that one pill we recovered."

"And the hospital can tell us how much the other girls ingested. But the only deaths we've seen have occurred in Milk and Honey customers. We know Darcy hated her job and the way a lot of people treated her. After tonight, we know she's distributing Red Rabbit and two tainted samples came directly from her."

"Sylvia and Paul Gwynn."

"Yeah."

"Don't forget Carla. We placed Darcy at the bar the night Carla was found dead. That's three."

"She's killing them." I blew out a breath. "We still don't know where she's getting the bad pills or how she's finding her targets at the clubs."

"Paul publicized his actions. I bet Carla did too. She had a fake ID and was super stoked about seeing the band. Darcy must have heard about it. The same's probably true of tonight's birthday party."

"What about the list? Do you think she went to all of those clubs, and we just happened to miss her?"

"I don't know, Liv. I wish I did."

"What about the other victims? We couldn't find anything on Macy."

"True." Brad fidgeted, rubbing the stubble on his cheek. "I'd say Darcy overheard the victims talking about their plans while she was serving them, but she quit her job a month ago. So that's out."

"Maybe not. She still hangs around there. She must gossip with her former coworkers. You saw how she behaved on the footage. She acts like she still works there. Most people, when they leave a job they hate, don't spend all of their spare time at that place."

"You're right. If she wanted to stay there, why did she bother quitting?" We drove in silence for a time before Brad asked, "How do you think Jimmy figures into this?"

"I'm not sure."

"Do you think Darcy's the one turning Red Rabbit into red rum?"

"What?"

"*The Shining.*" His eyes grew wide. "Murder." He waited, but I didn't say anything. "Based on what her roommate said, she has motive. And possibly means. Wasn't she a chemistry major? She might have mixed something up in one of the chem labs. I'd bet a school that size has plenty of rat poison on hand."

"Someone at that school would have noticed. And again, none of the ODs happened on campus. I don't see why she'd go through that much trouble when she could just deliver the pills to the residence halls."

"Okay, so she's getting the pills from somewhere else. But I think she's dousing the pills in rat poison."

"Dealers can't profit without repeat business. Killing customers after one dose detracts from the profit margin."

"Darcy's not doing this for money."

"Someone is." I turned to him. "Jimmy has something to do with this. He's a delivery driver. He was at the bar, and he's involved with Darcy."

Brad parked in front of the hospital. "That's more than three strikes."

Inside, we spoke to the hospital staff. Sylvia was in serious condition, but she was stable. The pills had been coated in what the hospital referred to as superwarfarin in a highly concentrated dose.

"We've never seen anything like this," the doctor said. "Most poisonings we see are accidental. Even the intentional ones usually require repeat exposure. This is some serious shit. One dose doesn't usually cause massive bleeding and damage to the internal organs. But this does."

"Do you think Sylvia will pull through?" I asked.

"You got her here just in time. A few more minutes, and I don't think we would have been able to get the bleeding under control."

"What about the others?" Brad asked.

"They need treatment, but they should be fine. We ran blood panels. Depending on other factors, they might have been facing the same crisis as their friend. It's a good thing you brought them in too. We have them all on vitamin K1 IV therapy. We'll see how they respond and reevaluate, but they'll probably need to continue to take K1 for a while until the superwarfarin runs its course and they are able to clot normally again."

"Thanks, Doc." Brad peered into the ER patient rooms. "May we speak to them?"

"I think they are asleep, but you can try."

We spoke to each of the girls, who appeared to have gotten off easy. The IVs they received had blunted the more serious side effects of their hangovers. None of the girls remembered seeing anyone else with Darcy. They just happened to bump into her at one of the clubs. According to Janice, they invited her to join them. Darcy said she was supposed to be partying with some friends, but they stood her up. So instead, she shared her "party favors" with the birthday girl. No one recalled exactly where Darcy went after that.

The security footage from the club had been pulled. The techs had already identified Darcy on the footage, but just like the night she dosed Paul, she left the club and vanished. She had to be traveling on foot since she had no car, didn't call for a ride, and didn't scan her metro card. By moving on foot, we were unable to track her using traffic cams or other citywide surveillance.

It was mid-morning by the time we called it quits. Brad and I were fast-approaching the twenty-four hour mark, so Captain Grayson forced us to go home.

"I don't want you going home alone," Brad said.

"You just want me to invite you for breakfast." I jerked my chin toward our parked cars. "Dad's making almond pancakes. I bet if you ask nicely, he'll make some sausage patties too."

"Sounds great." Brad opened my car door and held it for me. "I'll follow you."

"Okay."

My parents had already eaten by the time we got there, but Dad had made enough to feed an army, or my starving partner. I set the food to reheat while I cut up some fresh fruit. When we finished, Brad helped me clean up. Then we settled into the living room.

"Don't you want to get some sleep?" I asked.

"Not yet. Why? Do you want me to leave? I can go. You

should get some rest. You look beat."

I looked around, but the living room was empty. Dad was in his office, on the phone with a city council official. They were discussing security upgrades for an event, and my mom had gone to get her hair and nails done. She called it a spa day, which meant she might splurge and get a massage too. "I'm tired and wired. I just..." I let out a sigh. "I have so many questions and no answers."

"Me too."

Gunnie ran into the living room with the ball Brad had gotten him and bumped into the back of my leg. I sat on the floor to play fetch, and Brad dropped down beside me. He put the TV on, flipping channels until he found an old movie to watch.

When Gunnie got bored of fetch, he sprawled out on the floor. I turned to find that my partner had done the same. I grabbed two pillows off the couch, handed one to Brad, and stretched out beside him.

"What's going on with you?" I asked.

"What do you mean?"

"Ever since Gallagher, you've had storm clouds over your head. I worry."

"Don't. I'll be fine."

"Which means you're not fine now."

"After everything that's happened, how can I be?"

"We'll figure out this shit with Matthews." But that wasn't what had put the storm clouds over my partner's head.

"How? I went after Gallagher, and that wasn't enough." Brad swallowed. "Killing him wasn't enough. Nothing will ever be."

"He didn't leave you a choice. He would have killed you. Us. Both of us. And Emma, once he found her. It was a clean shoot."

He stared at the TV. "I know, but he was a cop. Things like this aren't supposed to happen. I don't understand why it's not over yet. I just want to wash my hands of this and be done. I hate thinking the things I do about the people around us. But every time we turn around, something else is going wrong. I can't take it."

I reached for him. "Hey, you got me. When things get too heavy, let me take on some of that weight. What can I do?"

"Nothing. I have to make my peace with this, with shooting Gallagher. He deserved it. I know it up here." He tapped his temple. "But it doesn't feel right in here." He pointed to his chest.

"You're not supposed to feel good about it, but you can't carry it either. You don't need that burden."

"I'm working on it. If it were just that, it'd be easier. Instead, I have to worry about the ramifications, how it impacts my career, your career, our lives, our safety. I made this decision. Me. I went to IAD. You shouldn't have to pay for any of this."

"I go where you go. That's our rule. Do I need to have that tattooed on my forehead so you don't forget?"

"It might help."

I picked up my pillow and hit him.

He held up his palms. "Clobbering me with a pillow isn't helping."

"Are you sure?" I hit him again.

He laughed, a mischievous grin on his face. "Okay, that's it." He picked up his pillow and bopped me with it.

By the time we were done, we were both laughing and breathless. I flopped onto my back, watching Gunnie excitedly circle around, letting out little yips, his tail wagging a million miles an hour. "Truce."

Brad dropped to his elbow, turning on his side to look at me. He reached over and gently pulled a wayward feather from my hair. "Thanks, Liv. I needed that."

"I didn't do anything."

"Yes, you did." He leaned in, smoothing my hair back into place. "You always make things better."

THIRTY-TWO

For days, Wilson Matthews waited for his chance. Being constantly watched by the cops was almost as bad as being stuck in jail. But they couldn't follow him forever. When the car outside pulled away from the curb, Matthews didn't waste any time. He had to go. Now.

He grabbed his netbook and whatever else he thought he might need and left his apartment. He knew better than to take his car. The police would be able to track his movements more easily.

After he made it a few blocks, he ducked into an alleyway, changed his jacket, lost the hat, and put on some sunglasses. He'd never thought of himself as paranoid, but since they were watching him, he had to be careful. More than likely, the police wouldn't even realize he was gone. That was another reason he left his car. But if they did, they'd come looking, and he didn't need them to interfere.

Emerging at the other end of the alleyway, he continued heading in the same direction he'd been traveling. Days before his arrest, he'd moved his collection and several necessities to a secure location. The police didn't know about his RV. No paper trail linked him to the bulky tin can. He'd paid cash and left the registration in the original owner's name. This would be his safe haven and base of operations.

He flagged down a cab and had the driver drop him off near the RV park. Rows of vehicles lined the area. The vast majority had out of state plates. When he finally got to his spot, he reached beneath the front bumper and felt around for the magnetic box. Inside were the keys. After removing the key, he returned the box.

The paint had faded, peeling in areas, from years spent baking in the Arizona sun. Even the license plate still had granules of sand stuck in the grooves. No one would give the RV a second look.

Opening the side door, he took a deep breath. The inside smelled like leather and metal. After pulling the door closed, he made sure the window coverings were secure before he turned on a light to admire his handiwork.

The interior had been custom-designed. He'd gutted the insides and remade it with everything he'd need for his crusade, but he'd never used the RV for any of his kills. The lying whores he punished would never have agreed to come here. And dragging them from a hotel or bar would have been too complicated. So he'd always done the deed elsewhere. But this was the perfect place to teach Detective Liv DeMarco a lesson.

The polished black metal of the saltire cross gleamed, begging Matthews to run his fingers over the cool surface. The metal rings attached to the built in cabinets would also work great for restraining her. He smiled. So many options, but which would he choose?

Crouching down, he opened one of the cabinets and pulled out the box containing strips of silky fabrics. A familiar tingling sensation coursed through him. He picked up a torn piece of red fabric and held it to his nose and closed his eyes. Memories flooded over him of the woman who'd worn that dress, bound with shreds of it, the blood pooling around her as the tears streamed down her face. He wondered if Liv would cry or beg. He liked it when they begged.

"Enough." He caressed each strip of fabric before lovingly closing the box and tucking it away. He could still remember the deceptive detective clad in a coral dress. That's what he wanted to use to tie her to the cross. But that was a minor detail. More importantly, he had to figure out how to trap her. She was scared, and when cornered, animals often became violent. He'd need to surprise her. That would require research. Lots of it. With the others, he studied them, followed them, and figured out where they were most vulnerable.

Opening another cabinet, he pulled out one of the dozen burner phones he'd hidden inside. He powered on the netbook and searched for a wi-fi signal. The RV park provided community wi-fi, so he logged on. He already had her address memorized, but he had to make absolutely certain he had the right place. The concussion had made his memory fuzzy when it came to details. But he knew where she lived. It was time he paid her a visit.

* * *

The entire police department was searching for Darcy Kolado. It had been days since the incident with the birthday party. But I knew she wasn't done yet.

Brad swiveled in his chair. "I don't understand why no one's looking for her."

"We are."

"Besides us. You would think someone would have reported her missing."

"Who's going to report it? Campus security knows we're looking for her. The dean of admissions has been briefed on the situation. I've spoken to Darcy's roommate. If anyone sees her on campus, they'll notify us. She doesn't have a job, so that's out. We haven't let Jimmy Stark out of our sight. He's the only other connection we know about."

"Surely, she must have other friends. A young woman can't just disappear."

"They do all the time."

"Not like her. She has established roots. Until a month ago, she had a job. Even now, she's still enrolled in college. She didn't just up and leave. She's gotta be close." He tapped his pen against his notepad. "What about her parents?"

"Sullivan spoke to them. They didn't know she was missing or anything else about her life, for that matter."

"Are we sure? Maybe she reached out to them. Maybe they're covering for her."

"Doubtful."

Brad quirked an eyebrow. "Why would you say that?"

"Ask Sullivan. That's the impression he got." My phone rang, and I picked it up, not recognizing the number. "Hello?"

"Is this Detective DeMarco?"

"Yes."

"You told me to call if Darcy came home. I didn't see her, but when I got back from class, I noticed more of her stuff was missing."

I gestured to Brad and mouthed, "It's the roommate."

Brad picked up the phone to notify campus security to be on alert and contacted dispatch to get the nearest patrol car to assist.

"What time was that?" I asked.

"I just got back from my eleven o'clock class. So like five minutes ago."

I got out of my chair and grabbed my jacket. "Darcy could still be on campus." I tossed the keys to Brad, and we ran down the stairs for the car. "Can you tell me what's missing?"

The roommate hesitated for a moment. "Um...some of her clothes. I don't see her black or purple dresses. Hang on." I heard shuffling through the receiver. "Her duffel bag is gone too."

"What did she keep in there?" I'd checked all of the bags and purses in her closet, but I didn't remember a duffel bag.

"Nothing. She bought it to use at the gym, but we only went once."

"What gym? Does she have a membership?"

"The gym on campus. It's in the student rec center."

"Did she take gym clothes?"

"I don't think so. Maybe some shirts and a couple of pairs of jeans. Oh, and her black buckle boots, and the sneakers she always kicks around in." The roommate continued searching. "That bitch."

"What?"

"She emptied out the fridge and pantry. I had a brand new pack of double-stuffed oreos in there."

I laughed in relief. "Did she leave a note or anything?"

"Let me look. We used to write stuff on post-its and put them on each other's corkboards. But we haven't done that in a long time."

With the siren on, we were making good time getting to campus. Brad was on the phone with campus security again, who were on their way to the residence hall. They hadn't seen Darcy return to campus, which meant she must have slipped past them, or someone else had gone to her dorm.

"I don't see a note."

"Is anything else missing?" I asked.

"I can't be sure. I didn't take an inventory of her things."

Luckily, we did.

By the time we arrived, campus security had already pulled the security footage. Darcy had entered the residence hall at 11:07 and left just minutes before her roommate returned. While officers and campus security asked the other students if they'd seen her, Brad and I searched Darcy's dorm.

"Was this here before?" I held up a flyer for a club re-opening.

The roommate squinted at it. "I've never seen that."

Brad pointed to the date. "That's two days from now."

"Are you sure she didn't leave a note?" I noticed a blank space on Darcy's corkboard. "Maybe you left her a note."

The roommate shook her head. "I love Darcy, but like I said, we haven't been on the best of terms lately. I still can't believe you think she's involved in drugs."

"You told me about the pills she had. Didn't you say she called them party favors?"

"Yeah, but it was just molly. I've never known Darcy to do the scary ones."

"What would those be?" Brad asked.

"Heroin or coke. Y'know, the ones people get addicted to

and die from."

"People die from taking party drugs all the time," Brad said. "We see it."

She swallowed. "I know, that was a stupid thing to say. Paul just died from taking molly. Do you really think Darcy gave it to him?"

"We need to find her. Even if she didn't give it to him," which I didn't believe, "she had the same pills on her. We need to know where she got them."

"Did Darcy ever mention Sylvia Trisk?" Brad asked.

"Not by name, but she wasn't a fan of any sorority sister."

"Why? What happened?"

"Pledge week, our freshman year, Darcy tried to get in. She thought joining a sorority would be great. They had the best parties, and the food and housing is way better. But the sororities only take so many girls, and to get in, you have to jump through major hoops. The senior girls treated all the pledges like shit. They made fun of Darcy's hair and clothes. They even cut off her long hair. Ever since then, she's avoided the houses and everyone affiliated with them."

"What about at work?" I asked.

"She'd try to get someone else to cover the counter for her if they came in."

Brad sat down in Darcy's chair. He leaned forward, resting his forearms on his knees while he opened his notepad. "Who else made Darcy's life miserable?"

The roommate turned to me. "Originally, you said Darcy was in danger. But you don't think that. You think she is the danger."

"New facts have come to light. We don't know anything for sure, but that is a possibility."

"If she is hurting people, we need to stop her before this gets worse," Brad said. "Please."

"There's the TA I already told you about."

"Anyone else?"

"I don't know. She complained all the time, mostly about customers."

"Any other groups who annoyed her? What about the

football team or cheerleaders?" Brad asked.

The roommate shook her head. She was done cooperating. Even if she knew someone else who might be at risk, she wouldn't tell us. She didn't want to believe her best friend was a killer.

Brad closed his notepad and tucked it into his inner jacket pocket. "We just want to find her before she hurts anyone else or gets herself hurt."

The roommate nodded, staring holes at the floor.

I patted her arm. "Your friend needs help. We'll get her that help."

She looked up with anger in her eyes. "By arresting her?"

"We won't arrest her unless she's committed a crime," I promised, coming up with a potential play on the fly. "But that loser boyfriend you mentioned, he's committed several crimes. He might have gotten her involved in something shady. Something sinister. She probably can't get away from him or the situation without someone stepping in."

"I hope you find her. I just want her to be okay."

"Did she ever talk about going somewhere with him? You said she spent the night with him sometimes," Brad said.

"Have you tried his apartment?"

"She isn't there. Maybe they hung out somewhere else? A friend's house? A hotel? Somewhere like that?" I suggested.

"I really don't know."

"Is there anyone else off-campus she'd stay with?" Brad asked.

"I don't think so."

"What about friends from high school?"

"None of them are in the city. And even if they were, Darcy hasn't kept in touch with any of them."

"What about on social media?" I asked.

"She doesn't do a lot of that." Her expression turned grim. "Darcy didn't have a lot of friends before she came here. She was kind of an outcast. She thought college would be her chance to reinvent herself. She thought she'd have a ton of friends and be popular, but that didn't happen. We went to a lot of parties and stuff on campus, but she never really clicked with anyone. She just hung around with me and my friends. Sometimes, she'd hang out with the people she worked with, but that was about it."

"It's always the quiet ones," Brad whispered as we headed down the stairs.

"Something must have happened to cause her to lash out like this."

"It sounds like a lot of terrible things happened. She was ridiculed. Bullied." He sucked in a shaky breath. "It's a good thing she didn't resort to gun violence. We'd be looking at a mass casualty event."

"Isn't this a mass casualty event?"

"You know what I mean."

"Women are significantly less likely to go that route. Poisonings are more common."

I debated searching the rest of the campus for signs of Darcy. But I knew we'd never find her. She spent three years of her life exploring this place. She knew how to get in and out without detection.

"She doesn't have a car. She hasn't accessed her bank account or used any credit cards. Her phone's still out of service. Jimmy's secondary phone, the one we believe she has, is turned off." Brad ticked off our usual methods for tracking down suspects. "Where is she staying? We know it's not with Jimmy. The surveillance team would have spotted her."

"Plus, Marietta's there."

"What about her work friends?"

"The rest of the task force explored that option. They ran background checks on everyone, went to their homes, spoke to the neighbors. They're clean."

"This doesn't make any sense." Brad opened the car door. "We issued a BOLO. We've checked area shelters and hostels. Where would a twenty-one year old female with limited resources go?" He peered at me over the roof of the car. "Where would you have gone?"

"Home."

"Not an option, Liv."

"I don't know. The library." I saw the confusion on my partner's face. "Whenever Emma and I had a fight, usually over someone staying overnight, I'd camp out at the library. It was quiet. It stayed open all night, and they had this great overstuffed couch in the reading room."

"I doubt Darcy's hiding out at the campus library."

"No, but she probably went somewhere familiar." I thought back over everything we knew. "We still haven't identified the source of the pills. Someone is supplying them to her. My gut says Jimmy's involved in distribution, but he doesn't have the brains or lab equipment to cook them up himself. He must get them from somewhere."

"Probably that bar, but we don't have enough to get a warrant to search the place. Too bad Axel won't ID the source," Brad said pointedly. "The lab couldn't tell us anything about the manufacturing."

"That's not true. The sample I took from the birthday girl had been coated in superwarfarin. Some of it had leached into the pill, but the highest concentration was on the coating."

"What does that mean?"

"It means the rat poison was added after the pills were made. Darcy must have modified them. Maybe you're on to something, Fennel."

"I'm sure I am." Brad grinned. "But you're referring to what exactly?"

"Darcy would go somewhere she feels safe. Somewhere familiar. She started out as a chemistry major."

"Yes, but you said someone would notice her hanging out in the chem labs."

"What if she found one no one was using?"

Brad and I raced back through the gate. The science building had undergone renovations over the last two years. State-of-the-art equipment and brand new labs had been built. A few of the smaller, older ones had been left empty.

The guard I'd spoken to on my first trip escorted us across campus and into the building. He led us down the stairs to what he called the tombs. The bottom floor had been a basement, converted into additional classrooms when the student body increased substantially.

"Gross anatomy used to meet down here. The floor has drains. It's some pretty creepy stuff." The guard glanced at us. "The kids like to tell ghost stories. Around Halloween, a couple of campus organizations stage this big haunted house thing down here as a fundraiser. It keeps the kids out of trouble and brings some of the community in. It's a lot of fun."

"What about the rest of the year?" Brad asked.

"Ever since the new addition was added, classes haven't been held down here." He opened one of the doors. "As you can see, the professors are using it for storage."

Old, dilapidated tables and stools filled half of one of the rooms. On the other side were open boxes with chipped beakers, test tubes, eyedroppers, and other lab essentials. The next room contained more furniture and projectors, a few chalkboards, and a couple of podiums.

Five rooms later, we found something. A sleeping bag and a pile of blankets were hidden behind the built-in counter. Brad peered down at the pink and purple bedding. "I think we found out where she's been staying."

"A student's been sleeping here?" The security guard looked appalled. "How could this be?"

"You said no one comes down here. Based on the layers of dust we observed in the other rooms, I'm going to guess that includes the janitorial staff." A duffel bag sat beside the makeshift bed. After putting on a pair of gloves, I unzipped it. "Double-stuffed oreos." I held up the package for Brad to see. "I've also got a purple dress, some jeans, and a few other clothing items."

"This is where Darcy's been hiding." Brad turned to the security guard. "Do you have security cameras?"

"Not in the tombs."

"What about covering the rest of the building?"

"The only cameras inside cover the new addition. We didn't want anyone to walk off with thousands of dollars' worth of equipment."

"Dammit." Brad rubbed his mouth. "How about outside? I thought I saw some cameras on the doors."

"The doors are covered."

"Get us the footage for all the entry points. Everything you've got for the last few weeks." Brad eyed him. "And make sure you don't disturb anything on your way out. We don't want her to know we've found this place."

"Yes, sir." The guard practically saluted before jogging out of the room and down the hallway.

"She must have dropped this stuff off and left," I said.

"She'll be back." Brad put on some gloves to help me search the rest of the room. "When she comes back, we're gonna grab her."

I pulled open the cabinet door, expecting to find more of Darcy's belongings. Instead, I found boxes and boxes of pesticides and rat poison. I'd never heard of the brand, and when I checked the label, I realized the stuff was ancient. It had expired at least a decade ago. "Take a look at this."

I handed one of the boxes to Brad while I took a photo of the rest.

"This one's open." He peered inside. "It looks almost empty." Brad put the box down and checked the trash can in the corner. "Liv, come see this."

After photographing the stockpile of rat poison, I crossed to where Brad was standing. "Are they all empty?"

Brad reached into the trash and checked each of the eight boxes. "I guess we know how the pills got tainted."

"She must have lab equipment set up somewhere to melt this stuff down or do whatever it is that gets the poison to coat the pills. You were right. We should have looked into this sooner."

We searched the rest of the room, but it was mostly discarded furniture and the few items Darcy had taken from her dorm. She even had an old TV set up on a table. In front of it, she'd placed one of the professor's chairs. Duct tape covered a rip on the back, but it looked comfy.

Brad pressed the power button. The set turned on. Hooked to it was a converter and a streaming device. He picked up the remote, not surprised to find it filled with various streaming service apps.

"How does that even work?" I asked.

"The school's wi-fi." He checked the settings, just to make sure. "How long do you think she's been living down here?"

"I don't know, probably ever since she and her roommate had a falling out."

In the lab across the hallway, the counter was covered in a very elaborate set-up. Freshly washed glassware sat on top of a towel. "This is where she does her work," Brad said.

I took several more photographs and forwarded them to our lab. They'd be able to figure out what exactly she was doing. "Have you found any baggies with Red Rabbit?"

"No pills."

"She cleaned up after her mess. If she planned to taint more of the stash, why would she go through the trouble of washing everything?"

"Maybe she has to clean up. We'll need the guys in the lab to tell us more about how this process works."

"CSU should check this out."

"If a crime van pulls up to the door, she's going to know her hideout's been compromised. We can't risk it." He checked the cabinets and searched the rest of the room. We photographed everything, but it looked like whatever chemistry experiment she had running was now over. "There's one other thing I want to see." Brad continued down the hallway to the last three rooms we hadn't checked. The two bathrooms and the gross anatomy lab.

The classroom was empty. The smell of formaldehyde and bleach continued to linger. The freezer was no longer cold or powered up, and from the thick layer of undisturbed dust covering all the plastic sheeting, I knew Darcy hadn't been inside.

Brad didn't wait for me before entering the men's room. He came out a moment later and opened the door to the ladies' room. I followed him inside.

The counter had been wiped down and a shower caddy sat on top, filled with everything from shampoo to lotion. Brad peered into the nearly empty trash can. "Jimmy's been here."

"How can you tell?"

He took a few photos before removing an evidence bag from his pocket and pulling out a discarded condom and wrapper from the garbage. "That's how."

THIRTY-THREE

Wilson Matthews stood outside Liv's apartment. He'd been watching the place for days. This was her address, but he'd never seen her come home. Even when her car wasn't parked at the precinct, she still wasn't here.

She really is a whore, like the others, Matthews thought. That was the only explanation he could come up with for her constant absences. A part of him wondered if all women were whores. He had yet to find one who wasn't.

When she first arrested him, he thought she might have been different. That Gallagher had lied to him about the type of woman Liv DeMarco was. But from the things he'd seen, he knew she was just another lying, cheating bitch, intent on destroying people's lives. She'd destroyed his. And he wasn't going to let her destroy anyone else's. It was time she paid for her sins.

As quietly as possible, he made his way to her front door. None of her neighbors were around, but he didn't want to make any noise and alert them. They wouldn't take kindly to a masked man sneaking around.

Before doing anything else, he knocked on the door and waited. He knew she wouldn't answer, but he wanted to make sure she didn't have any pets. He imagined a woman like her would have a German Shepherd or Rottweiler guarding the place. But he didn't hear any barking. That answered one question. Now for the next one.

Her door had two keyholes. One was a shiny silver deadbolt. The other was the doorknob. But this wasn't just any doorknob. The brushed stainless steel looked brand new and super heavy duty. He crouched down to examine the brand imprint. He snapped a few photos of the locks. Before leaving, he checked beneath the welcome mat and felt around the doorframe, but she hadn't hidden a spare key.

He'd bumped locks before, but he didn't want her to realize the intrusion. He wanted time to study her from the inside out, to see how she lived. Jogging back to his car, the junker he found for sale on the side of the road, he drove to the nearby coffee shop and found a parking space. They offered free wi-fi.

As fast as his fingers could type, he searched for those exact locks and ways to gain entry without a key. He found an online tutorial on how to deal with the deadbolt. With a little time and patience, he should be able to manipulate the tumblers. The doorknob was another story.

However, if he could wedge something between the frame and the door, creating a space, he might be able to force his way inside. As long as he took care of the deadbolt first, that might be an option. After two hours of searching, he came up with a plan. Now all he had to do was collect the tools he'd need and come back.

Tomorrow night, he promised himself. He'd need the cover of darkness while working on picking that lock. He couldn't afford for one of her neighbors to come home and spot him. So he'd pick a time when the building was quiet. Based on the days he'd spent observing, he should be okay any time after nine.

He didn't want to wait until the middle of the night because there would be no excuse for his presence if he were spotted. Nine was early enough in the evening for him to say he was visiting a friend or on his way out.

This was it. He'd done as much prep as he could stand. The yearning was becoming too great. He had to act soon, or he'd go insane.

It was decided. As long as she wasn't home, he'd break in tomorrow night, search her house, study every aspect of her he could find, and get that coral dress. He was determined to have it. He could still remember the way the fabric felt between his fingers, how he'd already pictured her bound and gagged by it. *Tomorrow*, he thought happily as he headed back to his RV.

*　　*　　*

Brad hung up the phone, his gaze still focused out the window. We were set up in the arts building, which overlooked the science building. From our current position, we could see both entry points into the science building, along with everyone who came and went. A few promising rookies dressed in plain clothes were keeping an eye out, in case we missed anything.

"That was the lab," Brad said. "The boxes of rodenticide you found contain high doses of anticoagulants. That particular poison was banned a few months after it hit the markets for posing too great a risk to humans and pets. The college had made a bulk purchase and never got around to using it."

"Why didn't they discard it?"

"They have to justify their budget and spend. Waste is frowned upon."

"That's how Darcy got the superwarfarin. Do the techs have any idea how she coated the pills?"

"They tried to explain it to me, but I didn't have my science to English dictionary handy."

"We should have called Emma to translate."

"I'd say this is beyond her capabilities too. Suffice it to say, Darcy somehow removed the fillers, purifying and concentrating the poison and turning it into a liquid state. From there, the pills were soaked in the solution and dried."

"Our case just became murder."

"I'd say so," Brad said.

"What about the condom?"

"The prints on the wrapper match Jimmy Stark."

"He's seen the set-up. He must know what Darcy's been doing."

"I don't know. We didn't dust the lab. We don't know if he ever went in there."

"Is Jimmy getting picked up?"

"Grayson wants to wait to see if he'll lead us to the supplier."

"Are we sure Darcy isn't manufacturing the pills here?"

"We didn't find any of the necessary ingredients. Narcotics thinks the bar we followed Jimmy to is the source of the pills. They're thinking Red Rabbit might not be local, after all. Narcotics heard a rumor raw product is getting shipped in from a Canadian lab, branded here, and redistributed."

"That's where Jimmy comes in."

"And Darcy. They finished going over Jimmy and Darcy's phone records. It sounds like Jimmy might have recruited her to help him distribute the pills at the college hangouts."

"How solid's our case?"

"It's getting there, but until we can grab Jimmy while he's in possession of the pills, everything we have on him is circumstantial. We need Darcy. She's our killer."

"That's why we've been staring at the science building all damn day." Just as I said that, a flood of students walked out. Classes were over for the day. I got up to stretch while Brad continued to stare out the window. "At least this is one stakeout that has indoor plumbing and central heating and air."

"True. The chairs could be softer though."

"Cap probably told them not to give us comfortable chairs or we might fall asleep."

Brad laughed. "Yeah, probably." He reached for the bag of almonds. "We should have the rookies pulled. It's after nine. It's dark. Not that many people are hanging out in the quad anymore."

"You're right. Tell Marcos and Bearing to circle twice more. The rest should call it quits."

Brad picked up the radio and relayed the message. Two

couples got up from different benches around campus and headed for the parking lot while the other two plain clothes officers continued to jog around the campus. "Next time, remind me to tell them to stagger their retreat."

"Don't worry about it. Every student who just got out of an evening class is in a huge rush to get to the cafeteria or to get off campus. If Darcy's down there somewhere, she won't notice." At least, I hoped she wouldn't. "I just don't understand why she hasn't come back yet. She dropped off the supplies she picked up. Where did she go?"

"I don't know. We have a unit on Jimmy. Another one is covering the bar where you spotted her. And we have people camped out at Milk and Honey."

I sat back down, taking the offered bag of almonds from Brad. "I only saw one dress in her bag. Her roommate said she took two dresses. A black one and a purple one."

"You think she's going clubbing?"

"I think she has plans. You saw the flyer."

"That re-opening isn't for another two days."

I stared out the window, glad that the paths around campus were so well lit. If they weren't, we'd never see anyone from up here.

Officer Marcos finished his run. He stopped to stretch near a large tree close to the science building. Five minutes later, he left. Bearing followed two minutes later. At least two of the rookies had paid attention when learning how to conduct surveillance.

The next three hours dragged. By the end, Brad and I had cleaned out our emergency stash of snacks. My back and shoulders were sore, and my butt was numb.

"Knock, knock," Loyola and Sullivan called from the doorway. "Your relief is here."

"I hope you brought a cushion to sit on. These chairs would make great torture devices." Brad stood, shaking the feeling back into his legs.

"Any sign of our suspect?" Sullivan asked.

"Nothing," I said.

Sullivan tested out the seat Brad vacated. "Once we close the case, I'm gonna recommend we replace the chairs inside the interrogation rooms with these."

"Great plan," I said, "except that might fall under cruel and unusual punishment."

"They can't be that bad. Worst case, they'll keep us on our toes," Loyola said, "perhaps literally." He laid two pizza boxes down on a desk and placed a large takeout bag on top of them. "Did you guys eat?" He looked at the empty bags of nuts and dried fruit. "Help yourselves to a slice."

"That's okay," I said.

"Right." Loyola opened the takeout bag. "You only eat rabbit food. I got a salad here if you want it."

"We'll pick up something on our way back." Brad unrolled his sleeves, buttoned the cuffs, and put his jacket back on. "Thanks, though." He patted Loyola on the shoulder.

"You gentlemen have fun," I called.

"We're gonna try." Sullivan turned around to look at us. "The two of you aren't scheduled for tomorrow. By the time you come back to work, we'll have put this thing to bed."

"I sure hope so."

"Night, guys," Brad waited for me to exit before following me out. "I forgot we're off tomorrow. I'm surprised they didn't ask us to work."

"We pulled too many doubles this week. The union wouldn't like it."

"What are your plans?"

"Sleep, yoga with Emma, and some grocery shopping. Someone has to replenish our stakeout snacks. The last time I let you do it, we ended up with nothing but jerky."

"You're never gonna let me live that down, are you? It was grass-fed with only natural ingredients. I thought you liked it."

"It's okay, but I'm an omnivore."

He fished out two twenties and handed them to me. "While you're picking up bear food, get some of my jerky snacks too."

"Bear food?"

"Nuts and berries."

I laughed. "You got it."

After we finished the paperwork, Brad followed me back to my parents' house like he'd done every night since we encountered Matthews at the café. But he didn't stay. After spending most of the day staking out the science building, we were both tired. It didn't make sense, but doing nothing was exhausting.

I ate dinner, took a hot bath, and went to bed, relieved to sleep soundly. When I woke up the next morning, Mom and Emma had a million activities planned for me. By the time I even thought to go to the grocery store, it was already dark outside.

"Do you need anything from the store, Mom?"

"I think we're okay."

I picked up my keys. "I'll see you later. I have a couple of things to take care of at home, so I'll probably be gone awhile. Don't wait up."

"All right, Liv. Just be careful. Don't forget to reset the alarm when you come in."

"I won't."

The city seemed quiet tonight. Peaceful. It normally didn't feel that way. But I might have been projecting. A day off had done wonders, even if my thoughts kept drifting to our current case. I wondered if Darcy had been arrested, but I resisted the urge to call and find out.

After parking my car on the street in front of my apartment, I got out and took a deep breath. Despite everything, it was good to be home. I jogged up the stairs and down the hall. I put the key for the deadbolt into the lock. For once, it didn't stick. I unlocked the bottom lock, noticing a few spots where the paint was chipping. As soon as my lease was up, I wouldn't have to worry about that anymore.

I swung the door open and stepped inside. I was finally home.

THIRTY-FOUR

Wilson Matthews froze in place when he heard the key scrape in the lock. As quickly and quietly as possible, he closed her dresser drawer. She couldn't know he was here. He'd already explored the rest of her apartment, saving the best for last. But now, he wished he'd moved faster. What was she doing home?

Grabbing the coral dress off the bed, he peered out her bedroom door. Maybe this was a sign he should act now. But he didn't have a knife on him. His favorite had been taken away as evidence. He had others in the RV, but while grabbing the rest of the tools required for the break-in, he had neglected to take one with him. He felt the weight of the picks in his pocket. They would shred her flesh with enough pressure, but he didn't want to do this messy. He wanted nice clean cuts. Maybe something shallow, so it would take a long time for her to exsanguinate.

He thought about the knives in her kitchen. One of those might do the trick. But how would he subdue her? She was a cop. Surely, she was armed.

Liv put her bag down near the door and went into the kitchen. He heard the refrigerator open and close, followed by the cabinets. For the briefest moment, he wondered if he put everything back where he found it. She would notice if he didn't, but she remained in the kitchen.

He held his breath and tiptoed out of her room, hoping to find she had stowed her gun. He could take that and force her compliance. But two steps later, the phone in her bag rang.

Quickly, he backtracked into her bedroom. Again, that trapped feeling came over him. He was the hunter. Why should he feel cornered when his prey was in his sights?

"Hey, Em," Liv said. "Did you remember what you wanted from the store?" She picked up her bag and headed back into the kitchen. She stopped in the middle of the hallway. "Hang on a second."

She knows I'm here, Matthews thought. He couldn't attack her when someone was on the phone listening. That would ruin everything. He had to hide. But where?

Based on her soft footfalls, she was moving slowly toward the bedroom. She probably had her gun out and ready. That gave her the upper hand.

Her bedroom was small and fairly sparse. *The closet*, he thought. He reached out to open it, but a moment later, he retracted his hand, recalling the annoying squeak. Hiding in there would be a fatal mistake. Instead, he dove under the bed just as she entered the room.

He didn't move. He didn't breathe. He waited, watching her feet move closer. Slowly, she approached the closet, yanking it open. Her foot position told him she was in the Weaver stance. He'd been right to think she was armed.

The metal hangers scraped against the bar as she moved her clothes from one side to the other. She let out an audible exhale before moving to the window and pushing the curtains away. Relieved, she put her gun down on the nightstand and sat on the bed.

The springs above him barely moved. He listened to her breathe, calming herself before tucking her gun at the small of her back and returning to the kitchen.

"Sorry about that, Em. That nagging feeling just came back. For a second, I thought I heard something," she said. "Yeah, I stopped off at home to see if I had anything in the cabinets. Brad really loves that snack mix you make. Would you mind? I want to do something for him. He's just dealing with a lot, and I have no idea what to do to help." She laughed. "You don't have to make it. Just send me the recipe." She laughed again. "Fine, I'll let you make it. I don't see why you and my mom are so opposed to sharing your recipe secrets. I know how to cook." She paused for a beat. "Did you know Mom's teaching him to make lasagna? What is that about?" She let out a sigh. "How many times do I have to tell you we aren't like that? He's my partner. That's it." She laughed again. "Okay, maybe you're right. Maybe he's vying for position as best friend, but you have nothing to worry about. You're more than my best friend. You're my sister."

Matthews let his forehead drop to the floor. That was a close one. Once his heart stopped hammering in his ears, he listened to the rest of her conversation. After she hung up, Liv returned to the bedroom. Again, he held his breath.

She moved slowly, cautiously, through her room. Again, she approached the closet with apprehension. After sliding her clothes back and forth, she pulled out a small rolling suitcase and tossed in several outfits. She put the bag on top of the bed and went to her dresser.

He'd already searched her underwear drawer, surprised he didn't find many lacy little nothings. He had found one teddy, which she left in the drawer as she continued to pack.

The thought sunk in more deeply. She was packing. She must be staying elsewhere, like he assumed. She'd told her friend she wasn't interested in Brad. But that didn't mean she wasn't shacking up with him. Or was she seeing that Detective Voletek, the one who'd put the handcuffs on too tightly? While he debated the merits of slaughtering her at another cop's home rather than the RV, she dropped one of her socks. He watched it land.

For a moment, his heart stopped as she knelt down. Would she see him? He clutched her coral dress even tighter in his hand. If push came to shove, he'd act now. But she picked up the sock so effortlessly, he'd barely glimpsed her slender fingers and thin wrists as she lifted it off the ground.

Visions of bright red dripping from her fingertips made him so giddy his mind got a little lost in the daydream. By the time he blinked back to reality, she had taken the bag and left the bedroom. The lights went out, and the front door closed. He was safe.

Without wasting a second, he rolled out from beneath the bed and went to the window. She loaded the bag into her trunk and got behind the wheel. He couldn't see exactly what she was doing, but she hadn't moved. Now was his chance to follow her and find out where she was staying.

Tucking the balled up dress beneath his sweatshirt, he left her apartment and raced down the steps. He stopped before exiting the front door, hoping she wouldn't notice. Even if she did, she wouldn't recognize him with the cap and hood, not to mention the face mask he wore.

He exited the apartment, walked down the block, and got into his new car. She hadn't moved from her spot, but given the age of his new vehicle, that was a blessing in disguise. It always took a few tries before the engine turned over. As soon as it did, he was ready to follow her. Like his father always told him, failure was another opportunity to learn. Tonight, he planned to learn everything he needed to know.

*   *   *

I checked the time, wondering if Brad would be awake. Deciding I'd call him after my trip to the grocery store, I left my apartment and headed for my car. But the moment I stepped foot outside, my heart rate skyrocketed. Something wasn't right.

I looked around, but I didn't see any signs of danger. Most of my neighborhood was already home for the night or coming back from a late dinner. It was just another normal night, but someone was watching. Wilson Matthews was close. I could practically smell his pungent aftershave.

My fingers grazed the scar at the back of my neck. *Stop it,* my internal voice warned. I was safe. Matthews wasn't here. In fact, ever since our encounter outside Milk and

Honey, he hadn't left his apartment. My eyes darted back and forth as I jogged to my car. No matter how irrational it was, I knew someone was watching.

Safely inside, I locked the doors and called work. They patched me through to the patrol unit sitting outside Matthews' apartment. "We haven't seen him at all. His car hasn't moved. He hasn't gone anywhere."

"Thanks."

I hung up, convinced I was going crazy. To distract myself from my paranoid thoughts, I replayed the evidence and facts we had against Darcy Kolado. More than anything, I hoped Sullivan and Loyola had found her and taken her into custody. Even if we couldn't make a case against Jimmy or stop the distribution of Red Rabbit, we'd stop one woman from poisoning people. Hopefully, that'd be enough of a win for my partner. Because like he said, he needed a win.

The supermarket wasn't very crowded at this time of night, and I found a great spot among the nine other cars. By the time I made it to the doors, another car pulled into the lot. I took a shopping basket and headed for the organic section.

I grabbed a few bags of crunchy snacks, splurging on some kale chips. The store had just restocked the grass-fed jerky, so I picked up a couple of flavor varieties. Brad liked the spicy one, while I preferred the sea salt. We both liked the Italian blend.

I was examining the various types of dried fruits when the hairs at the back of my neck prickled. "Seriously, Liv, get a grip," I hissed. As if I weren't crazy enough, now I was talking to myself in public. If I wasn't careful, someone would haul me in on a fifty-one fifty. It was probably a good thing I had an appointment with the department psychologist on the books.

Still, better safe than sorry. I searched the aisle for signs of danger. But no one else was nearby. I tossed several bags of fruit into my basket and went to check out the nut selection, which would have made me chuckle had I not been convinced there was an imminent threat.

Movement in the periphery caught my eye. I pivoted on

my heel. My hand slid toward my off duty piece, which was tucked in the holster at the small of my back. While I pretended to scratch an itch, I turned to face the coolers, using the reflection in the freezer doors to study my surroundings.

At the very end of the aisle stood a man in an oversized sweatshirt and jacket. He kept his head down, studying the different flavors of ice cream. Every few seconds, he'd glance in my direction.

"Excuse me," I said. "Would you happen to know where I'd find the cherry vanilla?"

"Only one brand makes that kind." He pointed to the section. "It looks like they're out."

"Thanks, anyway."

He finished getting his ice cream and walked away. As the door swung closed, I spotted Wilson Matthews' reflection on the shiny metal frame. I spun just in time to glimpse a figure retreating into another aisle.

I reversed direction, hurrying after the fleeing figure, but by the time I got to the next aisle, it was empty. I continued, checking one aisle after another. But the figure had vanished. Deciding it'd be best to get the hell out of here, I went to pay for my items.

While the cashier scanned the groceries, I peered around the store. I saw the man from the ice cream aisle leave, but he was of no concern. He was just another customer.

I took the bags out to the car and placed them in the trunk. On the ground was a receipt. I picked it up, examining it under my trunk light. It was from Milk and Honey, dated the same morning I ran into Wilson Matthews. The order was for a cup of tea and nothing else. It wasn't mine.

Turning, I searched the parking lot, but I didn't see Matthews' silver sports car or anyone else. The bastard had been here. He had followed me and wanted to make sure I knew.

Patrol told me he hadn't moved, but I didn't believe them. All of Brad's worries and fears played through my head as I drove toward Matthews' apartment, expecting to find his car gone or that the patrol unit had been called away.

Instead, the silver sports car was in the same exact spot it had been in for a week. The patrol unit remained outside, close enough to have a good view of the apartment building in its entirety. Matthews wouldn't be able to leave without them noticing, assuming they were paying attention.

I thought about stopping, but accusing officers of not doing their jobs wasn't the way to go. For Matthews to have followed me to the grocery store, he would have needed a car. Another question came to mind. How could he have known I was going to the store?

My phone wasn't compromised. I was sure of that. I'd mentioned it to Brad, but I never told him which store. In fact, I hadn't even told Emma which store when she called. He had to have followed me from home. Was he staking out my place? I'd felt him there.

I looked down at the receipt, which I'd tucked into my cupholder. That proved I wasn't crazy or hallucinating. Matthews didn't drop it by mistake. He left it on purpose. He wanted me to know he was watching. That he could get to me anytime he wanted. But everything indicated he was at home.

More than anything, I wanted to ring his doorbell and prove he wasn't there. But I knew better. If he answered at this time of night, he'd take it to a judge and say it was police harassment. Winters had already warned me about this. There was also another possibility. Matthews might be working with someone else to try to shake me. Given that his previous accomplice had been a corrupt cop, I feared Gallagher might have volunteered another one of his associates to stalk me.

Unsure if Matthews was tailing me, I circled around for a while. Several residential streets didn't have any traffic, so I turned down one of those, parked on the end, and waited. When no one came down the street for ten minutes, I knew it was safe. But I didn't go back to my parents. Instead, I sent them a text saying something came up and I wouldn't be home, and then I went to Brad's.

"Liv?" He squinted at me, keeping half his body

concealed behind the door while he leaned his right forearm against the doorjamb. "What are you doing here?"

I could smell the booze on his breath. "I was hoping we could talk."

He glanced behind him, looking at something in his apartment that I couldn't see. "Now's really not a good time."

I took a step back. "I didn't realize you had company. I should have called first. I'm gonna go. I'll see you tomorrow at work."

I was halfway down the hall when Brad let out a quiet curse. "Liv, wait. Come in and tell me what's going on."

"Are you sure?"

"Yeah. Come on." He left the door open for me and went back inside.

I closed his door and flipped the locks. When I turned around, he was shoving empties into a plastic bag.

"I can't believe you threw a party and didn't invite me."

He gave me a look over his shoulder before giving up and dropping to the couch. "Don't bust my balls. You know damn well there was no party."

Brad's apartment had never been this messy before. Empty beer and hard cider bottles covered the counter. Tequila, rum, and bourbon bottles littered the table. They were all empty. Despite the evidence, my partner didn't seem drunk, even if I could smell the liquor on him.

"Are you okay?"

He shook his head. "You first."

Having this discussion now seemed like a bad idea given the state of Brad's apartment. But he tucked his hands into his pockets and stared at me expectantly. So I told him about my trip to the grocery store and everything else.

"I can't believe the brass ones on this prick. Leaving the receipt, following you to the store," he shook his head in disbelief, "he's not going to give up, is he?"

"Once I spotted him, I'm pretty sure he left. He's not ready for direct confrontation."

"It didn't seem that way outside Milk and Honey." Brad saw how shaken I was. "Are you okay?"

"Just rattled. I didn't know where to go. I didn't want to

go home to my parents. What if he followed me there? But I just couldn't go back to my apartment."

"You were right to come here."

"I made sure he wasn't following me. I watched for a tail. He wasn't behind me. His car's still at his apartment, but he must have other means of transportation. It's possible I missed him, but I took every precaution. The last thing I want to do is lead him here."

"I know. It's okay. I'm glad you came over."

"It didn't sound that way when I knocked on your door. It looks like I interrupted quite the rager."

He sighed, ignoring the obvious question. "Do you want to crash in my room? I can take the couch."

"No, I'm okay out here."

"All right. I'm gonna get some sleep. We'll talk more in the morning. If you need anything, let me know." He stopped in the doorway. "Night, Liv."

He left his bedroom door cracked open. I looked at the time. It was early. Brad just wanted to get away from me before I could question him about the bottles again. I knew I couldn't force him to talk about it, but I wished he'd open up.

As quietly as possible, I straightened up his apartment, gently placing the empty bottles and cans into the recycling bin. I opened his liquor cabinet, finding it empty. He had four beers in the fridge and a bottle of wine. I didn't find anything else in his apartment. More than anything, I hoped he wouldn't replenish his stock.

I'd just spread the blanket out on his couch when I heard a muffled cry come from his bedroom. "Brad?" I moved closer to his bedroom door. "Are you okay?"

"Fine, go to sleep."

Hoping I wasn't going to walk into an embarrassing situation, I pushed his bedroom door open. "You don't sound okay. What happened?"

He swallowed, and that's when I realized the perspiration on his face, his shallow breathing, and his pinprick eyes weren't because of the alcohol. My partner was having an anxiety attack and had been having one for a while. "Nothing," he gulped, "I just can't get it to stop." He held up his left hand which shook.

Based on the disarray of his bed, he must have had a nightmare, possibly before I arrived. "Hey, I'm here. Talk to me." I sat on the edge of his bed. "What triggered it?"

He closed his eyes for a moment, wincing as his eyeballs raced from left to right beneath his lids. "Whenever I close my eyes, I'm back there. The ambush. Hearing the shots. The screams."

I grabbed his shaking hand. "Do you feel this?" I squeezed.

"Yeah."

"Good." I gave him an encouraging smile. "What do you hear? The sound of my voice? The neighbor's TV? Right?"

He nodded a few times.

"What do you see?"

He named a few things in his apartment as I guided him through the same anti-anxiety techniques Dr. Sloan had taught me. Brad's therapist must have done the same with him, but Brad's focus had been too narrow for him to step back and get out of his nightmare. He let go of my hand and reached for some water. The tremor hadn't completely gone away, but he was able to lift the glass and drink without it spilling.

"When's the last time you slept soundly?" I asked.

"I don't know."

"Lie back."

"Liv, I can't."

"Shh. Get comfortable."

An amused grin crossed his face, even though his eyes still looked terrified. "What are you going to do?"

"Not whatever it is you're thinking. Try to focus on your breathing. Four counts in. Four out. Slow and deep."

He snickered, a sure sign he was feeling more like himself. He tapped his hand a few times against the mattress, hoping to shake out the nervous energy.

I lay down beside him and gripped his hand in both of mine. "Just concentrate on your breath and the sound of my voice. The feel of my hands."

He nodded, shifting onto his side and putting his other hand over mine. We watched each other in the quiet. He matched his breathing to mine. Eventually, the panic ebbed and his eyes closed. Every part of him relaxed, erasing the tension from his face and causing the tremor to stop. I watched him sleep, afraid I'd wake him if I pulled my hands away.

THIRTY-FIVE

Wilson Matthews woke from a dreamless sleep. Last night hadn't gone the way he hoped. He thought by following her, by leaving her the receipt, he'd scare Liv DeMarco into running straight into the arms of her lover. The man's identity was still unclear, but Matthews had seen this situation play out enough times in bars and clubs to know that master manipulators, like Liv, would seek help from a man in the face of danger. It was all part of the charade— just more lies, expressing disingenuous affection and convincing the unsuspecting man that she wanted and needed him. At least, that's what Matthews had seen happen time and time again with his own mother and father. And the pattern repeated itself every time he observed an escort in a bar or club. Why was the damsel in distress so enticing? He didn't understand, but he fully intended to take advantage of it.

Unfortunately, Liv didn't behave the way he had hoped. Instead of going for help, she cruised around the city. He figured she might take a few precautions, which is why he left the store before she did and moved his car out of the parking lot and onto the street. As soon as she pulled out, he followed her. But when she literally drove in a circle, he realized she wanted to trick him.

He went back to her apartment, hoping she'd return. But after three hours, he realized she wouldn't be back. She was with him—Brad, Jake, or some unknown. So he returned to his RV to finish planning.

He didn't know where she went, but after such a close call tonight, he couldn't wait any longer. He wanted her to suffer. He had to do it. Before going to sleep, he promised himself that in twenty-four hours, Liv DeMarco would be bound and begging for her life.

He tore her dress, turning the skirt into five thick strips which would serve to bind her limbs and gag her. He selected the knife he intended to use, made sure the saltire cross was ready. Now all he had to do was find her and wait for the perfect opportunity to take her.

Despite the desire to get revenge for her deceit, he wanted to make sure the world saw her the same way he did. He wanted them to understand why he'd been forced to act. If everything went according to plan, Matthews would convince Brad to watch as Liv crumbled, confessing her sins while she begged for her life.

Capturing two cops instead of one would be a lot more dangerous and require more planning. Matthews wasn't sure he could wait for that. His cells were itching with anticipation. He'd just have to prepare for everything. Instead of taking his car, he started the RV. It sputtered and wheezed before rumbling awake.

He drove carefully, unfamiliar with the mechanics of operating such an unwieldy vehicle. He turned into one of the parking lots near the precinct which allowed temporary parking for recreational vehicles. The RV slipped in, just inches beneath the height clearance bar. He circled around to a spot that overlooked the precinct and parked.

At some point, she'd show up. And then he'd make his move.

* * *

"What is Brad doing here?" Emma asked as I unrolled my yoga mat.

"He's joining us for yoga."

"Since when."

"He's been here before."

She watched as he signed in at the front desk. "I don't like it. He ruins the class."

"How?"

Emma gave me a pointed look. "You can't possibly be that oblivious." Several women had already clustered around him, smiling and flirting. Emma jerked her chin toward the growing crowd. "They're already starting to stampede."

I rolled my eyes. "They're just being friendly."

"Friendly my ass."

"Are you jealous, Em?"

"God, no."

"Then don't worry about it. Brad asked if he could tag along. I said it'd be okay. Should I have checked with you first?"

"No," she let out a little grunt, "I'm just saying, with the way these women act, you'd think they'd never seen a man before."

"Brad's not the only guy here." I nodded to three others scattered around the room.

"He's the only straight one."

"Greg's straight. Didn't you go out with him?"

"We went for smoothies after class once. It was most definitely not a date."

"Whatever you say, Em."

"If Bradley wasn't so ridiculously flexible this wouldn't be a problem. He and his stupid perfect standing splits. Men should not be able to do that. Physiologically, it should not be possible."

I laughed. "You're jealous."

She glared at me. "Maybe."

"Be nice. He didn't come here to show you up. He just wants to center himself and calm his mind. Don't give him a hard time about this. Please."

"Fine." She stretched into downward dog, peddling her feet to loosen up.

Another woman spread her mat out beside mine, taking

the spot I'd tried to save for Brad. He waved me off before I could say anything to her and spread his yoga mat out in the back corner of the room. Despite what he'd said this morning, part of the reason he came with me was to make sure Wilson Matthews didn't show up. By staying near the back of the room, he'd have a better vantage point. Plus, it limited the number of women who could surround him.

Halfway through class, my phone buzzed. I grabbed it from where I'd tucked it beneath my towel. It was work. Darcy's phone just turned on. Units were already mobilizing.

"Em," I whispered, "I have to go. I'll see you later."

"You owe me breakfast," she grunted as she shifted into warrior three.

"Ask Greg."

"I hate you."

"Next time. I promise." I rolled up my mat, nodded to the instructor, and tiptoed around the rest of the students. Brad was waiting at the door.

Leslie, the woman who'd been practicing beside him, turned and waved. He winked at her before pushing the door open for me to walk through. "This was good," he said, climbing behind the wheel. "Maybe I'll join you more often."

"I can see why."

"Not because of her. Because I need something to help quiet the voices. Last night's the first time I've slept through the night in weeks. If it hadn't been for you, that never would have happened. I owe you."

"I fully intend to collect."

"I bet you do. But I don't care. That's probably because I'm feeling so good today. And now, we have a lead on Darcy. Things are definitely looking up."

"Can we talk about last night?"

"Only if you promise to drop it once we get to work."

"Deal." I took a breath. "What was up with all those bottles? I thought you weren't drinking like that anymore."

"I'm not."

"Your recycling bin says otherwise."

"I wasn't drunk, Liv. I just told you I haven't been able

to sleep. Drinking takes the edge off. With everything going on, you shouldn't be surprised I'm having sleep issues. We have more than enough to be anxious about."

"Are you dealing with that?"

"Trying."

It didn't seem that way last night. "I shouldn't burden you with the Wilson Matthews stuff. I should have realized you were already stretched too thin. I'm sorry."

"Hey, it's not a burden. That's something I need to know. Matters that concern you, concern me, especially when we're dealing with a killer."

My phone buzzed again. Darcy turned off her phone, but we'd intercepted a few text messages she and Jimmy exchanged. "Matthews isn't the only killer we have to worry about. You shouldn't have to deal with both."

"Neither should you." Brad pulled into the lot beside the precinct and found a spot. "But that's the job. We knew it when we signed up." He grabbed his clothes from the back seat, and I pulled my suitcase out of the trunk. After what happened at the grocery store, he thought it'd be best if we rode together. Since Matthews knew my car, taking Brad's would make it harder for him to track me. "We'll finish this conversation later."

After changing in the locker room, I met the rest of the task force in the conference room. Brad was already there, giving Loyola and Sullivan a hard time for not arresting Darcy the day before. But she never returned to the chemistry building.

"She might know we're on to her. Between campus security and our presence in her dorm, something probably got out. Someone must have made a mention of it on social media or she heard whispers from the other students and took off before we got eyes on her," Loyola said.

"It doesn't matter." Grayson put the text message chain up on the screen for us to see. "Thanks to our friends at the phone company, we know Darcy's supposed to be meeting Jimmy at the club tonight at eleven. Unfortunately, neither of them mentioned which club."

"It must be the one that's re-opening. We saw a flyer for it in her dorm room," I said.

G.K. Parks

"That's a possibility. It's also possible she could be meeting Jimmy at one of the other clubs from that list you found, or she might be hooking up with him at that dive bar."

"I wouldn't call that a club," Brad said.

"Regardless, I'm not pulling the unit assigned to monitor that bar. They might just show up there." The captain picked up a stack of folders and handed them out. "Those are your undercover assignments. I've spoken to narcotics and homicide. For tonight's op, we'll need all the manpower we can get. Every potential location will be covered. Since the five of you are the most familiar with this case, you'll be assigned to the most likely targets."

"What about Jimmy?" Ashmore asked. "Why can't we just follow him?"

"We will," Grayson promised, "but you know how quickly things can pop off. It'd be best to have officers already waiting for him when he arrives." Grayson nodded to Ashmore. "That's why I want you to sit on Jimmy. DeMarco and Fennel, you'll cover the club opening, and Loyola and Sullivan, I want you to hang out at that dive. No one knows you as cops. If we're right and Red Rabbit is being moved through that bar, tonight might be our best chance to catch them in the act."

"Do you think Jimmy's gonna make a pick-up before meeting Darcy?" Sullivan asked.

"I don't know, but I hope so." Grayson looked at our ragtag team. "If that's the case, the three of you should be able to take Jimmy and the supplier at that bar. Liv and Brad will wait for Darcy and take her at the club. Any questions?"

"What happens if no one shows?" I asked.

"Then we hope one of the dozens of cops out looking for our suspects finds them hanging out at one of the other clubs." He looked around the room. "I want everyone in position by eight o'clock. Let's not be tardy. In the meantime, you have today. If you need to get some sleep or find something to eat, go do that. I want you alive and alert."

An echo of affirmatives rang out. And then we were

dismissed.

THIRTY-SIX

"Ashmore just spotted Jimmy and someone else getting into the car," I said. "No ID yet on his companion, but based on the build, Ashmore thinks it's a woman."

"Darcy?" Brad asked.

"Possibly." I slipped the phone back into my pocket and looked around the club. "Unless it's Marietta."

"That would make more sense." Brad pointed to the staircase leading to the balcony. "We should be able to see everything from up there."

"All right."

He took my hand and led me through the club. As far as anyone was concerned, we were just another couple out to have a good time. Despite the early hour, most of the upstairs was occupied. The tables were filled with groups enjoying drinks and each other's company. The music seemed even louder, probably since we were closer to the speakers.

Several people clustered around the railing, cheering on the DJ, waving to friends, and getting frisky. After we circled, making sure Darcy wasn't up here waiting, we found an empty spot near the railing. Brad put his hands on my waist and pulled me against him, already moving to the beat. I swayed, putting my hands over his.

"Do you think she dyed her hair?" I hoped not, since the red would stick out in the crowd.

"It depends on where she's been these last two days. Let's hope she didn't get the chance."

My phone buzzed again. "Jimmy just dropped the unknown woman off at the waterfront. Ashmore's going to maintain eyes on her. Nearby patrols should be able to intercept Jimmy in two blocks. They'll follow until an unmarked takes over."

"That's a bad play."

"Grayson made the call," I said. "He must think the unsub is Darcy. She's the priority."

"She's killing people. That's how the Cap sees it. I'm surprised Ashmore's going along with it."

"He follows orders. Grayson's got rank. Ashmore will do what he's told."

Brad moved his hands so I could put my phone back in my pocket. "He's a good cop. They both are."

"Have you decided you trust them?" I asked.

"I always trusted Cap."

"And Ashmore? Don't the two of you have issues?"

"Nah, we're good. Ashmore was part of my cover. He doesn't know that, but he wouldn't have been if anyone suspected him of anything. He's clean."

I rested the back of my head against Brad's shoulder and turned so my mouth was near his ear. I wanted to make sure he could hear me without screaming. Since we were conducting surveillance, I couldn't turn around to have this conversation. "Why did you suddenly change your tune? Did something happen yesterday that I don't know about?"

"Not yesterday."

"Today?"

"Yeah." He nodded to another large group that just entered the club. "We've already seen everyone who's inside. Why don't you head down to the dance floor and find a spot with a good view of the front door? I'll keep watch from up here."

I spun in his arms, continuing to dance. "Don't look at me, Fennel. Watch below us." I ran my hands through his hair and trailed them down his shoulders before letting go and continuing to sway back and forth. Spending six months dancing in a cage for Axel Kincaid had left me with a few tricks. "What happened today? Is this about the call you took this afternoon?"

"Liv, you promised. Later."

"Fine." I dragged my fingers across his clavicle and down his arm as I walked away. He hooked his fingertips on mine, giving a slight tug for just a second. To anyone observing, they wouldn't think twice about my departure.

By the time I reached the bottom of the stairs, Brad had a drink in his hand. More than likely, it was club soda or iced tea. From here, I couldn't even see the color. But he wouldn't jeopardize our integrity, not when we hoped to arrest a killer.

I found a spot in the middle of the dance floor that allowed me a clear view of the door if I bobbed and weaved to see around the other clubgoers. With the pulsing rhythms, finding a partner wasn't necessary. With over two hundred people clustered together, we moved as one, bouncing and gyrating to the music. I kept my eyes on the door, letting my body move along with the surrounding wave. People bumped and brushed into me, but no one lingered.

My phone buzzed again. Patrol had yet to pick up Jimmy's car. "Dammit."

Do you have eyes on Darcy? I texted Ashmore.

Negative, pursuing on foot.

I let out a sigh, edging away from the center as more and more people blocked my view of the door. By the time I found another vantage point, I was on the outskirts of the crowd. Someone knocked into me hard. At the last second, he gripped my arm, either to balance me or himself. I turned to see who it was, but he disappeared into the throng.

I kept my eyes peeled, but the colors were starting to blur. Any of these young women could be Darcy. With so many people crowding inside, I was overwhelmed.

Moving away from the dance floor, I was glad the swirling lights had stopped their assault on my eyes. I went to the bar and asked for a bottle of water. Brad met me a minute later.

"Are you okay?" he asked.

"Yeah, but I couldn't see through the lights and the crowd."

"Based on the line outside, the club's at full capacity." He pulled out his phone. It was a few minutes after eleven. "Darcy might be stuck waiting in line. We should request units check outside."

"While they're at it, see if they spot Jimmy." I checked my phone, figuring I might not have noticed if it buzzed with the constant vibrations on the dance floor. "Sullivan and Loyola haven't reported anything." I sent them a text, asking for their status. "Nothing to report," I read.

Brad cursed. "This entire thing could be a ruse. The texts might have been meant to distract us. Jimmy knows we've been watching him. He probably knows we're monitoring his calls. He wouldn't be stupid enough to text with Darcy, would he?"

"She initiated. You saw the text chain. It was short and vague. He might have figured it was safe enough. It's possible that's their only means of communication after we crashed their meeting at the bar."

"I guess." Brad ordered another club soda. "But units were mobilized. We pinged her phone. We should have found her this morning."

"You know how that works. By the time we narrowed the pings to a few blocks, she shut off her phone. That's too large of an area to search."

"It was near that bar where you chased her down, right?"

"Yeah..." I wondered what my partner was thinking.

"That probably means she already picked up whatever drugs they're moving tonight. Did anyone leave the bar around that time?" Brad didn't know, and neither did I. He pulled out his phone and dialed. He plugged his other ear with his finger, hoping to hear over the music. "Can you repeat that?" He squinted, concentrating hard on the words. "Run 'em. If you can come up with something, bring 'em in."

"What's going on?"

"The delivery guy left the bar ten minutes before Darcy's phone went live this morning. No one followed him when he left. But we stopped his truck a block before he made it to the bar and asked if we could search it. Patrol didn't find any contraband inside, which is why we didn't pursue. I'm guessing he picked up contraband from the bar to distribute elsewhere."

"You think he met Darcy and gave her more pills to move?"

"Given the timeframe, it fits."

Was that a stretch? I sipped more water and wiped the perspiration off my face. A moment later, my phone buzzed. It was Ashmore.

ID's been made. Marietta Linley.

"Dammit," Brad cursed, reading over my shoulder. "We have no idea where they are."

"They're supposed to be here." I checked the time. "Do you remember what the birthday party said? Didn't they encounter Darcy in the bathroom?"

"They weren't clear on that."

"No, but that could be where she's dealing. It fits. Think about when she poisoned Gwynn. The handoff wasn't caught on camera. She took him somewhere private. Most clubs have lots of cameras, but we've never seen her accept cash or pass product inside any of the clubs."

"Every club has plenty of blind spots. She could have been anywhere."

"It's worth exploring, don't you think?"

"Yeah, just be careful."

I slid off the barstool and tripped over my own feet. Brad grabbed my arm before I toppled over. He raised an eyebrow.

"I'm fine," I said. "Keep your eyes peeled. Text me if something happens."

"You do the same."

I made my way across the dance floor and down the narrow hallway that led to the bathrooms. A large line had already formed with women screaming to one another to be heard over the din.

"Have any of you seen a woman with red hair?" I described Darcy. "I'm supposed to be meeting her near the bathrooms."

"Sorry," one group shouted back.

I moved past them. "I'm just looking for a friend. I'm not cutting in line," I said to the woman who gave me a dirty look when I pushed in front of her. I entered the bathroom and looked around, but I didn't spot Darcy.

"What does she look like?" the woman at the front of the line asked me.

"She has short red hair. She's thin. Young. Have you seen her?"

Before the woman could reply, my phone buzzed. I tried to pull it out of my pocket, but my fingers couldn't quite grab it. Finally, I wrestled it free, blinking at the blurry display. *Possible Jimmy sighting. I'm following him upstairs now.*

"Brad," I mumbled, turning to leave.

"Did you hear me?" the woman asked.

"What?"

"I think your friend went that way. She was talking to some guy. She looked upset."

"What did he look like?"

"Kinda tall. Greased back brown hair."

"Where did he go?"

She shrugged. "He headed to the bar or upstairs. I'm not sure."

I nodded my thanks. How did Jimmy and Darcy get inside without us noticing? I headed in the direction the woman said Darcy had gone. The utility room was empty, but I wondered why it wasn't locked. That didn't make much sense.

A back staircase led to another part of the upstairs. I sent an update to the task force, informing them of a potential sighting, gave the location, and approximate time. Support was on the way.

Do you have Jimmy? I texted to Brad.

He didn't reply. This wasn't good. Nervous energy burned through me. I raced up the stairs, which led to a small balcony and a locked door. I tried the knob, but it didn't budge. I banged against it a few times, hoping someone on the other side might hear me and open up, but they didn't. Did Darcy lock the door from the other side? Had she even come up here?

I jogged down the steps, feeling dizzy from the sudden height change. My phone buzzed as I reached the bottom and I grabbed for it. It slid right out of my hand.

A sudden hot flash came over me, followed by a wave of nausea. I sucked in a breath. What was happening? My legs felt weak. I reached for the banister, watching as my hand fell short of connecting with it. My limbs felt like they were tied down with heavy weights, and my movements were sluggish. I sat down on the bottom step and put my head in my hands.

"You've had too much to drink, sweetie. Let's get you out of here," a familiar voice said as he sunk beneath one of my arms and slid his hand around my waist.

I turned, my reaction slow and my vision growing increasingly blurry. "Matthews?"

"It's about time we finished what we started all those weeks ago. I've been anxiously waiting. I know you have too."

"Help." I tried to call out, but my voice was weak. No one heard me over the music. As he moved me past the line of women, I tried to scream. The sound came out a gurgle. I tried again, realizing I had no control over my body. The darkness was coming fast. When my eyelids closed, I couldn't force them open again.

THIRTY-SEVEN

"Don't you fucking touch her, or I'll kill you," Brad snarled.

"I'm doing you a favor," Wilson Matthews said. "Why can't you see that? She deserves to be punished. Just wait. You'll see."

Metal chains rattled, and Brad let out a guttural scream. "I'm gonna kill you."

A blinding headache tore through me. This had to be the worst hangover in the history of hangovers, but I wasn't the one with all the empty bottles in my apartment. I could barely open my eyes, let alone get my limbs to move.

Matthews hurried to my side. "It looks like she's waking up."

My eyelids fluttered. Once they were open, it was less of a struggle to keep them that way. Brad was handcuffed to a large, dark metal ring near the floor. He met my eyes from across the room, rage burning in his. He tugged even harder against the chains, pushing against the frame with his feet while he tried to pull his hands free. His wrists were bleeding from the effort, but he didn't seem to notice.

"Liv." Matthews moved closer, inhaling my scent like some sort of animalistic lover. "Let's get rid of this, so the fun can begin." He reached for my outstretched arm, plucking a clear plastic adhesive pad from the crook of my elbow.

How did that get there? I tried to speak, but my tongue wouldn't cooperate. He must have been the guy on the dance floor who'd grabbed my arm. Why didn't I notice?

"It's a paralytic. It takes time to absorb through the skin. I wanted to make sure I had plenty of time to get you out of there. Of course, I had to pick up this guy first, which as you can imagine, wasn't particularly easy." He looked over his shoulder at my partner. "How's your head?"

Brad's scowl should have killed Matthews on the spot. Did he drug Brad too? I looked at my partner, still desperately trying to get free, but Matthews didn't care. He circled, a giddy laugh leaving his lips.

"Don't worry," Matthews said, "you didn't miss anything. I waited for you to wake up before the fun could start. I didn't want you to miss any of my process."

"Get away from her," Brad ordered. "You want to punish someone, punish me."

Matthews glanced at my partner. "She really has you fooled, doesn't she? You need to wake up and see things for what they are. She manipulated you into thinking these situations are your fault. That you're the cause of her pain. When in actuality, she's the cause of your pain. Stop fighting and think about it. Think about every time you've been hurt. Who caused that? It was her. Every damn time. Every broken promise. Every look. Every touch. Nothing but lies."

Matthews was projecting his childhood experiences onto Brad. The killer actually believed the shit he was saying. Brad fell silent, the wheels turning in his head. He was formulating a plan, but he'd need time to enact it.

"Does this look familiar?" Matthews held a coral piece of fabric in front of my face. "You wore it on our first date. It's only fitting you wear it now."

"How?" I managed without moving my mouth.

"I was there. Right there. You were so close. But I made you wait, just like you made me wait." He stepped away from me. I followed his movements with my eyes. From the counter in what looked like a kitchenette, he picked up a knife. "I think we should take things nice and slow."

Brad hadn't spoken in a few minutes. He had stopped tugging at the bindings. Instead, he had moved closer to the metal ring and worked his way to his knees.

Matthews turned to him. "Get comfortable. You don't want to miss the show. This is the first time I've had an audience, so I'm not completely prepared. Frankly, I almost didn't bother, but you need to see this."

"What are you going to do afterward?" Brad asked.

Matthews put the knife down. He crossed his arms and stared at my partner for a long few seconds. "That is a very good question."

"You could escape. Disappear. You'd be safe," Brad said. "You should go now."

"No." Matthews slammed his palms down on the counter. "I know what you're doing. You're trying to save her. You're going to tell me to spare her. To leave now. That you won't chase me. You still don't see." He picked up the knife, stabbing in Brad's direction. "You have to listen. You have to see. I want you to see." He slammed the knife back down and plucked a handcuff key off the counter and moved toward me.

"Wilson," I said, surprised when my tongue cooperated, "let him go."

"I'm not going to hurt him." Matthews looked me straight in the eye. "You're the only one who deserves to be punished. You took away my family. You turned Casey against me. He was my best friend. He was like a brother. But you poisoned his mind with your lies." He unlocked the handcuffs that held my left arm in place.

I tried to pull my hand away, but my reactions were slowed. He grabbed my hand, looping the coral sash around a few times before tying it into a complicated knot. He tugged, making sure it wouldn't come loose. Then he tossed my cuffs onto the counter.

"Why would she ask you to spare me?" Brad asked. "You said she manipulates me. Why would she ask you to spare my life? Doesn't that contradict your theory?"

Matthews turned to my partner, displeased with the question. "More manipulations. You have to learn to tell the truth from the lies. Don't they teach you these things in the police academy?"

"I was never very good at that part."

"Clearly. How long have you been her partner?"

"Two years. Shouldn't I know her pretty well after two years?"

"No, she lies. Years can pass. She acts like you're her world. That you matter. That she loves you. She says you're her good little boy. That she would never leave you." Matthews let out a huff, his hands balling into fists as he circled me. "That's just so she can inflict more pain."

I sucked in a breath, realizing Brad was trying to buy time. Now that the patch had been removed from my skin, I was regaining muscle function. But it was slow. I couldn't even make a tight fist, but I could move my eyes and mouth.

"I don't know."

"Two years is a long time to get inside someone's head. Trust me. I understand. It's no wonder you're confused." Matthews turned back to me, releasing a thick leather cuff that had bound my other arm to the cross.

"I remember you. You had the problem that I was supposed to help Gallagher fix. But I couldn't." Brad's words caught Matthews off guard. "Is that why you brought us here?"

"You couldn't fix it because she wouldn't let you." Matthews grabbed a fistful of my hair and yanked hard.

"Take it easy, man. Just tell me, is that why we're here?" Brad asked. "Isn't this my fault? Don't you want to punish me for failing to help you?"

"No, it's all because of her. I gave Gallagher the money. He said he'd take care of it, but he didn't. He told me it was her investigation. She wouldn't let it go. So he handed me her instead." Matthews' voice trembled with anger. Spit flew from his mouth. He picked up another strip of coral fabric, pulling it taut between his hands.

"I hate to break it to you," Brad said, "but Gallagher hung you out to dry. He set you up." Brad shifted, fighting to convince Matthews the anger he had shown toward him was now aimed at Gallagher. "The bastard set me up to."

Matthews didn't react. "I killed him. Did you know that?"

Matthews put the strip of fabric down and turned to Brad. "Why?"

"He tried to kill me." Brad glanced at me, but I shook my head. The last thing I wanted was for my partner to give this lunatic another reason to kill us both. Like Jake said, I checked all the boxes. Brad checked none of them. There was a chance Matthews might let him live.

"Why?"

"He got greedy."

Matthews snorted. "Sounds like Gallagher. That fucking bastard. Do you have any idea how much money I paid him? I could have bought a house in Nowheresville and disappeared on my own without his supposed help. I'm glad the bastard's dead." He smiled down at my partner. "See, we have enemies in common. Annoyances that have to be dealt with. We can help each other. You need to listen to me. Open your mind to what I'm showing you." Matthews grabbed the fabric strip and turned back to finish changing out my bindings. Using an article of my clothing was part of his ritual. Despite the added danger, he couldn't stop himself from following his obsession to the letter. He brushed his fingers through my hair. "The prettier the package, the more dangerous. The more deceitful."

He moved his fingers behind my ear, brushing my hair off my neck. I turned away, other villains and nightmares coming to mind. His hand froze for just a second, and he traced the scar that ran down the back of my neck and toward my shoulder.

Excitedly, he shoved the top of my blouse down to follow the jagged lines. "Someone's cut you before." He ran to get the knife, caressing the tip of the blade over the scar. The cold steel licked my hot flesh, leaving the memory of the icy tip behind. I couldn't see if he was cutting into me or not.

My heart pounded against my ribs, my breath growing more frantic. Now was not the time to panic, but I couldn't shake the memory of almost dying. The fear took hold.

"Liv, look at me." Brad wouldn't let me fall down that

hole, even if it ruined the rapport he'd been building with our captor. He made a show of sucking in a breath and blowing it out, just like I did for him last night. "You're okay. Just breathe."

Matthews didn't even appear to notice. He was enthralled by the jagged pink lines. He ran his fingers over them again, spreading my flesh out to see it better. "Turn around." He tried to yank me around, realizing he'd trapped my feet on the cross.

He knelt down, making quick work of the leather cuffs. My feet hit the floor. My knees threatened to buckle, but the adrenaline from my panic must have kickstarted something inside of me. My muscles held. Matthews reached for my free hand, so obsessed that he didn't realize his mistake.

He spun me around, my one arm bound to the cross while my other three limbs remained free. As he moved to cut my shirt off so he could see the extent of the scarring, I pulled back with as much force as I could muster and drove my elbow into his ribs.

The knife fell to the ground, and I scooped it up. I slashed at the fabric binding me to the metal. I'd only gotten it to fray when Matthews tackled me. The force caused my wrist to break free. He slammed me into the side of the counter, knocking the wind out of me.

"You're gonna pay for that." He reached for another knife he had laid out. This was a kitchen knife. The blade long and thick. Tucking his thumb over the top of the handle, he jabbed downward. I jerked, feeling the sharp edge skim across my side before becoming firmly planted in the countertop.

Matthews yanked hard, desperate to pull the knife out and stab me. My partner didn't waste a second. He kicked Matthews hard in the leg, just below the knee. Matthews veered sideways, almost losing his balance. Brad lunged forward, scissor-kicking into the air and wrapping his legs around Matthews.

"Liv, go," Brad yelled.

I scrambled to keep my legs beneath me as I tore free from the lodged knife. Matthews elbowed Brad hard, over and over, hitting him in the side. My partner grunted, but he held tight.

I grabbed the first thing I could find, which was a small cast iron skillet. It felt so heavy, I nearly dropped it. Matthews hit Brad again, breaking free from my partner's legs. With every ounce of strength I had, I swung the skillet at Matthews' head. It made contact, and he went down.

Without wasting a second, I grabbed the handcuff key and dropped to my knees. My fingers were too unreliable between the after effects of the paralytic and the adrenaline dump. Luckily, my partner's hands weren't shaking nearly as much as mine. He unhooked the handcuffs with ease, his bloody wrists nothing but an afterthought.

Quickly, he grabbed the gun off the counter. "Can you cover him?"

"I'll try."

He handed me the gun, and I forced my aim to steady while he handcuffed Matthews. Blood had started to soak the side of his shirt.

"Are you okay?" I asked.

"I will be if you will."

"Deal."

Brad took the gun from my unsteady grip and wrapped one arm around me and hugged me hard. "Liv, let's not do this again. Okay?"

"No problem."

He kissed my temple before letting go. While keeping one eye on Matthews, Brad searched the drawers and cabinets until he found our phones. He powered his back on and called it in. "This is Detective Fennel. We need a couple of ambulances. One suspect in custody."

I made my way to the door and pulled it open. "Brad, where are we?"

THIRTY-EIGHT

"Sit down, man. You're bleeding." Loyola watched my partner dab at the gash on the back of his head. "I can't believe the hospital released you like that. I saw the footage. That asshole swung for the stands. You're lucky we're not picking pieces of your melon off the dance floor. Did they check you for a concussion?"

"They did." Brad pulled the towel away, inspecting it for blood. "See? It stopped. That's just dried blood. No big deal."

"His head's too hard," Sullivan said. "How about you, Liv? Are you all right?"

"I'm fine."

"You sure?"

"Just a little shaky, but I'm okay. The paralytic's extremely short-lived. Matthews didn't want it to impede his fun. It'll be fully out of my system in twenty-four hours. But we don't have time to wait. We have to find Darcy and Jimmy." I turned to Captain Grayson. "Medical cleared us. We're good to go. We just need you to sign off."

Grayson assessed me for a moment. "All right, but I better not regret this."

"You won't, sir."

Brad put the towel down. "What did we miss?"

"Unfortunately, not much. You and Liv were right on top of them—Darcy and Jimmy," Grayson said.

"I remember," Brad said. "I was just a few feet from him when everything went black."

"Wilson Matthews snuck up behind you, smashed you over the head with a bottle and dragged you into a private VIP space. That area wasn't ready for the re-opening, so management put some temporary partitions up and covered them with velvet drapes. You probably assumed it was another wall. As soon as you walked past, Matthews hit you and dragged you inside. From there, he took you out the side entrance, where he had his RV waiting. Then he went back inside, found Liv, and walked her out of the bar."

"What does this have to do with Darcy and Jimmy?" I didn't want to relive those events if I could avoid it.

"If that hadn't happened, you would have arrested them." Grayson played the footage from the club. "Instead, Darcy and Jimmy spent the next ten minutes passing out Red Rabbit. When backup arrived, they bolted. We chased them for four blocks before they got into Jimmy's car. Twelve blocks later, they ditched the vehicle. We're still trying to find them."

"Shit." Brad rubbed a hand down his face.

"Any more poisonings?" I asked.

"None have been reported yet. We shut down the club. Those who admitted to taking the pills were brought to the hospital for evaluation. So far, no one's tested positive for superwarfarin."

"At least that's a plus." I looked at the map. "Where's Ashmore?"

"He's still keeping tabs on Marietta." Sullivan pointed to a red X on the map. "That's their current location. She's staying with a friend."

"What about tracking their phones?" Brad asked.

"Turned off," Loyola said.

"But they're together," I said. "Darcy and Jimmy."

"We don't know that," Grayson said. "They could have split up once they ditched the car."

Brad looked at me. "What are you thinking?"

"Marietta must know something. She was in the car with Jimmy. If she had any idea he was going to meet Darcy, she never would have gotten out of the car or let him out of her sight." I reached for the stack of files on the table. "Do we have her phone number handy?"

"Here." Sullivan handed it to me. "What are you going to do?"

"Call and ask if she knows where Jimmy is." I looked around the room. "Stop me if you have a better idea."

"Go ahead." Grayson folded his arms over his chest. "Put it on speaker."

Marietta answered on the third ring, so I told her who I was and asked if she knew where Jimmy was.

"He had deliveries to make. A whole slew of them."

"Are you sure about that?" I asked.

"What are you talking about?"

"Three hours ago, my partner and I spotted Jimmy at a club." I told her which club. "Any idea why he might have been there?"

Marietta's voice sounded like nails on a chalkboard. "None." She swallowed. "Where is he now?"

"I don't know. That's why I called you."

"Jimmy said he had a dozen deliveries to make tonight."

"Is that strange? He brings people food. Are there really that many places that need delivery at this time of night?"

"You got anything else to say to me?" she asked.

"No, ma'am."

"Good, because I don't know why you think calling me and causing trouble is a good idea. Good night." She disconnected.

"It was worth a shot," Loyola said.

I stared at the map. The clubs and bars we had covered were marked. Every location from the list I'd found and the suspected locations Ashmore had come up with were all represented. Darcy's secret lair and her dorm were being closely monitored. A squad car was parked outside Jimmy's place. They had to be somewhere.

"We should get back out there," Sullivan said. "Maybe we'll stumble upon them."

Grayson waved them off, and Loyola and Sullivan headed out. "Are you two going too?"

Brad rubbed his cheek as he studied the intel. "We almost had them, Cap. Liv followed Darcy. I was on Jimmy. If that son of a bitch hadn't interfered..."

"It's okay, Fennel. You couldn't have known. The unit watching Matthews was supposed to have been shadowing his movements. We didn't know he'd snuck away one night, paid cash for someone's old clunker, and had an RV waiting for him. There was no paper trail. I'm just relieved you survived. None of his victims did."

"He screwed up," I said. "He could have pulled it off if he'd just taken me and hadn't had to stick with his ritual."

"You threw him a curve ball," Brad said. "He didn't know you'd been injured. He was intrigued. That's what gave us the upper hand."

"On the bright side, CSU's processing the RV. They've found a box of torn fabric."

"Trophies from his previous kills," I said.

"In light of everything, his bail's been revoked. He'll be brought up on additional charges, and assuming he survives, the evidence is far too damning for him to ever see the light of day again. Chalk it up to a win," Grayson said.

"How is he?" I asked. "I don't think I hit him that hard, but with the pre-existing skull fracture, I don't know."

The captain looked at me. "This is why you shouldn't be working right now."

"How is he, Cap?" Brad asked.

"He's out of surgery. His scans were clean, but the doctors won't know for certain until he wakes up."

Brad stared out the door. "He's lucky I didn't hit him, or he wouldn't be waking up."

"You and me both." Grayson gave my shoulder a squeeze.

"How did he know where we were?" I asked. "Or who we were tracking?"

"I don't think he knew anything about the second part," Grayson said. "We checked DOT footage. The RV's been staking out the precinct all day. When you and Fennel left, it followed you to the club. The club cameras show him entering soon after you did. He was watching you the entire time."

"He's been watching Liv," Brad said. "He broke into her apartment. He followed her to the grocery store."

"Why didn't you report it?" Grayson asked.

"I mentioned it to several people, but stalking's hard to prove. Matthews knew that. It's why he didn't come at me directly. I didn't know he was inside my apartment." I shivered. "He was there the same time I was."

Grayson blew out a breath. Before he could offer some sage words of advice, the phone rang. Marietta Linley just borrowed her friend's car and took off like a bat out of hell. "Stay with her. Do not let her out of your sight." Grayson picked up the radio. "All units, be advised." He provided a description of the vehicle and read off the plate number. "Do not pull her over. We want to see where she's going."

"She's going to lead us to Jimmy," I said. "She'll find him, even if we can't."

Brad grabbed the radio off the desk. "Let's roll."

We listened to the reports, racing to catch up to their locations. Brad slowed when we approached a shut down restaurant. Marietta left the grey sedan parked out front, but she was nowhere to be seen. Ashmore had parked across the street.

Brad rolled down his window. "What's the situation?"

"She got out of the car and went around back. I noticed a light on inside, but I haven't seen any movement. I'm waiting for further instructions."

"Did you run the address?" I asked.

"The health department shut the place down six months ago."

I compared the address to the intel in Jimmy's file. "He used to make regular pick-ups from here. He must know this place pretty well."

"Could it be a cover?" Brad asked.

"If it is, narcotics doesn't know a thing about it." Ashmore reached for his phone. "I'll check with the DEA and see if it rings any bells."

While we waited, I stared at the restaurant, watching

the dim interior light flicker. Someone was definitely inside, and since Marietta hadn't come out, I had to assume Jimmy was still in there. I shared my suspicions with Brad, who agreed.

"Stay here," he said to Ashmore. "We'll check it out. If we need backup, we'll radio." He held up the handheld. "Channel three."

"Copy that." Ashmore nodded to us.

Brad turned the car around and pulled in front of the restaurant. Silently, we exited the vehicle. The front door was locked, so we went around the side. Brad tucked the radio into his pocket, the gun already in his hand. I was just as prepared. It'd been that kind of night.

When we made it around back, the door to the kitchen was ajar. Marietta's angered shrieking echoed around us. "How could you do this, Jimmy? Do you think I'm an idiot? Did you think I wouldn't find out?"

"It's not what you think," Jimmy said.

"Shut up," she snapped. "Shut your fucking mouth."

Brad slipped inside first. His gun aimed in front of him. I flicked on my flashlight and followed, conducting a sweep of the kitchen. "Clear," he whispered.

We continued moving forward.

"Please, baby, listen to me," Jimmy begged. "Take it easy. I love you."

"You're a whore, Jimmy. You sleep with whores. You are a whore." Something slammed down, followed by a pained gasp. "Don't even, you little bitch," Marietta said. "You knew damn well Jimmy had a girlfriend. What did you think? You could just move in on my territory with your perfect little tits and your tight little ass. I hate to break it to you, but he likes his women with a little more meat on their bones."

"Darcy," I mouthed to Brad.

We split up at the doorway and peered around the corner. Marietta had a gun pointed at Jimmy. Darcy was beside him. Her eye was swollen, and her lip was bleeding. Brad made a few hand gestures, but I shook my head. I'd take point. Brad gave me that defiant look. *Trust me*, I mouthed.

He tightened his grip and strengthened his stance. When he nodded, I stepped out of the kitchen.

"Marietta, what's going on?" I asked. She spun, surprised, her gun moving with her. "Take it easy."

"What are you doing here?"

"I told you we've been looking for Jimmy. We tracked him here. He's in a lot of trouble."

"You're telling me." She turned back around, aiming at him. "This son of a bitch thinks he can step out on me and there won't be consequences. I found him here with his little skank." She aimed at Darcy. "How many others have there been, Jimmy? Is this the bitch you brought to our house? The one who left her thong in our bed?" She shifted back to him. "Answer me."

"Answer her, Jimmy," I said, taking small half steps closer.

Brad kept his distance, drawing down on her. If she so much as flinched, he'd shoot her.

"I'm sorry."

"You're sorry?" Marietta screeched.

"Marietta, wait," I said. "You don't want to do this."

"The hell I don't."

"Look at me," I raised my hands a little higher and stopped aiming at her. "I don't want to hurt you. Neither does my partner. You made a deal with Detective Ashmore. He granted you immunity, but that doesn't include murder. Everything else, you'll walk away. But if you shoot Jimmy or the girl, I can't help you."

"I don't need your help."

"Listen. One of two things will happen if you pull that trigger."

"Jimmy will be dead."

"And my partner will have to put you down. If you live, you'll spend the rest of your life in prison. Do you really want some asshole like Jimmy to ruin your life? Think about it. Right now, you haven't done anything wrong. You won't get in any trouble. We'll cut you loose. Jimmy won't be that lucky. We have a solid case against him. He's going away for decades."

"What about her?" Marietta asked.

"Life," I said.

Marietta met my eyes. "Are you lying to me?"

"No, ma'am."

She turned back around, her eyes on Jimmy. The gun pointed at his head.

"Ask yourself one thing," I said. "Is Jimmy worth dying for?"

Marietta cursed, getting even more agitated. She put the gun on the table. Brad radioed for backup while I put her in cuffs. "What are you doing? You said I wouldn't get in any trouble."

"We have to take you in," I said, hoping to avoid the drama of telling her I lied.

"They fucking played you," Darcy hissed. "You should never believe anyone."

Once I had Marietta secured, Brad cuffed Jimmy. Just as Brad was tightening the cuffs, Ashmore joined us. He arrested Darcy and examined the injury sustained. He looked up at the two of us. "It looks like we can finally call it a night."

THIRTY-NINE

"Is that everything?" I asked.

ADA Logan Winters reread the confession Darcy submitted. "It looks like it. I still don't understand how any of this happened."

"It's not that hard to understand. Darcy was miserable. The assholes around her bullied and taunted her into feeling worthless. She didn't have a big enough support system to pull her through. Her parents cut her off, thinking that would get her back on track. Her only friend was her roommate. But one person wasn't enough. Darcy needed real professional help."

"She was raped," Brad said. "Her freshman year. Paul Gwynn attacked her at a party during pledge week. I'm guessing based on her hatred for the sorority, she must have blamed them for putting her in danger. For whatever the reason, she didn't report it, like a lot of women in her position. She probably hoped to forget it."

"Except Paul wouldn't let her." Winters frowned. "Assholes like him are the reason the world's as screwed up as it is. It wasn't enough for him to take advantage of her. He had to harass her every day on top of it. He wouldn't let her forget."

"It pushed her over the edge," I said. "She wanted to

find some way to escape it. Her grades suffered. She lost her way. The things she had in place to help her cope turned out to make matters worse."

"She struggled with her class load and had to cut back. She didn't have any friends she confided in. Even her roommate didn't know what Paul did to her. Then when her parents cut her off, she finally decided to quit her job to avoid seeing him. She figured it'd be a clean slate. But that's around the same time she met Jimmy," Brad said.

"Jimmy preyed on her vulnerabilities. He exploited them for his own gains." Winters read the confession where Darcy had underlined certain words. "The poor kid. I wish she'd reported what happened. We could have prosecuted, gotten her help, therapy, some kind of support."

"It's not always that easy," I said. "Victims are often blamed. Proof isn't always easy to find. The entire process of reporting can be almost as traumatic as the attack."

"I know," Winters agreed. "But it would have been better than the alternative."

"She bought pills from Jimmy, figuring she'd end it all. She never expected him to take an interest in her. He convinced her they'd make a great team. It's why we couldn't get our hands on any of the Red Rabbit pills. Jimmy dealt those exclusively, and he only sold them to people Darcy recognized."

"Do you think he knew Darcy was killing people?" Winters asked.

"I'm sure he did," Brad said. "I don't think he cared. She wasn't killing everyone, just the people who hurt her or failed to help her. The ones who made life harder for her to live."

"It doesn't make it right. Murder is murder," Winters said, "but in this case, I can't tell the victims from the perpetrators."

"What about Wilson Matthews?" I asked.

"No," Winters said. "Sickos like him deserve what they get."

"His mom screwed him up," I said. "He thought he was saving mankind from women like her."

"Trying to kill you isn't helping anyone," Winters said. He nodded to Brad. "I'm glad you're both okay."

"What'll happen to him?" Brad asked.

"He's been advised that a plea deal is the best he's going to get. He has time to think about it. If he won't confess, I'll nail him at trial. Either way, he's not getting out again. No bail. No parole. Nothing." Winters looked at me. "If he pleads, you don't have to testify. That's why I'm pushing for that."

"I'll be prepared either way."

Winters sighed. "You shouldn't have to face him again. You've already dealt with enough."

"It's the job."

"What about Jimmy?" Brad asked.

"With Darcy's confession, he's facing extensive drug charges and accessory for the murders. We're hoping to convince him to tell us who he's working for. If we can get the supplier, we can actually get these drugs off the streets."

"Yeah, until someone else fills in the gap," I said.

"It's better than nothing," Brad said. He glanced into the third interrogation room. "And Marietta?"

"Assault with a deadly weapon. The gun she had was unregistered. She'll be facing charges. She doesn't even care about a deal. She wants to tell us everything she knows about Jimmy and his business."

"According to Ashmore, narcotics already busted two stash houses where Jimmy made his alleged food deliveries. Even if he doesn't cooperate, I think the intel Marietta can provide will be invaluable," I said.

After Winters left, Brad and I packed up for the day. It had been a very long few weeks. "Are you ready for dinner?" Brad asked.

"We could grab a pizza."

"We could do that, or we could eat the tray of your mom's lasagna that's in my fridge. I thought it was your favorite."

"When did she have time to make it?"

"When she was teaching me the recipe. What do you say?"

"Are you driving?"

He nodded.

"Good, because I'm beat. These last few days have felt like one nonstop shift. I'm not even sure I've slept since the RV. Have you?"

"Yeah." He didn't say anything else until we were inside his car. "Agent Anderson called. The FBI cleared Lt. Winston. I saw the list of names still under investigation. It's no one we know. I finally feel like that's over. The secret's out. The LT knows. He hasn't retaliated. If anything, he's been up my ass trying to support me. It's weird."

"Good weird, right?"

Brad nodded. "And now that we know how Matthews snuck away and tracked you, a weight has been lifted. How are you feeling about this?"

"I'm good."

"Are you sure?"

"I'm still worried about you."

"Since you're so worried, maybe you should stay the night."

I rolled my eyes. "Brad, be serious."

"Who says I'm not?" He chuckled. "I'm okay, Liv. I just needed to sleep. My cortisol was through the roof. It was fueling the mental turmoil and creating this feedback loop. The doc prescribed some sleep aids in case it gets out of control again, but I really do feel better." He looked more at ease, more like himself before the world went crazy. "I've got cooking classes with your mom, yoga with you and Emma, and therapy three times a week until the nightmares are back under control. I have a support system. I'm not going to let things get out of control, especially when I know I can always call you to come over and hold my hand." He smiled. "I love you, Liv. You keep me sane and safe."

"Is that why you wanted to learn how to make lasagna?"

"Well, it is your favorite, and you deserve something special for putting up with all this shit. But it doesn't hurt that it's also damn good."

Don't miss *Mistaken Identity*, the next book in the Liv DeMarco series:

Are these crime scenes pranks or murder?

Halloween always brings out the crazies. The tip hotline has never been so busy with reports of bodies and body parts. Detective Liv DeMarco and her partner, Brad Fennel, have been running themselves ragged, investigating these staged scenes. So far, they've all been bogus, until now...

A killer is about to go on a rampage. He didn't get his happily ever after, so he wants to make sure no one else does either. So far, he's murdered one couple, but he's just getting started.

Available in print and ebook.

Imminent Threat

ABOUT THE AUTHOR

G.K. Parks is the author of the Alexis Parker series. The first novel, *Likely Suspects,* tells the story of Alexis' first foray into the private sector.

G.K. Parks received a Bachelor of Arts in Political Science and History. After spending some time in law school, G.K. changed paths and earned a Master of Arts in Criminology/Criminal Justice. Now all that education is being put to use creating a fictional world based upon years of study and research.

You can find additional information on G.K. Parks and the Alexis Parker series by visiting our website at
www.alexisparkerseries.com

Made in United States
Orlando, FL
19 April 2023

32248678R20181